Cupid

and the Silent

Goddess

Other novels by Alan Fisk

The Strange Things of the World

The Summer Stars

Forty Testoons

Lord of Silver

Alan Fisk

Cupid
and the Silent
Goddess

PAGE D'OR
MMXXII

Page d'Or is an imprint of Prosperity Education Limited
Registered offices: 58 Sherlock Close, Cambridge CB3 0HP,
United Kingdom

First published 2003 by Twenty-First Century Publishers
Second edition published 2022

A catalogue record for this book is available from the British Library

ISBN: 978-1-913825-56-0

Typeset in Palatino Lynotype by ORP Cambridge
Cover designed by ORP Cambridge
Cover photo and frontispiece: *An Allegory with Venus and Cupid* by Bronzino
(1503–1572), painted about 1545 in oil on wood (146.5 x 116.8 cm),
reproduced with permission from The National Gallery.

For further information visit: www.pagedor.co.uk

Ad infinitum et ultra.

An Allegory with Venus and Cupid
by Bronzino (1503–1572)

Preface

This painting, which is now in the National Gallery under the title *An Allegory with Venus and Cupid*, has been, and still is, known by many other names. Its original name, if it ever had one, is not known.

Painted in Florence, in 1544, it is one of the earliest examples of the artistic style called 'Mannerism', and was presented to King François I of France as a diplomatic gift. After various travels over the centuries, it was purchased by the National Gallery in 1860. At some earlier time, it had been bowdlerised with various decorous overpaintings of its most explicit details, and was not fully revealed until 1958.

King François, like his contemporary Henry VIII, was a cultured and educated king. He might have found it easier than we do to work out the meanings of the various allegorical figures in the painting. Many interpretations have been offered over the centuries, some of them almost as bizarre as the painting itself.

My narrator Giuseppe's view of Bronzino is a narrow one, seen by a teenage boy of limited horizons and intelligence. Anyone who wants to learn more about Bronzino should read his biography in Vasari's Lives of the Artists.

Pontormo did keep a diary, and the surviving extracts are just as odd as the fictional entries I have made up in this story. Bronzino, Pontormo, Duke Cosimo de' Medici, and

Baccio Bandinelli and his son Clemente were real people. Every other character is imaginary, but Father 'Fleccia' appears under his English name of Father Ralph Fletcher as the main character of my novel *Forty Testoons*, which tells the story of his winter in the island of 'Terra Nuova' (Newfoundland).

I would like to thank the following people for their invaluable help during the preparation of the original edition of *Cupid and the Silent Goddess*: from the National Gallery, Lucy Harmer, who was the Information Desk Manager; Dr. Nicholas Penny, then the Curator of the painting; and in particular Carol Plazzotta, Assistant Curator, who supplied me with the results of her latest research into how the painting was made; the Bronzino scholar Dr. Deborah Parker of the University of Virginia; and the hairstyles expert Moyra Byford, author of *Hairstyles in History*.

Alan Fisk, 2022.

FIRENZE

1

When I was a young man, King François of France greatly admired my bare buttocks. I have that information only by hearsay, of course, because my buttocks were in the king's château of Chambord while I was here in Italy.

None of that would ever have happened if Duke Cosimo de' Medici of Florence had not caught me naked in my master's studio on the hot afternoon of Wednesday the 21st of May, 1544.

I had been modelling for a study which my master was making. He was beginning to transform a vision in his mind into a painting on wood or canvas, and had made me stand in a contorted and painful pose for an hour after lunch. When my master decided to stop work and join the rest of the city in its heavy afternoon sleep, he did not give me leave to sleep as well. He let me relax from my painful Classical posture and stretch my twisted limbs, and then, once he had relieved me of the task of being a model, he sent me back to my tasks as his apprentice.

'The last layer of gesso should be dry by now, Giuseppe,' he told me.

'You may now apply the first layer of *gesso sottile*. Keep the door closed so that the smell doesn't wake me up.'

He turned his dark staring eyes away from me and strode off to his bedroom as stiffly and smartly as one of the Duke's soldiers marching in a parade. I heard him collapse

1

onto his bed with a long sigh, and then he was silent. He could fall asleep instantly, like a cat. I took out the bucket and spatula, and began mixing the plaster with the glue to form more gesso. My job was to apply it to a rectangular wooden panel, upon which my master was going to paint his next picture. Because of the heat, and because I believed that I was the only human being still awake in all of Florence, I did not bother to dress again.

The smell of the liquid gesso beat back the smells of the city, which were trying to force their way in through the open window. As I began to apply the first layer of *gesso sottile* to the panel, I was nearly gagging from the stink of the glue. It is made by boiling down the coarsest parts of dead animals. One of the first lessons I had learned as a painter's apprentice was that great art is often begun by handling low and humble substances. The sculptors must often feel this. They create the most elegant and graceful statues by hammering away in clouds of dust like common labourers, which, indeed, some painters consider them to be.

I was pondering these elevated matters while my afore-mentioned bare buttocks slowly heated up and moistened with sweat in a shaft of cruel sunlight that was shining upon them. Suddenly, I heard the street door on the floor below being wrenched open, taking the strong iron bolt with it. I then heard the sound of boots and men's voices coming up the stairs, at a time of day when neither footsteps nor voices should be heard.

Duke Cosimo believed in the sanctity of the afternoon siesta. He had been known to have a man publicly caned for tuning a lute at an open window during the hours set aside for the siesta, and quite rightly too, I say. Now the door to the studio opened. I found myself facing two of the

Duke's personal guards in their distinctive uniforms and helmets, while they found themselves looking at a naked, curly-haired youth holding a bucket of something white and stinking in one hand, and a spatula in the other. The two guards said nothing, so I spoke first, in a compulsion to explain myself.

'I'm applying a layer of gesso to this panel so my master can paint a picture on it,' I said.

'We don't care what you're doing,' one of the guards replied. 'The Duke has come to see Bronzino. Where is he?'

Everyone called my master 'Bronzino', meaning 'the little bronze man'. He always used it himself, and had done so since he was a boy.

'My master is asleep,' I replied, putting down my bucket and spatula. 'I'll wake him.'

'No need,' said my master from inside his bedroom. He spoke the words wearily, as though he were continuing the long-measured sigh with which he had abandoned himself to sleep. Bronzino came out into the studio looking as tidy and composed as if he had been waiting within for an hour for just such a call. They called him 'the little bronze man' because he was short and had a dark, swarthy skin. I had always suspected that he had Moorish or Jewish blood, but I had never dared to say so.

Now we heard two more men coming up the stairs. The first man of the pair was hurrying. I guessed that it was another ducal guard, and I was right. The guard snapped to attention as soon as he was inside the studio door, and, staring over our heads, announced:

'His Grace Duke Cosimo of Florence!'

The other set of footsteps, slow and deliberate, approached the top of the stairs. The first two guards had also come to attention. Bronzino was standing in a civilian

3

position of respect, with his arms clasped behind his back. As for myself, I, like our ancestor Adam after the Fall of Man, became unbearably aware of my nudity.

The Duke of Florence, disguised in the uniform of his own guards, stepped round the door and joined us in the now overcrowded room. He took off his helmet. As always whenever I saw him, I noticed the wart on his left cheek, and the way that every whisker in his beard was immaculately in place. He had all the manners and carriage of a natural ruler. He ignored the heat and smells of the room, he ignored his guards, and he ignored me as if he saw naked youths every day. There are men in Florence who do.

'Bronzino,' he said in that voice of his that somehow absorbed your attention entirely so that you forgot all other sounds, 'I want you to paint me a picture. I know that you will have questions.'

'It is not for me to question my Duke,' Bronzino replied.

'Then I will put your questions to myself on your behalf,' Duke Cosimo declared. 'First of all: why has the Duke come to your house instead of summoning you to the Palazzo della Signoria?'

'It is a remarkable honour,' Bronzino replied.

'No, it isn't,' Duke Cosimo retorted. 'I pay honour only to God, to the Pope, and to the Holy Roman Emperor. I am a duke, and I expect to receive honour, not to bestow it. I am here not to honour you but because this is a matter of secrecy.'

'I am nevertheless glad that you should judge me reliable at keeping secrets,' Bronzino replied.

If indeed there was ever a man to whom you could entrust the most valuable and weighty of secrets, it was the silent and impassive Bronzino. I was one of only three citizens of Florence outside the Palazzo who knew that Bronzino had painted a nude picture of Duke Cosimo as Orpheus. I never found out why the Duke had commissioned that secret painting, and I was certainly not going to ask him.

'You had better keep my secret,' Duke Cosimo told him, 'or I'll have you flung alive into the river Arno without your skin.' There could be no answer to that, so Bronzino said nothing, and the Duke continued.

'I have decided to send a diplomatic gift to King François of France,' he announced. 'The gift is to be a painting, and I have chosen you to execute it.'

'I am at your service,' Bronzino replied.

'No, you are in my service,' the Duke corrected him, 'as my court painter. If you please me in this task, I may consider formally appointing you to that title. You will finish this painting within the next four months.'

'What is to be the subject?' Bronzino asked.

I had thought that the post of court painter which he held, although unofficially, was almost a title of nobility, but now I saw that Duke Cosimo regarded Bronzino as simply a particularly skilled servant, like a musician or a cook.

'The subject?' Duke Cosimo exclaimed. 'I have not thought of one in detail. I leave that to you, but it is to be a Classical subject. I thought of a mythological scene, or perhaps one with Classical figures.'

The Duke looked at me. I became conscious of the sweat that was trickling all down my body. I could not have been the only one in that crowded studio who was sweating in the gloomy and breathless heat, but all the others were fully dressed. They must have been sweating more, but they were showing it less. Duke Cosimo looked powerful enough to stop his body from doing anything as gross as sweating. The three guards looked as though they would not sweat unless they were ordered to. Bronzino always looked as though he was too refined to put out any kind of body product whatsoever. Now the Duke turned his attention to me.

'I may have a use for this creature. Who is he?'

My sweat seemed to turn into the rushing torrents that one sees plunging down the mountainsides around Lake Garda. Even the three guards could not prevent their eyes from widening. The Duke was a harsh man, but nobody had ever accused him of perversion: he had the sins of great men, not the mere vices of petty men. Bronzino answered him with his customary assured politeness.

'This is my apprentice, Giuseppe. In what way may he serve you?'

Bronzino was such a dry man that I am still wondering whether his offer was meant as a lewd joke. Then again, until I met Duke Cosimo, I had never grasped the real meaning of the expression 'not a man to be trifled with'.

'Does he model for you as well?' Duke Cosimo demanded.

'Why, yes.' Bronzino replied. 'In fact, he –'

'Good. He'll do,' the Duke decided.

'Do for what, Your Grace?' Bronzino asked with a bluntness which was quite uncharacteristic of him.

'For the painting, damn you!' the Duke shouted. 'Am I served only by idiots? You must use him as a model. He can model for Cupid.'

'Cupid?' Bronzino asked. 'Do you not think him somewhat too old –'

'Will you shut up and let me give you my orders without interruption?' the Duke bellowed. 'I leave the design of the painting up to you, but it must have something to do with

Cupid. There you are. There's your Cupid.'

'Your Grace shall have his painting incorporating Cupid,' Bronzino said. 'Are there any other specifications?'

'Just make it a fine and beautiful painting, fit to be presented to a king,' the Duke told him. 'This is to be kept a secret, do you understand? Make sure that your Cupid here understands that too, or he'll be modelling for St. Sebastian, out in the piazza.'

'I believe that Giuseppe understands,' Bronzino replied, and Giuseppe certainly did. I had no doubt that Duke Cosimo really would have me shot full of arrows like St. Sebastian if he were to suspect me of giving away the secret of the painting.

'My chamberlain will send for you when I have time to give you an appointment to discuss this further,' the Duke informed Bronzino. He beckoned to his guards. 'Come on, I'm going back to the Palazzo. I've given up my siesta for this. So have you. So has Bronzino,' the Duke added, as he stepped out and went down the stairs. As he was descending the staircase, we heard his voice again. 'Only Cupid has not given up his siesta! Try to find the allegorical meaning of that, Bronzino!'

The street door slammed shut like a thunderclap, shaking the house.

Obviously at least one of the guards had forgotten that they had smashed the bolt off it.

'Cupid never sleeps,' Bronzino said, apparently to himself. I looked at him, waiting for his orders. 'Well?' Bronzino responded. 'Why are you staring at me? Mix up the *gesso sottile* again, and get back to what you were told to do. I'm going back to bed.'

By the time I had begun preparing the gesso again, Bronzino was already asleep once more. As I spread the *gesso sottile* slowly and carefully over the coarser, earlier layers of gesso, I felt like someone awakening from a dream, still confused over whether the events of the dream are real or not. Had Duke Cosimo really come in person to Bronzino's house, passing in and out like a storm?

As if the Duke had summoned it, a storm was in fact beginning to organise itself in the spring sky. I looked out through the window, which was angled to direct light onto whatever painting Bronzino was working on. The wooden panel that was my task now seemed dark grey as the clouds built up over the valley of the Arno. Thousands of Florentines would be woken from their afternoon slumbers by the first clap of thunder, and I hoped that Bronzino would be, too. He slept through the storm, of course. I had to nearly close the window to stop the rain coming into the studio. That made the room even more hot and stuffy. The stink of the gesso mixture spread from wall to wall like a disease.

When I finished applying the bucket of gesso, the rain was just ending. I flung some clothes onto my wet and clammy body. I may have looked like Cupid, but must have smelled more like the goat-god Pan. I took advantage of Bronzino's continuing unconsciousness to take the bucket down to the well out in the courtyard. There, I rinsed the bucket out and then washed myself down. By the time I had drawn a final bucket of clean water and carried it upstairs, Bronzino had woken up. I found him inspecting my work on the wooden panel.

'You've applied the gesso unevenly,' he informed me. 'Look, here and here. Remember, this is the *gesso sottile*, not the rough gesso foundation. You'll have to plane down the rough spots before you apply the next layer tomorrow.'

I was astonished that he had said nothing about the

Duke's visit, or about the painting that he was going to execute for the king of France.

'Master,' I ventured, 'why do you think the Duke wanted me to be the model for Cupid?'

'Because he evidently thinks that you look like his idea of Cupid,' Bronzino replied.

'I'm too old, Master,' I objected. 'You told him so yourself. I'm seventeen. Cupid is always represented as a small boy.'

'Yes,' Bronzino agreed, 'he is always represented as a small, curly haired boy. You have curly hair. If Cupid were ever to grow up, he would resemble you. You can be the first grown-up Cupid in art. You'll have to be. The Duke has insisted upon Cupid appearing in the painting, and he has insisted upon you being the model.'

'At least I'll be able to model for a real finished painting,' I said, 'instead of only for studies and sketches. I shall appear before a king. Well, the painted image of me will be presented to a king, anyway.'

'Your father told me that you were arrogant, Giuseppe,' Bronzino replied. 'Before you become too pleased with yourself, remember that you are still my apprentice.'

I have to admit that Bronzino treated me no worse than any other Florentine painter or sculptor would have done, and far better than many that I had come to know of. My father was a carpenter of rare skill. He had four sons of whom I was the youngest. I was a burden not only because of my need, like any other boy, for my father to provide me with food, drink, clothes and beatings. My father judged, rightly, that I had no aptitude for carpentry, and he looked out for another calling to which I might be better suited. One day he overheard two of my brothers bullying me because of my liking for drawing. I had found a scrap of wood and a tiny stub of charcoal, and I had drawn a quick portrait of my father's bull-like face upon it. My father flung my two brothers aside in opposite directions, like a pair of quarrelling cats, and picked up the hopeful little drawing.

'Why, Giuseppe, this is me!' he exclaimed. 'Isn't it?' My father went to the ancient bronze mirror into which he never looked. It hung on a neglected wall in a particularly dark corner of our crude little house. My father squinted at the drawing in his hand, and then studied his face in the mirror. He looked back and forth from one of the images to the other, and then proclaimed his judgement. 'It is indeed me, Giuseppe. Would you like to work for a painter?'

'Yes, I would,' I said, although the idea had never occurred to me. The next morning, my father dressed me in the suit of clothes that my oldest brother, then two years dead, had worn at his wedding. (My father had made my brother's shattered widow give them back.) Having dressed me in my brother's clothes, my father took me around the city in search of a painter who wanted an apprentice. I cannot remember how many studios and workshops we visited. Every artist that we called upon told us to try someone else. Even then, I suspected the each of them was giving us the name of someone against whom he held a grudge, in the way that artists and poets all do – except for Bronzino, that is, who never considered any man to be his enemy, or his friend.

All through that day my father kept producing my little wooden drawing to show to another prospect as evidence of my artistic bent. None of them was impressed. They were not seeking a juvenile assistant to train up. They wanted a servant to do the dirty jobs that make art possible. While my father and I were passed around Florence as hastily as two false coins discovered in a purse of ducats, I knew that

I was living through a day that would always matter to me, and that I would never forget it. I certainly never forgot the scene when my father knocked forcefully upon that very door through which Duke Cosimo would make his fateful entrance four years later. A thin, nervous old man opened the door and raised his wiry twitching eyebrows at my father, who responded with his now well-practised flourish of my portrait of him.

'My son drew this picture of me. Will you take him on as an apprentice?'

The old man shook his head. 'I'm not the owner of this studio.'

Another voice interrupted him from above. 'I'll talk to them, Master. I'm coming down.'

Master? If the old man was not the artist, then of whom was he the master? I could not ask him, because he had scuttled indoors, and a short, dark-complexioned man with great deep eyes came to the door.

Although I did not know it at that moment, the ancient man who had first answered us was in fact then only forty-six years old.

'Are you Il Bronzino, the artist?' my father inquired.

'I am,' Bronzino replied. 'Is this the boy you are offering?'

'This is my son Giuseppe, Messer Bronzino. He is good at drawing. Look, here's a drawing that he made of me only yesterday.'

Bronzino took the scrap of wood. He held it up to his eyes and peered at it with interest. 'It is a surprisingly good likeness, and done in only a few lines,' he said, 'but I need to know what the boy himself says. Do you really want to learn to be a painter, Giuseppe?'

'Yes, sir, I do,' I replied, and by then it was true. I had had time to imagine the other alternatives which fate might choose to present to me, and the life of a painter sounded the most attractive of the possibilities.

Bronzino spotted that my interest was real. 'It can be hard, you know,' he warned me. 'I shall require you to do all kinds of unpleasant jobs preparing materials for me. I shall also require you to help with all the domestic tasks, because there are no women in this house.' That statement was another warning, of which I failed to grasp the meaning, because I was so eager to be accepted. Because I had no experience then of the life of an artist in Florence, I did not know that Bronzino should already have had other apprentices serving in his studio.

'I would be glad to serve you, sir,' I replied.

'Good!' Bronzino responded. 'I myself served as an apprentice to the distinguished painter Jacopo da Pontormo. He is the gentleman who first appeared at the door to you. I therefore stand here as proof that a boy can survive his apprenticeship to a painter.'

My father, who probably did not care whether I survived or not, provided he got rid of me, was desperate to strike an agreement with Bronzino. 'I commend my son to you, Messer Bronzino,' he declared.

'Then please come inside the house so that we can discuss the arrangements,' Bronzino replied. 'Giuseppe, please wait here until you are called for.'

Bronzino took my father into the house, and closed the door, leaving me in the sunlight of the street, hot and uncomfortable in my late brother's heavy best clothes. I did not feel any nervousness about my apprenticeship. At that moment, I was more worried about my personal safety. I might be robbed and murdered only for my clothes. It has happened many times on the streets of Florence. I looked around for possible assailants, but I was alone. I wondered who lived in the houses nearby. It was obvious that some of the buildings belonged to shopkeepers, because of the shutters that were pulled down over their counters. At least one was inhabited by lazy servants, because a collection of long-dry washing hung from the poles that must have been thrust out of the windows early that morning. I could see no other clues to who my new neighbours were to be.

Bronzino's door opened again, and my father strode out happily into the sunshine. 'Signor Bronzino has agreed to take you on, Giuseppe,' he said. 'You are very lucky. Be a good boy, and work hard.'

With that, my father turned from me without waiting for a reply, and strolled away, tossing up and catching my little wooden sketch which he still held in his hand. He walked off along the shady side of the street, tossing up and catching that little piece of wood over and over again. As it rose to the top of its trajectory, it escaped from the shade and caught the sunlight, so that it glinted for a moment like a star before it fell back again.

I wish I had kept that first crude drawing, because it was that last time that I ever saw my father, and I never heard from him or my brothers again. I could have found my way back to our house at any time, of course, and knocked on the door, but I never did. I would walk the long way round rather than pass down our street. One thing upon which my father and I were in complete agreement was that there was no bond between us.

My new family had already gathered to welcome me. Bronzino and Pontormo drew me inside, and led me up to the studio which was to be the very centre of my life for years to come. Bronzino began with a few basic instructions for me. 'You are to call me Master. I will see that you are properly enrolled as an apprentice in the records of the

Guild of St. Luke, to which all we painters are unfortunately forced to belong.'

Pontormo spoke to me for the first time. 'Damn the Guild of St. Luke! Damn them all! Except for the painters, of course, but damn the physicians and the apothecaries!'

Bronzino interrupted him. 'Those are the same curses that you made when you took me on as an apprentice, Master,' Bronzino said. 'I had no idea then what you were talking about.'

'Pill-rollers!' Pontormo replied.

Bronzino ignored him, and gave me the explanation that Pontormo had obviously failed to give him when Bronzino had been a puzzled boy like myself. 'The Guild of St. Luke comprises physicians, apothecaries and painters, Giuseppe. The connection is that we all use the pestle and mortar. I hope you have had enough religious education to know that St. Luke is the patron saint of physicians.'

'Damn them, too,' commented Pontormo.

'It is the dream shared by nearly all the painters in Florence,' Bronzino continued, serenely ignoring Pontormo, 'that one day we shall escape from the Guild. Being members of the Guild keeps us in the social status of craftsmen. We hope that one day we will be recognised as real artists.'

'He's a poet, too,' Pontormo remarked, and I strained to work out what the point was of his telling me that. 'He didn't learn that from me. He taught poetry-writing to himself.'

'Poets are recognised as artists,' Bronzino explained. 'Painters are not.'

Four years after that first, frightening, exciting, baffling day, I had indeed never forgotten that I was Bronzino's apprentice, as Bronzino had been Pontormo's apprentice. We had worked out a way of living together just as if we had been a real family. Indeed, Pontormo had eventually adopted Bronzino as his son. I learned how to behave to my master, to Pontormo, and to all the important and fascinating guests who came to Bronzino's house. I was taught how to prepare and serve food to painters, sculptors, philosophers, and poets. I was taught how to speak pleasingly when I was spoken to, and how to be agreeably still and silent otherwise. Bronzino kept his undertaking to have me enrolled as an apprentice in the Guild of St. Luke. He had also not been joking about the pestle and mortar, the use of which united us in unwilling brotherhood with the physicians and apothecaries. How I ground that pestle against that mortar, hour after hour, day after day, year after year, grinding up pigments to produce the powder which we mix with oil to make paint. For some kinds of pigment, I had to grind one kind of stone upon another, kneeling as if in prayer. I suppose it helped to develop my muscles. Every painter in Florence made his paints himself, or, at least, his tired and perspiring apprentices did so. The mortar had deep grooves like plough-banks, no doubt bored out by Bronzino when he had been Pontormo's apprentice, and perhaps even by Pontormo when he had spent a brief and unhappy apprenticeship with Andrea del Sarto. The only colours that are bought ready-made are a few very rare and expensive ones, such as ultramarine blue. Ultramarine blue comes from somewhere in Asia, far away along the Silk Road, and quite literally costs as much as gold. Although Pontormo spent so much of his time at Bronzino's house that he seemed to live there, he had a house of his own that I had never seen.

As my growth and education proceeded, I began to grasp

my lost father's reasoning in finding an apprenticeship for me. He knew that, under the close tutoring of Bronzino, I would be trained fully in painting and sodomy; for, after all, as my father would have known, every man without private means should learn a trade that is universally recognised and always in demand. It was, I am sure, not with such thoughts in his mind that Bronzino looked me over as the model who had been forced upon him at Duke Cosimo's command to represent Cupid. God knows, as did our corrupt parish priest, that Bronzino could not have been more familiar already with my body. It is almost a tradition in Florence that painters and sculptors used their apprentices so. I had been shocked and terrified the first time that Bronzino had seized me in the night, with astonishing force and roughness for such a controlled and quiet man. I knew at once what he wanted, and that I would have to submit. When Bronzino had finished, he returned to his own bed and left me aching, bleeding and appalled. When I became accustomed to his assaults, they no longer hurt me so much. But one thing never changed. Bronzino always left me on my own afterwards, to clean myself up while he fell asleep at once in that feline way of his. He never spent the whole night with me, but he often did so with Pontormo when he was staying with us. Bronzino also never spoke to me of what we did together. It was as if these shameful acts were no part of our life, but happened instead in a special separate realm of which we know nothing, just as sleepwalkers know nothing of where they are or what they are doing.

I always confessed to our priest. He listened in bored silence, and always prescribed light penances. He made the ritual demand of me that I should avoid that sin in future, and I always promised to try to do so, but we both knew that I would be back in confession again telling the same story. My sins against nature recurred as regularly and unstoppably as the feast days of the saints. The priest was as lazy and slovenly as the servants in that house across the street, the ones who always hung the household linen up to dry late and brought it in again late.

Bronzino, in spite of his natural grace, was not a lazy man. He worked hard and incessantly, so that I did not greatly resent the way that he made me work long and hard as well. After he had given me his instructions on how I was to plane down the wooden panel in his studio, and re-apply the gesso where I had put it on too thickly, Bronzino stepped back across the room and gazed at the blank panel as though there were already a picture painted on it.

'Yes, Giuseppe,' he murmured, 'be sure to do a good job preparing this panel. You will appear on it, after all. Would you like the smoothness of your body to be disfigured by a lump of excess gesso somewhere?'

'Will you be using this particular panel for the Duke's painting, then?' I asked.

My reaction was not out of artistic interest in the project. I was frightened by the responsibility of preparing the panel for Bronzino's painting. The Duke knew very well that it was I who was doing the job. If he found some blemish in the final painting which could be traced to my faulty application of the *gesso sottile*, I would be for it. I did not know what 'it' was, but it would certainly be painful. My body would definitely not be fit to represent Cupid after the Duke's bullies and torturers had finished with me.

Bronzino continued to contemplate the blank panel. 'Yes,' he affirmed, 'such a painting will make a splendid diplomatic gift. The Duke will want to impress King François.'

Down below, I heard the door swing open once more. Surely it could not be Duke Cosimo again? I knew who it was when I heard the sound of a body falling against the tread of the staircase, followed by breathless curses. Bronzino smiled like one of those court portraits he often painted: a subtle smile that was almost a threat. 'That is my master Pontormo,' he said. 'No other man habitually falls up stairs instead of down them.'

2

After supper, Bronzino and Pontormo talked together far into the night. They both ignored me while I served them and cleaned up the house. Afterwards, I sat on a stool in front of the wooden panel which was slowly drying in the humid evening air. I lit two candles, which attracted the insects who dropped in inquisitively through the open window. I knew that one of my tasks the next morning would be to remove the tiny carcasses of the moths and midges which had alighted on the sticky gesso.

For the moment, I had nothing to do but sit and listen. Bronzino showed unusual animation as he expressed his worries about the commission that Duke Cosimo had given him. 'He wants a subject involving Cupid,' Bronzino said, 'and with a grown-up Cupid as well. It has never been done before.'

'This is the age of novelty,' Pontormo replied. 'You don't need to be apprehensive about producing something new.'

'Where can I find a subject for an adult Cupid?' Bronzino wondered.

'If only I knew what Cupid is to signify to King François. Why does our Duke want to send him a picture of Cupid?'

'Perhaps it is to be a scene of love,' Pontormo suggested.

'No,' Bronzino replied, 'the Duke would have told me that. He always demands of me that I shall produce what he wants, but he never tells me plainly what that is.'

'It is his way of ruling Florence,' Pontormo said. 'He never reveals himself. That's how he keeps everyone afraid of him. He shows only his implacable will. That's how he has brought peace and order to the city.'

'Well, he's created war and disorder in my mind,' Bronzino responded. 'He's never wanted a Classical picture from me before.'

'The picture isn't for him, but for the king of France,' Pontormo pointed out. 'The Duke doesn't want it for himself.'

'Why a Classical allegory?' Bronzino wondered again. 'He likes the way I do portraits of him and of his family. Sometimes he wants religious paintings.'

'You're no good at religious paintings,' Pontormo told him.

Pontormo often spoke to Bronzino as if Bronzino were still an apprentice, even though he knew I could hear.

'I'm not interested in religious paintings,' Bronzino admitted, 'but the Duke accepts my efforts. I'm still his unofficial court painter.'

'Many painters in Florence and elsewhere envy you for that,' Pontormo said.

'And I envy them,' Bronzino replied, 'because they never have to worry about having to meet the Duke's requirements.'

'They still have to paint what their patron orders them to paint,' Pontormo said. 'No painter can paint whatever subject he chooses. No painter can paint only to please himself.'

'Well, then,' Bronzino exclaimed, 'I must have Cupid in my picture. What can he be doing? Who else is to be in the painting? Giuseppe, go down to the well and draw us some water to drink. It's hot tonight.'

'Water, Master?' I asked. 'Not wine?'

'When I call for water, I mean water!' Bronzino snapped.

I went out into the courtyard to draw the water. While I was down there, I checked the wine stores in the cellar. We still had plenty, so I drank some myself before I brought a jug of water up to Bronzino. I poured out the water as ceremoniously as if it had been wine. Some say that the water from the wells and from the river Arno makes you ill, but Bronzino, Pontormo and I often drank it, and it never harmed us. Bronzino drank a cupful, and then asked me a question.

'Giuseppe, what are the attributes of Cupid?'

'Wings, Master,' I replied, 'and a bow and arrow.'

'We can't avoid the bow and arrow,' Bronzino said, 'but it will be difficult to give you a pair of wings that won't look ridiculous.'

Pontormo offered a suggestion. 'You could make the wings much larger than on a traditional Cupid. You could make them big enough for Cupid to fly with.'

'No,' Bronzino said, 'because then they would become the dominant feature of the painting. What's more, if Cupid had great wings like that, he would appear frightening.'

'Perhaps that could be your theme,' Pontormo said. 'After all, we all fear love.'

I know that in those days I certainly feared love. It made my bowels ache for days afterwards.

'An adult Cupid, with mighty wings, representing the terror of love, might make an arresting picture,' Bronzino conceded, 'but I'm sure that the Duke does not want to send King François a warning against love.'

Bronzino thought in silence for a few moments, and then he seemed to be struck by an idea. 'Love, though, that's the theme,' he decided. 'I can fill the painting with figures representing the joys of love, and the pain and terror, too.'

'You should spend most of your time planning the design,' Pontormo instructed him, reverting to the master–apprentice roles that they had played for so long.

'I must consult the poets,' Bronzino declared.

'You're a poet yourself,' Pontormo reminded him. 'Anyway, you're composing a painting, not a poem.'

'Yes,' Bronzino replied, 'but I need suggestions for the Classical figures to choose to represent all the emotions of love.'

'You cannot possibly show all the emotions of love in one single painting!' Pontormo protested. He and Bronzino went into the longest and most argumentative discussion fuelled by water that I have ever heard. By now I was becoming tired. The physical exhaustion of all the work I had done that day was overcoming the nervous tension caused by the Duke's visit. When the conversation paused for a moment, while I served more plain water, I asked permission from Bronzino to be allowed to go to bed, which he granted with a nod.

I climbed up to the little corner under the roof that I called my own. Bronzino had taken me up to it on the day when I had first arrived, and I was still sleeping there four years later. Why should he have moved me, after all? Those who think it romantic to live an artistic life in a garret have never experienced it. Being directly under the roof meant that I was hot all through the spring and summer, and cold during the days of snow and bitter winds.

Yes, I thought, as I undressed and lay down on my wide bed (Bronzino had bought it as its second or third owner, and it had been made for some unknown married couple), I spent every night in contact with the heavens that sailed over the city of Florence. When it rained, I was the first to hear the drops of water drumming on the roof like a thousand little angry fists demanding entrance. When it was hot, I felt the full force of the sun's power even in the middle of the night long after the sun had set. If it was warm and the weather was clear, I could open the window above me and watch the stars slowly turn, and wonder why the moon never, ever, shone through my window.

Sometimes I would wake up late in the morning, and have my dreams interrupted by the cry of the first sellers of provisions coming down our street. I would have to rush down to the studio, snatch up the coins that Bronzino set out every night for just that purpose, and lower them in the basket which hung beside the window. If I had only just woken up, it was difficult for me to find enough voice to shout down my order, so the sellers would guess it, and when I hauled the basket back up it would contain whatever assortment of loaves, fruits, vegetables and meats that those below thought we needed.

The heavenly sounds from above and the earthly sounds from the street were often balanced by hellish sounds from below, whenever Pontormo or some other close friend spent the night with Bronzino. On that night after the Duke's visit, I was not surprised to be kept awake by the noises of abominable and unnatural vice coming from the room under the floor, followed by hurried and agitated conversation.

I was surprised on that occasion to hear the intense talk, with words that were too muffled to make out, being followed by frantic weeping and the sound of a soothing, compassionate voice. Who was doing the weeping, and who was doing the comforting? I never found out.

This, then, is the life of a painter's apprentice in Florence:

to be a domestic servant, to spread gesso on wood and canvas, and to be sodomised by his master. It has been like that for hundreds of years, and will no doubt be so for hundreds of years more.

That morning, after Pontormo had returned to his own house, Bronzino seemed to have forgotten that he was a painter. He had fallen into one of those moods when he was interested only in poetry. I had expected him to order me to do more work on preparing that panel. The work is so monotonous because the final result must be as monotonous as possible. It must be perfectly flat, perfectly white, and with no features at all. Instead, Bronzino told me to collect together as many scraps of old paper as I could find about the house.

I came upon a dozen pieces of paper, all torn, and all having been brought into the house to serve some other purpose. I brought Bronzino the backs of bills that he had never got around to paying, rude ballads that had been sung under our windows and that Bronzino had sent me to buy so that he could sing them, too, and irregularly shaped sheets that had already been used a second time to wrap vegetables or blocks of colour that I had had to grind up.

Bronzino was sitting at the table as if for a meal. I served up the pieces of paper as gracefully as I could.

'Excellent!' he declared, taking out a stub of charcoal. 'Now, I am going to start my notes for this painting.' He took one sheet of paper and wrote CUPID upon it. He then took the next sheet from the pile and wrote VENUS on it. He laid the two pieces of paper next to each other on the table.

'The Duke has ordered that Cupid must appear in the painting,' he reminded me. Bronzino now picked up the sheet marked VENUS. 'If there is to be a full-grown Cupid, there must also be a Venus, so that we have a man and a woman. A male God – if Cupid is a god; I suppose he is – and a goddess.'

I thought that Bronzino would begin roughing out some sketches for the poses of Cupid and Venus, but instead he moved the two pieces of paper round and round on the table, like counters in a board game. He looked up at me for a moment, with those dark eyes that you see in the faces of all the subjects of all the formal portraits that he painted. No matter who Bronzino's sitters were, somehow all his portraits came out resembling himself.

'Giuseppe, I must spend more time studying you as a subject. I had never expected to use you as a model for an important painting.'

Another facet of Bronzino's character that you can see in his portraits is his simple directness. He was a surprisingly plain speaker for a poet.

'I will do my best, Master,' I replied.

'No, *I* will do my best, Giuseppe,' Bronzino responded, 'because I'm the one who will set the pose and put you in it. I had to do the same for my own master Pontormo, once.'

One of Pontormo's paintings that I would dearly like to see is called *Joseph in Egypt*. Pontormo placed the boy Bronzino on the steps of a building, with a basket. As I say, I have never seen the painting, but Bronzino often described it to me.

'There I sit for as long as the painting will last,' he had remarked, 'a small dark solemn boy. Nobody will never need to ask why I was nicknamed Il Bronzino if they see that little portrait of me.'

'What will they think I was nicknamed,' I asked him, 'if I go down to posterity represented as a nude Cupid?'

'That is not a question that bothers me,' Bronzino replied,

'any more than Pontormo cared what people thought of me as the boy with a basket.'

We both knew that it was not true. Pontormo was never indifferent to anything. It occurred to me that the painting in which Bronzino had appeared was called *Joseph in Egypt*. Well, I, Giuseppe, am of course a Joseph, too, but I knew that Bronzino's painting, whatever its final title, would not be called *Giuseppe in Florence*, even if that was what it showed.

Bronzino rearranged the two scraps of paper into ever-varying relationships with each other. He muttered to himself. I had already noticed over the years that whenever Bronzino was under stress, he would unconsciously start a restrained imitation of the odd habits of his master Pontormo. Many who knew Bronzino blamed mad old Pontormo for having made Bronzino what he was. He brought the two pieces of paper to a halt, with CUPID on the left and VENUS on the right.

'I have a Cupid, whether or not he is the one I would have chosen myself,' Bronzino said, perhaps to himself, or perhaps to me. 'Now I need a Venus. Oh, if only I had a Simonetta Vespucci!'

Simonetta Vespucci, who had died many years before either Bronzino or Pontormo had been born, was one of Bronzino's great obsessions. She had been the favourite model of the artist Botticelli, even though she belonged to a family of quite high-status merchants. She had been Botticelli's Venus, rising from a giant shell floating upon the waters of the Mediterranean. Botticelli himself had died when Bronzino was seven years old, and so Bronzino had never known him, but Pontormo remembered Botticelli and had often been told, by him and others, of the eerie beauty of Simonetta Vespucci.

'You could hardly believe that she was human,' Pontormo had once told me. 'Such beauty was almost a challenge to God, and yet she was not at all vain or arrogant.'

I wish I had asked Pontormo more about Simonetta Vespucci. She had never lost her beauty until the last few days of her life, because she died of tuberculosis at the age of twenty-four. It is said that nearly the entire population of Florence had turned out to see her funeral procession go by. They had all made the sign of the Cross upon themselves, but nobody had spoken a word. They had all been awed into silence by the knowledge that they had been privileged to see beauty such as had never been seen on Earth before and might never be seen again.

I could not ask Pontormo more about what he had heard about Simonetta Vespucci's funeral, because one of his eccentricities was a terror of death and of anything that reminded him of death. Pontormo often gave offence by not coming to the funerals of deceased friends and patrons. Indeed, the Guild of St. Luke had more than once tried to fine him for it. As he grew older, his friends and patrons aged with him, and more of them were buried without his attendance. Pontormo knew very well that he was expected to come to the funerals, but he just could not bring himself to come. He would walk far out of his way if he saw a funeral cortège approaching. If there were a corpse lying in the street outside the house, he would not come out until it had been removed.

One of the first rules of my apprenticeship that Bronzino had imposed upon me was that I must never mention death when Pontormo was around and might hear me. I greatly feared for Pontormo, because one day his own death would inevitably have to come, and I was afraid that when he realised he was meeting death he would experience horror beyond imagining. At least death had not robbed the world completely of the beauty of Simonetta Vespucci. Only a few people will ever be admitted to the private interior palace rooms where her portraits hang, but those few privileged persons at least will know why she was mourned so deeply by all those who had seen her in life. I mischievously reminded Bronzino of that.

'Perhaps you could copy one of the paintings of her by Botticelli or by Piero di Cosimo,' I suggested. 'You could place her in a pose of your own choosing, and so you would have Simonetta Vespucci as your Venus after all.' I expected Bronzino to rise to the bait and reply that the Duke would have him dissected in the piazza for doing such a thing, but his anger came from a completely different direction.

'Work from a copy? Use another man's painting? After four years with me, haven't you noticed that I always work from a live model? You can't create art from another man's art. Botticelli had the real Simonetta Vespucci, damn him, but I must find my own Venus, and I'm not looking for any more stupid suggestions from you.'

'There is no shortage of women in Florence who would be glad to model as Venus,' I said.

'Yes, and there is no shortage of vain young men who would like to model as Cupid,' Bronzino replied. 'I can find a model easily enough. The problem is to know where I can find a woman who can be presented to the king of France as the image of Venus.'

'Surely one of those women who model for artists can do that, Master,' I said. 'This must be the finest city in the world for finding a beautiful female model.'

'Yes, but I don't just need a beautiful woman,' Bronzino retorted. 'I need Venus. I need a woman who will pose as Venus, not one who just wants to show herself off.'

That was perhaps the only criticism one might have made of the late Simonetta Vespucci, for whom Bronzino yearned with such hopeless desperation. In all the paintings of her, one does not see Venus or Roxana or whatever figure she is representing. One sees the fascinating Simonetta Vespucci herself. I offered another suggestion that I hoped Bronzino would listen to, because I meant it seriously.

'Perhaps a sculptor's model would be better,' I began. 'When you see a sculpture, it never seems to represent the character of the model. The David of Michelangelo is only David. You never find yourself wondering who the model was.'

'Yes, I've even forgotten his name,' Bronzino replied. 'I'm told that he was stupid and brutal. A sculptor's model won't do, though. I'm a painter. I work in only two dimensions. I'm used to creating the illusion of a scene on a flat surface. Sculptors use three dimensions to represent reality.'

'You must find *someone* to represent Venus,' I said unnecessarily.

'Thank you for stating the obvious,' Bronzino replied. 'I shall just have to consider all the models in the city until I find one who will have to do.'

I thought that he, too, was stating the obvious, but I knew that even after four years of apprenticeship there were limits to how much I could get away with in arguing with my master. He still sat at the table, fiddling annoyingly with the pieces of paper.

Since Bronzino seemed to have nothing further to say to me, or to himself, I went back to mixing gesso for the panel, in the hope that the smell would drive him away. I had already resolved to do as good a job as I could on the panel. This might be my only appearance in a painting in my life, just as Bronzino, as far as I know, appears only in Pontormo's *Joseph in Egypt*. In that painting, Bronzino is preserved for ever as a young boy. I would be preserved for ever as a youth of seventeen or eighteen, and my painted image would never become old or fat or bald, no matter what ugly transformations the years might wreak upon my real body.

Bronzino still found daily fault with my work, and made me do it again to his satisfaction, but then, that was his duty as my master in the Guild of St. Luke.

Unusually, Pontormo did not appear at our house for several days. I wondered whether he and Bronzino had not had some sort of quarrel on that night when one of them had wept in the other's arms, or whether Pontormo had fallen ill. He often became sick, because he took no care of himself. He would not employ a servant, because it would mean allowing someone else into his house, and he had never taken on another apprentice after Bronzino. I believe that Pontormo would have died of malnutrition in his forties if it had not been for the meals that I served to him at Bronzino's house. Posterity will owe much of Pontormo's life's work to me for having kept him alive, and posterity will never know.

Duke Cosimo must have passed the word around the great families of Florence that Bronzino was working on an important painting for him, and was not available for lesser work. We knew that, because no servants and messengers arrived with invitations for Bronzino to come to dinner at some grand palazzo. It had become a point of prestige among the noble families and the grand merchants (who would become the noble families of the next generation) to have a son or daughter sit for one of Bronzino's cool and elegant portraits. Such commissions must have made Bronzino so rich that he could have bought a palazzo himself, instead of living in the comfortable but ordinary town house that we inhabited. He could also well have afforded more than one servant, because in reality that was what I was.

My life lacked money but not achievement. The gesso always ended up glowing white and perfectly flat, the house had no rats or spiders in most of the rooms, and I always hoisted our laundry over the street to dry hours before those slovenly people in the house opposite.

One evening after supper Bronzino gave me an unexpected order.

'Giuseppe, prepare a lantern and fetch my cloak. We're going to Pontormo's house.'

'Is that safe, Master?' I asked. I was tired from the day's work, and had been hoping to go to bed.

'Of course it's not safe!' Bronzino replied. 'That's why I'm taking you with me.'

I lit the lantern, put on my own cloak and put Bronzino's cloak across his shoulders. The Duke had granted Bronzino one of the special licences which a citizen of Florence had to possess in order to be out in the streets after curfew. Bronzino and I both buckled on our swords. He had paid for me to have the basic lessons in the use of the sword that every man must have if he wants to survive in the streets of Florence even by day, but I was not at all happy to face the night. I closed all the windows, in spite of the heat. It might delay any thieves who wanted to break in, although I am sure that word had got around the guild of thieves that there was nothing of value to be stolen from Bronzino's house. He kept nearly all his money with the goldsmiths, not at home.

As soon as we stepped out into the sticky blackness of the May night, all the mosquitoes in Florence rose up in a whining cloud from the river Arno and droned towards my lantern. The mosquitoes saw Bronzino and myself as a pair of walking feasts, and Bronzino cursed and slapped so loudly as we proceeded through the streets that voices from darkened windows told him with equal rudeness to be quiet. Bronzino should really have been carrying the lantern himself, because he was the one who knew the way. He gave curt directions such as 'Left, now, and watch out for the drain'.

He paused for another slap and oath, which were the last rites for yet another mosquito despatched out of this world. Those who did not know Bronzino well would be astonished that such a cultured man could swear like an Arno boatman. The lantern did not cast its light very far, and I was glad of Bronzino's curses. They mostly drowned out the terrifying sounds of muttering and rasped breathing which came out of dark corners as we passed. I did not fear spirits and demons, but I knew that there were savage and evil men out in the blinded city with us.

Terrible deeds of violence are done every day in Florence in the sunniest of light. Far worse is done by night. Bronzino suddenly announced that we had arrived, and he snatched the lantern away from me, waving it from side to side in front of Pontormo's badly fitting door as though the door itself had eyes to see it.

'Master!' he called out. 'Are you there? It's Bronzino.'

I wondered whether Pontormo had always called my master Bronzino, perhaps from the moment when that small dark-complexioned boy was first brought to him as a prospective apprentice. I heard sounds of shuffling and growling from within, as though we had disturbed a ferocious animal. While Bronzino continued to swing the lantern back and forth, I took advantage of the shifting pools of light that it cast upon the wall to try to make out details of Pontormo's house.

All Florentine houses, except for those of the rich and the great, have little to show from the outside, but what I could see of Pontormo's house was that there was, in fact, nothing to see. The outer walls were rough, and pockmarked with neglect. I did not dare to imagine what the interior might look like. Eventually Pontormo opened the door. I am sure that he would have opened it to no other man but Bronzino. The Pope or the Holy Roman Emperor or even Duke Cosimo would have knocked and shouted in vain.

'What do you want?' Pontormo demanded. He appeared even more unwell than he usually did, probably from having forgotten about meals.

'I want you to help me, Master,' Bronzino replied. 'Please come home with us. I will have Giuseppe prepare you a good supper.' So much for my hopes for an early night in my upstairs room under the stars. Pontormo stepped out and locked his front door behind him. He did not need to fetch or pack anything. Bronzino handed the lantern back to me. 'Walk behind us, Giuseppe,' he ordered, 'but make sure that the way in front is well lit.'

We all set off along the street. It was less frightening than the way out had been, because Bronzino and Pontormo chattered loudly to each other, so that I could hardly hear the alarming noises from the shadows. I could even hardly hear the abuse that they received from householders who wanted silence under their windows.

Bronzino kept expressing his fears about the painting to be sent to King François.

'All I've been told is that it must include Cupid,' he said.

'If the Duke doesn't like the picture, I'll lose my position as official painter to the whole Medici family.'

'You don't hold any such position,' Pontormo reminded him.

'Well, everyone thinks I do,' Bronzino replied. 'If the Duke stops employing me, what will I do then? Become a jobbing painter in some little town up in the mountains, painting formula religious scenes and portraits of tradesmen and their wives?'

'Many live happily doing just that,' Pontormo said, but he must have known that Bronzino could never have lived happily anywhere but in Florence. If he had had to leave Florence permanently, he would have had to give up painting and find another occupation. With his natural cool bearing, Bronzino would have made a fine major-domo in a noble's palazzo. Alternatively, he could have become a procurer of beautiful boys for gentlemen with lewd tastes. Either way, I am sure that he would have been a success and never felt any shame.

Bronzino repeated what he had said when Pontormo had come to the door. 'I want your help, Master. I want your ideas and advice. You are still my teacher, and more skilled and accomplished than I am.'

That was not true. Everyone rated Bronzino above Pontormo as a painter. Even Pontormo knew it, and, being Pontormo, he did not care. Pontormo was doubtful that he could give much assistance.

'Allegories on Classical subjects are not what I do best,' he protested. 'I'm a religious painter more than anything.'

This was really the opposite of Bronzino, who always did better with Classical subjects and with his formal portraits. His religious pictures never quite worked, possibly because he had no natural passion in his character, while

Pontormo probably had too much. Their conversation was enlivened with much arm-waving, most of which was to slap mosquitoes.

To my great relief, we arrived back at Bronzino's house, still alive, uninjured and unrobbed. I set to work making the supper that Bronzino had promised to Pontormo, while Bronzino continued to worry aloud about what he was going to do to carry out the Duke's commission. Just as I put the meal on the table, Pontormo lost patience with his former apprentice.

'Stop complaining to me about your problems with this painting!' he squeaked. 'You're worried about only one thing: who's going to be your Venus. All right. You asked for my help. All right, I'll give you my help.'

Pontormo was not angry enough to abstain from eating his supper while he continued his lecture.

'Tomorrow morning, we'll go out and look in all the places where we might find a model. We won't stop until we find her. Then you'll be able to start work.'

'Are we going to search all over Florence, then?' Bronzino demanded.

'Yes,' Pontormo replied, 'and then we'll search in Pisa, and in Bologna, and in Rome. Take some money with you in case we have to stay in inns and in case we need to travel. We won't return to this house until we've found a model for your Venus.'

For the first time Bronzino noticed my presence at the table. I was standing silently but attentively behind Pontormo, as an efficient servant should when he is waiting upon a guest at a meal.

'My master is right, Giuseppe,' Bronzino said, holding out his cup for me to fill with wine. 'He's deduced the problem and found the solution. I hope I can be half as good a master to you as he has been to me. Pontormo arranges my life in the same way that he composes a painting.'

I refrained from expressing my immediate thought that a life composed by Pontormo would be a disorderly, eccentric and dramatic one, but Pontormo was certainly right about Bronzino needing to remove the block to his painting by finding a model for Venus. Perhaps Pontormo was one of those people who give good advice on other people's lives, but who cannot manage their own. One thinks of the academics who criticise other men's paintings and sculptures, but who could not paint their own front door, or carve a chicken.

Bronzino and Pontormo retired to bed while I washed the dishes.

There was complete silence from Bronzino's bedroom below mine, at least until I fell into a strange blank sleep, so profound and unnatural that I awoke the next morning in the same posture as when I had fallen asleep. I could tell from the strength of the light that it would be a hot day.

The sun, like the moon, never passed over my window. Although all the familiar noises were already busy in the street below, our house was silent. It was as if real life were outside, and that we and our house were only a painting: a painting in the old style of two or three hundred years ago, with dull colours and no perspective.

I went down to the studio, opened the window and emptied the night pot as close as I dared to the loudest voices below. On a whim, I also opened the second window which Bronzino used only when he was painting. He would also set up plain boards covered with pure white *gesso sottile* so as to reflect light back into the shadows. That is why the faces and bodies in his paintings seem to be caught in a soft shadowless light coming from no particular direction.

Just as I had set out the cheese, bread and grapes for breakfast, I heard Bronzino and Pontormo getting up in the other room. They joined me at the table as if I were their host rather than their servant, and took their meal in uncharacteristic silence.

It was Pontormo who finally spoke. In the dusty hush of the house, his voice was like a clap of thunder. 'Giuseppe, lay out your master's clothes, as well as his purse and sword. Close up the house well. We may be out for days.'

When we were all ready, I shut all the windows and threw old sheets over the furniture. After that, Bronzino, Pontormo and I stepped out into the sunlit streets of Florence, which were full as usual of shouts and smells and curses and threats, and we set off to search for the Goddess of Love.

3

Of course, we bypassed the establishments like the one opposite our house, and tried the higher-class brothels first, but we would have had better luck there searching for the God of War, so fierce and hard-eyed were the women. Bronzino looked at them all.

As I say, it was the eyes that were the problem. The women often had surprisingly beautiful bodies. I had expected that they would have sores and spots, but I was struck by the perfection and grace that were put on show for us in one house after another. The proprietors knew very well that Bronzino wanted only to look at the girls, but they must have intended to charge him a high price for looking.

One short dark woman, who had inherited the house from her father, was exasperated by Bronzino's lack of interest. 'What's wrong with my girls?' she demanded. 'Aren't they beautiful enough to sit for a goddess, any one of them?'

Bronzino surveyed the pairs of glittering eyes that were watching him from a dozen lovely, well-proportioned faces, all set upon bodies that were just as perfect. Bronzino sighed, and dismissed the beauties' prospects with a wave of his hand. 'It's the eyes,' he said. 'I need a model who represents Love, not one who looks as though she would slide a dagger between your ribs as soon as you turned your back on her.'

I am surprised that, in the end, Bronzino was never charged for making the girls and their employers get up in the morning, a time that they must ordinarily rarely have seen.

We had wandered into an unfamiliar quarter of Florence. I began to feel that we really would have to go to Pisa, Bologna and Rome, and that we might never come home, wandering for ever in search of a woman who was the perfect embodiment of the Goddess of Love. Well, many men have perished in search of her, but this would have been the first time that three sodomites had done so.

At noon, Bronzino found a tavern and we went in for lunch, more to escape from the hammering heat of the sun than because we were hungry. It was the kind of place where both the owners and the customers are suspicious of you if they do not know you. I was conscious of hostile eyes inspecting us. They reminded me of the eyes of the girls in the brothels, who were no doubt the sisters and daughters of the customers in the tavern. The only way to deal with the lack of welcome was to ignore it, rather than to confront the men and cause a fight that we would certainly lose, and that we might not survive.

Bronzino had been doing more thinking. 'Perhaps what I need is a nun. They don't have those hard eyes.' That intriguing remark attracted the attention of the other drinkers, but we continued to ignore them.

Pontormo dismissed the idea. 'What Mother Superior would allow you to make a nude painting of one of her nuns? Anyway, you'd have to do a lot of washing and shaving before a nun could pose for Venus. They're as hairy as monkeys under their habits.'

Even the tough customers in the tavern did not dare to ask Pontormo how he knew that, but I was convinced that he was right. Pontormo had lived among monks and friars, sometimes for years at a time, and those are the men who would know.

'We've shaved models before,' Bronzino replied.

Indeed, he was quite accomplished at it, and had taught me to shave off all my body hair even before I had exhibited the beginnings of a beard. My hairless condition as Cupid is not my natural state. When I stopped being a model I gratefully gave up shaving, and I was soon covered as God intended, with reddish hair, so that I do look much like a monkey myself.

Pontormo had the final word in the argument. 'The Duke would never allow it. Can you imagine the scandal if he sent a nude Venus to the king of France, and it turned out to be a picture of a nun?'

'From what I hear of King François,' Bronzino replied, 'I think he'd be greatly amused.'

'And from what I hear of Duke Cosimo,' Pontormo retorted, 'he'd be enraged beyond the point of madness. We'd all have to spend the rest of our lives cowering in sanctuary with the Dominicans.'

This was a prospect that I could not face, and I said so. 'I'd rather seek sanctuary with the Franciscans,' I said. 'They're kind and jolly, and friendly.'

'They're popular, too,' Pontormo replied, 'and they want to remain popular with ordinary Florentines, so that they can keep preaching to them. The Franciscans would hand you over to the Dominicans, who would make you spend the rest of your life doing penance for your sins. Bronzino: forget the idea of employing a nun. This business has got you into enough trouble already.'

'And I didn't even volunteer for it,' Bronzino sighed. He pushed aside his empty plate and mug. 'Have we all finished?'

I could tell that he was not his normal self because he paid the bill for us all without arguing over the amount.

When we were out in the street again, we had to pause for a few moments while our eyes adjusted to the blinding early afternoon sunlight. I dared to speak first.

'Where to now, Master?' I asked. 'Do we try more of the brothels?'

'Unless you have a better idea,' Bronzino replied. 'My own master has forbidden me to try the convents.'

Because we did not know that part of the city, we did not know where to find suitable houses, and we had to be careful whom we approached for directions. It takes nice judgement to pick a man out of the passers-by and ask him where in the district one can find a good brothel. There were not many people of any kind to be met with, because sensible citizens were beginning to turn in for their afternoon siesta.

We tried turning left into another street, mainly because it was so narrow that it was almost completely shaded, and so it offered some relief from the sun. After a few steps, I paused to wipe my watering eyes on the sleeve of my sweat-sodden doublet. I blinked two or three times to stop my eyes from stinging, looked up, and found myself confronted by what the poets and prophets tell us about, but which men of our modern times are supposed never to see: a vision.

A young woman with loose hair, and bare arms and shoulders was looking down at us from a window on the top floor. It was not the beauty of her face that rocked me. I have seen beautiful women nearly every day of my life, although few of them have noticed me. The woman of my vision was gazing down with the smallest, the mildest of smiles, the kind of smile that you might fancy you were imagining. But the smile was not for me, nor for Bronzino, nor for Pontormo. It was not even for the otherwise empty street. Who knew for whom or for what she was smiling?

I clutched at Bronzino's sleeve like a small boy. 'Look up, Master! Look up at that woman! Couldn't she be your Venus? She's so beautiful, but with such a gentle face!' By the time I had finished gabbling, Bronzino was no longer listening. He was staring upwards with his hand roofing his eyes, and his jaw open, as I once saw men looking at an eclipse of the sun.

'My God,' he cried. 'Who is she?'

Pontormo had fallen on his threadbare knees, with his head bowed, begging the Virgin to pray for us. As always, he left out 'and in the hour of our death'.

The three of us must have made such a striking tableau that we would have been worthy of being painted ourselves. Bronzino was the first of us to compose himself. He seemed not to dare to address the vision herself. As for me, I was afraid that she would vanish if we spoke to her. Even Bronzino seemed to fear that, because instead of addressing the apparition directly, he pounded on the door of the house. I was still watching the woman. She continued to smile down absently upon us all, while Bronzino knocked again. Without any warning a shutter was slid aside and a pair of grey-brown eyes peered out through the aperture.

'What do you want?' a woman's voice demanded. The eyes slowly bobbed up and down, bafflingly and disconcertingly, as though the woman were floating in the air behind the door. Was this an unhallowed house of witches and spirits? Bronzino went straight to the point.

'I would like to speak to the beautiful young woman who is looking out of the window on the top floor,' he said.

'Oh, Mother of God, no,' the woman replied. She turned away, and snapped a few sharp words at some unseen person.

'Is there something wrong?' Bronzino asked, while Pontormo peered in at Bronzino's shoulder. It must have been an alarming sight for whoever might be looking out from within.

I could not stop looking at the vision in the upper window, but someone snatched her away from behind. For an instant I thought I caught a glimpse of bare breasts.

The dialogue through the door resumed. 'Whoever you are, go away,' the woman commanded. Her eyes were still floating up and down.

'Please, my lady,' Bronzino purred, 'I am the painter called Agnolo Il Bronzino, and this is my master Iacopo di Pontormo.' The floating grey-brown eyes seemed unimpressed. Bronzino persisted.

'I have been commissioned by Duke Cosimo de' Medici to paint a picture to send to the king of France,' he said. 'You may send to the Palazzo della Signoria for confirmation that I am telling the truth.'

'Go away and paint your picture, then,' the woman told him.

'That is what I cannot do without your help,' Bronzino replied. 'The painting will show Cupid and Venus. I already have my model for Cupid. That young woman, whoever she may be, is the image of Venus that I want to send to the king of France. May I speak to her?'

'There is no place for men in this house,' the woman said, causing Pontormo to remark: 'Well, we know it's not a brothel, then.' That finally drove the woman into a rage.

'Go away! I'm closing this door up now, and you can hammer on it for the rest of the day. You're not going to speak to her, or, for that matter, to me. Leave us all in peace!' She snapped the grille shut, so loudly that the sound actually echoed back from further down the street. Bronzino and I both looked hopefully upwards again, but the beautiful young woman had not come back. Pontormo shook his head.

'Well, that's that, then,' he pronounced. 'You must keep on searching for your Venus.'

'No, I won't,' Bronzino replied. 'I've found her now, and she's going to be my model, whether that witch likes it or not. Giuseppe! Look around you. Make a note of as many details as you can of this street, and of this house, so that we can describe it well enough to find it again.'

I peered about me, memorising all the details, while Pontormo argued with his former pupil.

'What good will it do you to come back? You'll only get the same answer.'

'Don't you think that woman who was up there would make a remarkable Venus?' Bronzino asked him.

'Yes, indeed,' Pontormo admitted, 'but –'

'– but then so will Duke Cosimo,' Bronzino replied with an air of triumph. 'I'll send a message to him and ask for an audience about the painting. He'll give me his time.'

That was how our long search ended, after only half a day, and after travelling only a little way across the city, instead of marching like pilgrims to Pisa and Bologna and Rome. There might have been material for a great epic poem in that.

I made a point of noting all the landmarks on our way

home, while Bronzino and Pontormo walked together in front of me, both uncharacteristically silent. My desire not to forget how to find that strange house again was even stronger than Bronzino's seemed to be. I cared nothing for the mysterious woman at the upstairs window, or for who she might be. I just wanted to see her again, to enjoy contemplating her beauty.

Once again I was denied my siesta on a hot afternoon. Bronzino made me dress up in my most formal clothes to carry his message to the Duke's court. Not only were my fine stuffed doublet and my tight hose very hot, I felt like a fool wearing them in the street on my own. The vile children who infest every street in Florence suggested as I passed by that I was acting as a character in a pageant, and had somehow taken a wrong turn and lost my place in the parade. I announced myself to the bored guards at the outermost doors of the Palazzo della Signoria. They passed me on to their more senior colleagues, and as I worked my way through the galleries, the successive sets of guards became less bored, more alert, and less dirty. Finally I was presented to some sort of chamberlain or manservant, who accepted the letter that I handed to him. He took the letter with a smart curving flourish as though it were a document for which he had yearned all his life. I knew that he would have spent years learning the graces of a courtier, and that his elegant gesture was a well-practised act, but it was pleasing to see it done so well. I tried to make sure that the letter would actually get through.

'My master is Agnolo Il Bronzino, the painter to the court,' I said, not claiming any official status for him.

'I know,' the elegant man replied.

'Bronzino has found the most beautiful woman in Florence,' I said.

'I didn't know he was interested in women,' the man replied.

'He isn't,' I admitted, 'except as subjects for paintings. I assure you that this matter will be of great interest to the Duke.'

'He will receive it as soon as he wakes up,' the man assured me.

I knew that there was no point in my waiting for a reply, so I withdrew all the way out through the Palazzo again. Time seemed to go backwards as I passed through successively less grand and important rooms and past successively less intelligent guards.

The reply was delivered to our house even before Bronzino woke up.

I carried the heavy paper scroll up to him, and handed it over. It was still rolled up and tied in a gold- and white-patterned ribbon.

'I'll keep this ribbon,' Bronzino announced to himself, while he unrolled the letter. 'It might make a good prop for a painting.' He scanned the letter. 'Jesus Mary!' he exclaimed. 'I have to attend the Duke at dinner tonight.'

'You mean you have to help serve it?' I asked.

'No, you fool! I mean that I have to report to him while he's having dinner.'

Pontormo stirred. He was lying on the other side of the bed. 'I hope I don't have to come, too,' he muttered. 'You know I hate formal occasions.'

'No, Master, you don't need to come,' Bronzino reassured him. 'The summons is only for me, but Giuseppe will need to come with me.'

'I'm not looking forward to going out at night for the second evening in a row,' I said.

'We won't be alone this time,' Bronzino told me. 'The

Duke will send over a detachment of guards at nine o'clock to take us there.'

'At least the mosquitoes will have to spread their attacks over more targets,' I remarked.

As it turned out, we made quite a busy and active group walking through the darkened city, while everyone else was sleeping or fornicating or sodomising. No fewer than twelve guards came to escort us. Four of them were carrying lanterns. The mosquitoes did swarm against us, but the lanterns also attracted bats, which swooped around our heads and swallowed mosquitoes by the dozen. It was like a summer evening up in Riva del Garda, when the little bats come down from the caves above the lake and flutter about the town, whirling around every lantern hung out over a tavern or garden.

Somehow the interior of the Palazzo della Signoria was more imposing by night. I wondered how many servants were employed to light all the lamps. As we passed through the rooms and halls and corridors, I noticed fragments of great art pass by: a glint of gold leaf, a dark limb of bronze reaching out from a statue, a clutch of faces engaged in earnest conversation in a fresco. I noticed that we were being conducted towards a muffled sound of music. Somewhere ahead of us, behind more closed doors, a voice was singing and strings were being plucked. As we came closer, I could make out the sound of voices busy with conversation and laughter. The unfortunate singer was evidently having to struggle against this background noise. It must be like trying to paint a picture while four fools with paintbrushes are amusing themselves by slapping random splashes of paint onto the gesso.

Finally, we reached the last door, which was opened

for us from within. I have never learned how the Palazzo servants always know when someone is arriving on the other side of the doors.

Bronzino hissed into my ear. 'Now, for God's sake, look serious and anonymous!' What he meant was that he wanted me not to be noticed.

In the great hall, my first impression was not of the light or the music, or the gold. The first thing that struck me was the extraordinary abundance of food that stretched like an ocean all the way to the impossibly long table, at which Duke Cosimo sat in his stately chair. He glowered at Bronzino and beckoned him forward. I stepped one pace ahead, but the guards gripped my arms in an implacable hold. Bronzino went to the Duke's elbow. The Duke gestured to him to bend down and speak. Bronzino said a stream of urgent words to the Duke, who answered with two or three words of his own.

Then, to my alarm, Duke Cosimo looked straight into my eyes and waved at me to come to him. I bowed as I had been taught to do in the presence of my betters, and, while I was still straightening myself up again, the Duke spoke to me.

'You're that naked creature Bronzino keeps in his studio, aren't you?' he asked. That remark caused the conversation to cease all the way down the table, and made the hapless singer fluff one of his phrases. I could have sworn that the hundred candles even flickered in unison. I had to reply.

'I am Messer Bronzino's apprentice, my lord. I am not always naked.'

'Don't take on, boy. If I hadn't seen you, I wouldn't have picked you out to model for Cupid.'

He turned to all the faces staring at him along the table. 'None of you heard that, do you understand?' he roared.

'You all heard nothing.'

The guests all turned their faces modestly downwards. I am sure that nobody would ever dare to repeat Duke Cosimo's private words outside his palazzo. I was relieved, because I had been terrified that he would order me to strip off there and then, so that he could exhibit his good judgement (as he saw it) in choosing me to be Cupid. It turned out that the Duke's thoughts were now on the other central figure in the painting.

'My painter Bronzino tells me that you and old Pontormo saw the perfect Venus here in Florence this afternoon. Is that true?'

'Yes, Your Grace,' I replied. 'The woman has an astonishing serene beauty.'

'Tell me where the house was,' the Duke commanded with quiet menace.

Luckily I could remember all the details, and as I described the route and the landmarks of the street, as well as the characteristics of the house itself, the Duke's expression became knowing and conspiratorial.

'I know of that house,' he told us. 'My people observe it all the time. I even infiltrated a spy in there once, disguised as a maidservant, but she lasted only a day before Sister Benedicta detected her and threw her out. Clever woman! It will be a great satisfaction for me to score a point off her.' The Duke grinned, always a sign that he was about to say something that would please him greatly, and that would probably bring great discomfort to whoever he was thinking about. 'I demanded to know the truth of the rumours of what goes on in her cellar. If what I hear is true, she is engaging in activities that the Church forbids, but somehow she's obtained special protection. I wanted her to work for me, but she refused, and damn it, even I can't pass the shield that the Church has given her.'

I remembered the angry grey-brown eyes bobbing up and down behind the grille in the door. They must belong to the formidable Sister Benedicta, whoever and whatever she might be.

The Duke snapped his fingers at the guard who was standing behind his right shoulder.

'Get me Captain Da Lucca,' he ordered, and the guard vanished into the shadows. Duke Cosimo turned his attention back to Bronzino. 'Be ready at your house at ten o'clock tomorrow morning, both you and the naked boy. Clothed, of course. I'm going to get that woman for you. I've found your Cupid, and I'll find your Venus. I can't paint, but I can help to assemble the figures in your painting.'

A dark lithe man slid silently out of the darkness like a snake and stood to attention without a sound. Few soldiers can do that. The Duke gave his orders.

'Be at the painter Bronzino's house at ten o'clock tomorrow morning with ten guards, and as many men as you need in order to carry a battering ram. Draw an old one from the arsenal stores, one that's been used in real war. Don't draw a fancy parade ram. They're too expensive.' The Duke smiled, always a frightening sight to those few Florentines who ever saw it. 'I assure you,' he promised Captain Da Lucca, 'that mounting an assault upon Sister Benedicta's house will be real war! All that will be missing will be blades and gunpowder, and it wouldn't surprise me if she's manufacturing gunpowder in there as well.'

As well as what, I wondered, but the Duke dismissed Captain Da Lucca, Bronzino and myself with one single flip of his hand. We left in opposite directions. Captain Da Lucca vanished back into the darkness, while Bronzino and

I walked backwards, as court etiquette demands, all the way down the hall to the door by which we had entered. As soon as we found ourselves outside, our escort reappeared.

I did not speak to Bronzino all the way back to our house, because the guards would have overheard us and reported every word back to the Duke. The guards themselves said nothing. Every so often a set of shutters would open as we passed, and then hastily bang closed again. Someone had wondered what the lights were, opened the shutters to shout down some remark, and then thought better of it when they recognised the uniform of Duke Cosimo's personal guards.

The officer in charge broke his silence when he left us. 'Be ready at ten o'clock, but don't wear your best clothes this time. In fact, bring out your oldest rags in case you have to fight.'

'Fight who?' I asked.

'Fight Sister Benedicta, of course! We'll need every guard in the palazzo to subdue her if she resists. You'll see! Make your confession before you go. You may be one of the fatalities.'

On that encouraging note, the guards marched away, while we went upstairs. Because we had brought no lanterns of our own, we had to feel our way upstairs in total darkness. Pontormo was waiting for us, nervously wringing his hands. It was typical of Pontormo to be worried about us, while not thinking of bringing down a candle to light our way up the stairs.

Bronzino reassured him. 'I shall have my Venus, Master. The Duke has promised it.'

I put in my own contribution to the news. 'The Duke is sending round a body of guards, and even a battering ram to make sure we get her. Apparently he knows of the house already.'

Bronzino waved at me to be quiet. During my four years as his apprentice, he had developed a repertoire of gestures which I understood perfectly. He took over the explanation to Pontormo.

'You remember that woman who argued with me this afternoon, Master?'

'I certainly do,' Pontormo replied. 'The Bishop should be told about her.'

'He already knows,' Bronzino replied, 'because she's some kind of nun. The Duke even knows her name: Sister Benedicta. He seems to have some kind of grudge against her, or some suspicion about what she does in her house.'

Pontormo snorted. 'I expect he failed to get his way in something. I begin to think more highly already of the woman.'

So did I. Whatever might be said of the other aspects of her character, Sister Benedicta must be brave.

Bronzino was already anticipating his victory.

'The Duke and I are agreed on one thing. That woman we saw at the upper window will be my Venus, the Duke's Venus, the Venus that we're going to send to the king of France.'

I could not keep myself silent any more.

'But, Master,' I said, 'what if she doesn't want to?'

'This is Florence, where Duke Cosimo rules,' Bronzino replied. 'Such questions are not asked here.'

That night I was glad that Pontormo was staying with us, because he would be Bronzino's bed partner and not mine. When Bronzino was in his triumphant mood, he usually liked to end his day by seizing and using me particularly cruelly. On such nights he would forget his elegant

Florentine speech, and bark and swear at me in the rough peasant dialect of the nearby village of Monticelli from which he had come. So, thanks to Pontormo's presence, I spent a solitary but mainly sleepless night in my room.

When I was sure that Bronzino had gone to bed, I hung a piece of gauze over my window to keep the mosquitoes out. Bronzino never knew that I had stolen that square of expensive filmy cloth from him. He had bought several arm's-lengths of it to be used as draperies in some painting that he had planned but never executed.

When I awoke in the morning, the first task I had to perform was to take down the gauze from the window and hide it away again. It was the only thought that occurred to me at first. It happens so often that when one wakes up in the morning, one does not at first remember that a crisis is to occur that day.

Bronzino and Pontormo were both still sleeping so soundly that I had to knock on the bedroom door many times, and call repeatedly, before I could wake them up. I could have opened the door and walked in, but I could not face the idea of the scene that I might discover. It would have been sickening to find the two of them in bed together, perhaps even in an obscene embrace.

It would have been an image that I could never have cleaned from my memory.

As it was, Bronzino also seemed to have forgotten what we were to do that day. 'What is it?' he called. He was angry because I rarely woke him up. I only did it when he had an important appointment.

'We have to be ready for the Duke's guards, Master,' I reminded him.

'Oh, yes!' he responded eagerly through the door.

He and Pontormo breakfasted as cheerily as though they

were going to a grand feast or celebration. Even Pontormo was in a good mood, laughing and joking, but because he was such an odd and melancholy man, his laughter was alarming to me. Neither of them noticed my own mood, but then they never did. I was eager to see the mysterious young woman again, just to gaze in rapture at her beauty, but I also knew that she was a person, not a painting or a sculpture to be looked at for hours simply for the pleasure of the viewer.

Nobody was going to ask her whether she wanted to be in the Duke's painting. He was using her for his own purposes as surely as he might take a woman into his household as a mistress. I imagine that any woman might feel honoured to be told that she was beautiful enough to be fit to serve as a model for the goddess Venus. The marvellous Simonetta Vespucci herself had done so in the last century, and she will be admired as Venus rising from the sea for as long as art endures. Yet there was a difference: Simonetta Vespucci came from a notable family, and must have given her consent freely to be Botticelli's model. Nobody had asked the beautiful young woman whom we had glimpsed at the upstairs window whether she wanted her nude image carried all the way from Italy to France, and put on display to anyone who might visit the French king. I kept silent, because my opinion would matter no more than hers. As the lawyers say, he who is silent gives his consent, so I have to admit that I was an accomplice of the Duke and Bronzino.

Bronzino and Pontormo were still sitting back in satisfaction, both contemplating the remains of their breakfast as though the crumbs and grape-seeds and cheese-parings were objects that they were going to arrange in an artistic composition, when we heard from the street a sound very familiar to all Florentines: a mixture of cheers and boos.

Bronzino stood up and went to the window.

'I believe that our escort is approaching,' he said. 'We must go down and meet them.'

The three of us trooped down the stairs to strike our poses in the unholy scene that was to follow: the Abduction of Venus.

4

Pontormo said that not since Florence had surrendered after the great siege of 1529–30 had he seen a battering ram carried through the streets. To judge by the stares we attracted, and the way people scuttled out of our path, I am sure he was right. I was particularly sorry for the guards who had to carry the thing. I had never seen a battering ram before, and had not realised how heavy one could be. The guards were soaked with sweat in the morning heat, and they had to march in perfect unison. If only one of them had slipped, or even broken step, they would all have lost control of the battering ram and dropped it, almost certainly causing broken bones. Someone should invent a long wagon for carrying battering rams to where they are needed.

Bronzino and I were walking behind the battering ram, with Pontormo muttering to himself behind us, and Captain Da Lucca and his two-man personal escort at the rear. At the very front, one guard carried Duke Cosimo's personal standard on a gold-painted pole. Bronzino was becoming unhealthily interested in the sight of the men carrying the battering ram in front of us.

At least people stood aside as we approached, in the same way as they stand aside when they see a man coming carrying a heavy, towering load on his back, and for the same reason: the unfortunate bearers cannot possibly swerve to the left or right. They can only aim the load in the direction in which they want it to go, and must then fight its reluctance to be turned aside from that course.

Bronzino kept wandering about, looking at the scene from different angles. 'What a study this would make!' he hissed to me. 'I can imagine putting it in a Classical setting, so the men can be nude.'

Sooner than I expected, we arrived in the street which held our destination, and Bronzino had to turn his attention away from the muscular young men marching in front of us. In fact, we seemed to have crossed an invisible frontier between a city of men and a city of women.

Out of every house, women were leaning from windows; but not, alas, the one woman we wanted to see.

Our group were the only men in sight, and I suddenly began to fear that we really had been bewitched and drawn into an evil fairy kingdom of female demons. Perhaps, though, the women were simply doing the same as Bronzino: looking with admiration upon the young men.

Captain Da Lucca obviously was not suffering from such superstitious fears. He strode up to that portentous door and pounded four times upon it. He thrust his face up to the closed grille and bellowed: 'Open the door, by command of the Duke!'

Bronzino, Pontormo and I gathered around him, but not too closely. The grille snapped open, and the familiar voice replied, giving no sign of being intimidated by being only a finger's length away from Captain Da Lucca's dark and harsh face.

'I see no sign of the Duke,' said Sister Benedicta.

'You see his power, you witch,' Captain Da Lucca told her in a calm voice. 'You see his guards and his battering ram. There will be a dozen cruel and filthy men in your

house a few minutes from now if you do not open this
door, because, by God, Sister Benedicta, no man refuses to
do my will, and no woman will ever defy it either.'

I do not think that Captain Da Lucca included we three
nervous, delicate sodomites among the body of men who
made up his threat.

'There are no weapons in this house, and not a single
man,' Sister Benedicta replied. 'There is no threat to the
Duke here.'

'No, but there is a threat to you out here,' Captain Da
Lucca told her. His polite tone did not match his words.
'Either open the door and let us in, or I'll have my men
break it in. This battering ram smashed down one of the
city gates fourteen years ago. Your front door won't stop
it today.'

'I never expected that this house would need to with-
stand attack from our own Duke,' Sister Benedicta said.
'Promise me, upon your honour as an officer of Florence,
that the guards will remain outside, and I'll open the door.'

'Only I and three artists will come in,' Captain Da Lucca
assured her.

I heard Bronzino say, 'two artists and an apprentice,'
as the bolts were drawn aside and the mysterious door
opened to us.

Captain Da Lucca walked in first. The Duke must have
ordered him to ensure our safety. He satisfied himself that
the house held no dangers, and beckoned us to follow him.
I stood aside to let Bronzino and Pontormo go in first, and
then I followed, closing the door behind me.

At first, of course, I could see nothing in the gloom of
the hall. My eyes were still attuned to the daylight of the
street. After a moment, though, I could make out doors, a
staircase and a woman in a nun's habit. I recognised her

grey-brown eyes from Bronzino's conversations with her through the grille in the door. Now I realised why her eyes had bobbed up and down. She was not very tall, and she must have been constantly stretching herself up and then sinking back down again. In spite of her lack of height, Sister Benedicta glared up at Captain Da Lucca.

'Well, now that you're in,' she said, 'who are you and what do you want?'

'I am Captain Da Lucca, in the service of the Duke. These are the artists called Pontormo and Bronzino, and the boy is Bronzino's apprentice.'

'Doesn't the boy have a name?' Sister Benedicta asked.

'I'm called Giuseppe,' I told her.

'Thank you for the introductions,' Sister Benedicta said to Captain Da Lucca, 'although your manners are unworthy of men who attend a Duke's court. To the point, then: what do you want?'

Bronzino gave her a direct answer. 'We require a woman whom we believe to live in this house. We saw her looking out of an upstairs window yesterday morning.'

'You insolent brute!' Sister Benedicta replied. 'This is not that kind of house.'

'We don't want that kind of woman,' Bronzino told her. 'If we did, we could obtain one with far less trouble than you have put us to. What we need – what I need – is a woman to model for a painting.'

'There are thousands of women in Florence,' Sister Benedicta retorted. 'Many of them would be willing to model for your painting. Why must you disturb the peace of this home?'

'This is no ordinary painting,' Bronzino told her. 'The Duke himself has commissioned it, as a diplomatic gift to send to the king of France. No ordinary model will do, either, because it is to be a picture built around Venus and Cupid. It needs a special woman to represent the goddess Venus.'

'Oh, this woman is special,' Sister Benedicta said, 'so special that when you meet her, you will no longer want her. I see that as the quickest way to get rid of you all.' She called to some unseen person up the stairs. 'Maria! Bring Angelina down here.'

So that was the name of the beautiful woman: Angelina. We four intruders stood in silence in the hall, while a voice muttered and cajoled somewhere upstairs, and shoes moved around on the floor above our heads, as though someone up there were practising dance steps. At last we heard two people, whoever they might turn out to be, coming down the stairs. I expected that Maria would be another nun, but the small dark woman who came down the stairs first was dressed in the rough plain clothes of a lay helper. Maria was leading by the hand the goddess Venus, who was wrapped in two blankets and stumbled her way down to us, frowning with painful concentration at each step that she had to descend. I had expected that I would be entranced by Angelina's beauty when I saw her close for the first time. She was still beautiful, of course, even swathed in old blankets, but I stared at her height. I had not realised that she was so tall.

Sister Benedicta stepped forward, took Angelina's hand from Maria's, and brought her forward to meet us. Sister Benedicta had not spoken a word to Angelina. Instead, she addressed herself to us, while keeping hold of Angelina's hand.

'There,' she said, 'Angelina is sweet and quiet. She is innocent and biddable. What could you want from her?' All the time, Angelina continued to stare into the shadows behind our heads, smiling at nobody, in just the same way as when I had first seen her at the window. Sister Benedicta repeated herself to Bronzino.

'What could you want from Angelina?' she asked again.

'I want her to be the image of Venus,' Bronzino replied, and he reached out and snatched the blankets off Angelina's shoulders, revealing her nudity.

Even Captain Da Lucca was shocked. 'Bronzino! What are you doing?' he shouted.

'Inspecting my model for Venus,' Bronzino told him, gathering up the fallen blankets. 'Yes, she is my Venus.'

Sister Benedicta stood transfixed, with her hand across her mouth. I heard a faint cry from Maria in the shadows. The only people in the room who made no sound were Pontormo and Angelina herself. She remained silent and smiling, as though she were a painted Venus already.

I guessed the secret before anyone else did. 'Master,' I said to Bronzino, 'there is something wrong with her.'

'Wrong?' Bronzino answered. 'Nonsense. Look at those graceful legs, and she has perfect breasts.'

'Not her body, Master!' I corrected him. 'There is something missing in her spirit. Look, she's not even shocked or ashamed.'

Sister Benedicta took her hand down from her face to reveal an expression of bitter triumph. Pontormo looked puzzled. Captain Da Lucca now looked interested. Angelina stood still, with her hands clasped together in front of her. She continued to smile at nothing. I noticed that her fingers were ceaselessly twisting. I hoped that Bronzino would now take us away and leave the poor woman to whatever strange but safe life she led in this place. Instead, he grasped Sister Benedicta by the shoulder and shouted in her face.

'What's wrong with her? Is she an idiot? Is she mad?'

Sister Benedicta took the opportunity to snatch up the two blankets from the floor. She wrapped them deftly around Angelina's body before answering Bronzino's questions.

'No, she is not an idiot. She looks after herself very well, and we have taught her to do many tasks. Angelina is not mad, either.'

Bronzino could not contain himself. 'Then why does she just stand there smiling?' he demanded.

'Yes, it is a beautiful, sweet smile, isn't it?' Sister Benedicta said. 'My poor Angelina. Yet really I do not pity her in the least. I don't think she's really here with us at all. Do you know that when angels appear to humanity on Earth, they never really leave Heaven? They carry it like a cocoon around them, so that they are never in contact with our corrupted world.'

Pontormo now managed to make himself speak. 'Do you mean to say that she's an angel?'

'No, she is as human as we are. She sees our world, and lives in it, and walks through it, but she is always somewhere else, alone. Angelina is so alone.'

Bronzino had a brisk answer to these revelations. 'If she is always in her own world, it will be no sin for me to take her away from here until my painting is finished.'

'What?' Sister Benedicta cried. 'Can't you see how we care for her?'

'We'll look after her,' Bronzino promised. 'She's more valuable to me that you can imagine. If she came to any harm, the Duke would punish me.'

'But my poor Angelina! You burst in here with no permission –'

'– by the Duke's order,' Captain Da Lucca reminded her.

'You are in this house against my will,' Sister Benedicta persisted. 'A few moments ago, Angelina was leading a peaceful and, I believe, a happy life with us. Now suddenly you demand to drag her away.'

Bronzino became more angry. 'I've already undertaken to you that she will be looked after.'

'But Angelina has always been looked after only by women, ever since she was first brought here as a little girl,' Sister Benedicta said.

'How is she to be looked after by men? Do you have female servants in your house?'

'No woman lives there,' Captain Da Lucca told her with a grin.

Sister Benedicta folded her arms and looked away from us. 'She will not be safe.'

'I promise you that she will be as safe as she is here,' Bronzino told her. 'She will be under the Duke's own protection.'

Captain Da Lucca intervened in the conversation again, but this time his face and voice were harder. 'Sister, we have given you the Duke's order. You will now release this woman to us. I am a Captain in the Duke's personal guard. I am not accustomed to being made to wait by people of low rank.'

Sister Benedicta unfolded her arms and clasped Angelina to her. Then she turned to the servant Maria.

'Maria, go and pack up whatever we can for Angelina,' she ordered, and then she faced us again. 'We never expected that she would go out of this house.'

The snuffling Maria took Angelina's arm, leading her toward the stairs. Bronzino stepped forward to stop her, but Captain Da Lucca held him back. 'Let them go upstairs. They can't get away from us by going up there.'

Maria led Angelina up the stairs, while Sister Benedicta wrung her hands and studied the tiles on the floor. 'My poor Angelina,' she said yet again. 'I know the Duke has long wanted to injure me, but why did he have to do it by hurting Angelina? She's never harmed him or anyone else.'

Bronzino ignored her, but Pontormo's interest was aroused. 'Why does the Duke want to injure you?' he asked. 'What have you done to him?'

'Why, nothing,' Sister Benedicta replied. 'That's my offence. I have secrets, you see, and Duke Cosimo de' Medici wants there to be no secrets from him in Florence.'

'What secrets do you have in your house?' Pontormo asked. 'Do you mean the strange woman?'

'No,' Sister Benedicta replied, 'he knew nothing of her until you told him, and brought armed men and uproar here. Even that stupid woman he sent as a spy didn't discover Angelina. In any case, this is not my house. It belongs to the Order to which I, in turn, belong.'

'Shouldn't you be in a convent?' Bronzino interrupted.

'Yes, but I have been placed here to care for these women who cannot care for themselves. There is a priest who comes in to say Mass. The Duke doesn't like him either, because the priest shares my secrets.'

Neither Pontormo nor Bronzino asked any more questions, but I could not restrain my own curiosity.

'What secrets do you have that could endanger the Duke?'

'None. What we do is not even a secret in itself. The priest and I are undertaking studies in alchemy.'

That brought Bronzino back into the conversation. 'Ha! Alchemy is dead. It belongs to the old Gothic world. Why are you wasting your time with the green lion and the peacock's tail?'

Sister Benedicta turned to him. 'An alchemist must have disappointed you once,' she said.

'The alchemists have disappointed everyone,' Bronzino replied. 'They promised to turn base metals into gold, and they have never succeeded.'

I interrupted them again. 'Master,' I asked, 'what is all this about a green lion and a peacock's tail?'

'Never mind, Giuseppe,' Bronzino replied. 'I've done my best to educate you in the modern way, in the spirit of humanism and the new learning. Alchemy is an outdated way of seeking for truth.'

'Truth,' Sister Benedicta declared, 'is never out of date.'

Captain Da Lucca spoke the words that ended the discussion. 'I'll take up alchemy when you show me man- or woman-made gold,' he said, as Maria led the newly dressed Angelina down the stairs to us.

I was surprised by the high quality of her clothes. They were of the best materials, and had obviously been made to fit her. Someone was paying the Order of nuns well for giving a home to Angelina. Sister Benedicta inspected her. 'Well, gentlemen,' she said, 'here is your prize of war. You have captured her, although not by fair means. Captain Da Lucca: where are you going to take her now?'

'My orders are to conduct her to Bronzino's house.'

'I cannot come with you,' Sister Benedicta cried. 'I have not left this house for years.'

'Well, I have no orders to forbid you,' Captain Da Lucca replied.

'Come if you want, and make your own way back.'

Sister Benedicta opened the door, weeping. 'Go then, and may God punish you all,' she ordered.

Captain Da Lucca was the last one of us out, but he turned at the threshold. 'If you shut the door behind me, my men will break it down, and when they get in they will break everything in your house.'

'I believe they would,' Sister Benedicta replied, 'and I'm not trying to play a trick on you.'

We waited in the street while Sister Benedicta pushed Angelina out into the sunlight. She was so pale from being kept indoors. No wonder that she liked to spend her time at the window which was her only viewpoint on the world. It occurred to me that she must be accustomed to seeing the world as a modern painter sees it, from a single viewpoint, with fixed lines of sight and a few receding planes to create perspective.

Angelina would have had only three things to look at: people and objects close at hand within the rooms of the house, the other houses on the opposite side of the street and the russet roofs of Florence with the green hills beyond. Now Angelina found herself in the strange environment of the street, and surrounded by men. For the first time she showed a reaction, clutching at Sister Benedicta, who was much smaller than she was. Angelina let out a faint soft whimper, and Sister Benedicta patted her arm.

'There now, my Angelina,' she said. 'Everything is all right.'

That may have been the greatest lie that Sister Benedicta ever told in her life, but it was well meant. She handed Angelina's bundle of possessions to, surprisingly, Pontormo, and then vanished quickly into the house. The door slammed and the grille slid shut. We all moved off in procession, with Angelina in the middle, as though we were escorting a princess. Well, she was going to appear as the image of a goddess, after all.

Captain Da Lucca marched in front of us this time. Behind came Bronzino and Pontormo, and then the guards with the battering ram, and, almost at the rear, myself and Angelina. The last few guards were following us, obviously having been ordered by Captain Da Lucca to watch out for any attempt by the two women to escape. Angelina set the pace. In spite of her height, she walked slowly and shufflingly, without rhythm, while I walked on her left.

I decided to risk trying to talk to Angelina. I came as close as I could without touching her, and spoke quietly.

'Hello, Angelina. My name's Giuseppe,' I said. 'I was taken to Bronzino's house myself, four years ago.' Angelina looked round, and for the first time those eyes rested upon me deliberately. I continued in the hope that she was listening to me. 'Bronzino took me for his own purposes as well,' I said. 'I hope you'll be friends with me.' Angelina's face broke into her faint smile again. She took my hand in a soft but firm grasp, and we walked on as though we had always known each other.

An unfamiliar voice behind me said, 'I thought you didn't like girls,' and I realised that it came from one of the guards who had been posted in the rear. I thought of making an answer, but I decided that I had little chance of winning a contest in ribald abuse with one of the Duke's guards, so I pretended not to have heard him. For an instant I had the even more foolish idea of making a break and running off with Angelina, but I immediately saw that they would catch us at once. Even if they did not, it would not be hard to trace a curly haired youth wandering the streets of Florence with a tall mute woman. Even if they never found us, where would I take her? I did not know anyone in Florence who would take us in and not betray us. Even if I had had such a place to go to, would we have hidden there for the rest of our lives? I contented myself with the knowledge that Angelina seemed to trust me.

Bronzino found his way home easily enough without my help. Captain Da Lucca brought our whole tragi-comic procession to a halt outside the door. Everyone was still and silent for a moment, and I remembered how I had waited outside that door while my father negotiated the terms of my apprenticeship with Bronzino. Captain Da Lucca briskly brought the pause to an end.

'I have carried out my orders, Bronzino. I've got you the woman and escorted her to your house. From now on, it's up to you to make sure that the rest of the Duke's orders are carried out.' With that, he called his men to him, formed them up into an organised body, and marched them away, back to the Palazzo della Signoria. I am sure that the guards were glad to return the battering ram to the ordnance stores, and I am equally sure that they never gave a moment's thought to us again.

Bronzino took charge. 'Giuseppe, take the woman inside and take her up to your room.'

I pulled Angelina as gently as I could towards our door. 'Here, Angelina, come with me,' I coaxed her. 'I won't hurt you.' To my surprise, she shuffled quite willingly into the house, and I was beginning to enjoy my relief at how easy it was proving to be, when Angelina must have suddenly realised that Sister Benedicta was not with us. Perhaps it set off some memory of the day when her parents had abandoned her to Sister Benedicta, just as I had been reminded of the day when my father had abandoned me to Bronzino. She let out a terrible long, loud wail, and then began to shriek over and over again.

In spite of her screams, Angelina was still holding on to me tightly. I was talking to her, trying to calm her, but I doubt that she was hearing me.

I had another of those mad, inappropriate and unseemly

thoughts: how is this to be resolved? Are we going to stand in this wild noisy tableau of figures for ever?

Just then, help came, as they say, from an unexpected quarter: Pontormo, who put down Angelina's pathetic luggage and began to stroke her. It was extraordinary to see. Pontormo did not say anything to her. His touch was not at all like an erotic caress. He was stroking her with a firm touch, as if he were grooming a beast. Angelina began to quieten down, and Pontormo slowly stopped touching her. She sank down and knelt on the cool tiles of the hall floor, so I put my arm around her. Angelina silently pressed herself into my embrace, while Pontormo watched us approvingly.

'There,' he said, 'now you know how to calm her when she's frightened.'

Angelina was now breathing calmly, and Pontormo took her other arm and gently persuaded her to stand upright again.

Bronzino put his head through the door and finally saw that Angelina was at peace again.

'What did you do, Master?' he asked Pontormo.

'I calmed her by putting my hands on her,' Pontormo replied.

Bronzino came in and closed the door. I remembered the door closing behind him on the day that he and Pontormo had taken me in.

Bronzino's thoughts were only about matters at hand.

'Giuseppe, I told you to take the woman up to your room.'

'It's hot up there, Master,' I objected. 'Can't I get her some water? Some to drink, and some to wash herself with.'

'I'll get the water,' Bronzino replied. 'You take her up.'

Pontormo went up the stairs in front of us, carrying

Angelina's possessions. I climbed up beside her, guiding her steps. Every tread of the staircase seemed to be a novel and unexpected obstacle for Angelina. She was so tall that she had to stoop so as not to bang her head.

Pontormo and I led her into my room, which was indeed very hot then in the middle of the day. Pontormo laid her bags down in the middle of the floor.

'Sit down, Angelina,' he urged her, but instead Angelina walked in a circle around the sad little bundle. Then she seemed to notice my window. She stood directly under it, put her head back, and contemplated the rectangle of pale burning sky which was all that one could see through it. I heard Bronzino coming up the stairs. He came in carrying a jug of water, and a basin with a mug rattling around in it.

Bronzino was also carrying a towel over his arm. He looked like a tavern servant, or like a barber about to shave someone. Bronzino looked inquiringly at me.

'Can we trust her with the water?'

I could not imagine why he thought that I would know the answer.

'Let's try, Master,' I suggested. 'I'm sure that Sister Benedicta has taught her to wash herself.'

As it happened, Bronzino did not need to offer Angelina the water.

She reached for the towel, and took the basin out of Bronzino's hands.

Angelina placed the basin on the little table which was my only furniture apart from the stool and bed. She took out the mug and set it down next to the basin, and then laid the towel down on my bed. Then Angelina took the jug of water from Bronzino, filled up the basin, filled up the mug, and handed the basin back to him. I was fascinated, but Bronzino was nervous. Pontormo was enthralled.

'Look how gracefully she moves, Bronzino!' he exclaimed. 'She really could be the goddess Venus herself.'

Bronzino said nothing, but he and I watched Angelina wash her long-fingered hands in the basin and dry them on the towel. Only then did she take the mug, in both hands, and drink from it.

'Well,' Bronzino said cruelly, 'at least we know you're right, Giuseppe: she has been thoroughly trained.'

'She's not an animal, Master,' I protested.

'Are you sure?' he replied. 'She has no power of speech, and she doesn't seem to understand us, either.'

Pontormo was outraged. 'She's beautiful, Bronzino!'

'So is a cat, Master,' Bronzino told him, 'but it has no soul.'

Angelina had ignored all this discussion. She finished the water and put the mug down on the table. Then, with perfect assurance, she sat down on the middle of my bed, and smiled up in turn at Pontormo and myself, who were standing on either side of her. As before, I was not sure that Angelina's smile actually meant anything. It seemed to be bestowed upon anybody and nobody. Bronzino, though, had no such doubts.

'Well, she's evidently taken a liking to the pair of you, so I hope we'll have no further trouble from her.'

It seemed to me that it was Angelina who had had trouble from us, rather than the other way round, and I found it painful to remember that it was I who had first pointed her out at the upper window.

Bronzino was utterly satisfied with himself. 'After lunch, we'll all have a rest, and then we'll start work. I'll put you through every pose we can think of.' He had one more thought. 'Her presence here must be kept a secret.'

Just then, we noticed a growing rumble of voices down

in the street, two storeys below. Pontormo rubbed at his fascinatingly disordered beard.

'I suspect, Bronzino, that it's already the best-known fact in Florence.'

5

For a Florentine mob, they were surprisingly polite. They did not break in and tear our limbs off. They did not carry us down to the banks of the Arno to be sewn into fresh donkey hides and then flung into the waters. They did not even cut our ears off. Bronzino was quite brave in putting his head out of the studio window to enter into reasoned philosophical discussion with the dirty and unshaven faces below.

'What do you want?' he shouted. 'What have we done?'

'Set that young woman free!' someone shouted, and others took it up as well. There was an ominous banging at the door downstairs. Bronzino had not spent as much as he should in having it repaired, and I knew that it would take much less force than Captain Da Lucca's battering ram to smash through it. Bronzino tried to deny the charge against him.

'My model is as free as she has ever been!' he protested. 'She was confined for many years in the house of that witch Sister Benedicta.'

That certainly silenced the crowd, but for the wrong reasons. There was quiet for a moment or two, and then a voice called out one word, questioningly and diffidently, as though the speaker were unsure that he had actually heard Bronzino say it.

'Witch?'

'A witch?' said another man.

'Sister Benedicta?' asked a woman, and the banging at the door became slower, but more forceful. The door-batterers were becoming serious, and the whole house shook with their efforts. Bronzino called upon all his verbal resources as a poet to try to soothe the anger that was being flung up at him.

'Please, my friends –' That produced a growl. No Florentine crowd would like to think that it could be bought with such a cheap rhetorical device. '– I was not accusing Sister Benedicta of witchcraft. I was only insulting her. What man can call himself a Florentine who does not hand out insults?'

'Sister Benedicta is a saint!' someone proclaimed.

The crowd began to chant 'A saint, a saint!'

Bronzino waved down the noise. The crowd obeyed him, but only to hear what provocative statement he might make next. Bronzino took a daring chance, by reminding them of why they had assembled outside his house in the first place.

'You are all hailing Sister Benedicta,' he told them. 'Have you already forgotten about my model?' That produced yet another silence. Bronzino turned away from the window. 'Quick,' he told me, 'bring the woman down here.'

I rushed up to my room to fetch her. She was still sitting demurely on my bed, still smiling, and still tractable enough to let me take her by the arm and lift her up. Angelina did not come down the stairs any more gracefully than she had gone up them. I was afraid that her stumbles would magnify until she would stumble upon her own stumbles and fall headlong all the way down to the cellar. It seemed somehow wrong that a woman of such beauty should be so clumsy. It was as if it were a sin or a character defect of which she was wilfully guilty.

When we came into the studio, Bronzino was still at the window, with Pontormo standing at his shoulder as though he had just introduced Bronzino to the crowd. It was like a parody of a Papal election, with Pontormo playing the role of a Cardinal bringing out a new Pope.

I pushed Angelina forward, and both Bronzino and Pontormo stepped aside so that I could thrust her between them. We then all took one pace forward so that the crowd could see Angelina as I had first seen her: at an upper window. Bronzino's training of me as an apprentice painter, which included taking me to palaces and great houses to see the finest pictures of our age and of the past, was responsible for my habit of seeing every scene as a possible subject for a painting. This one might have been called *Three Sodomites Presenting the Goddess Venus to the People*.

I was hoping that Duke Cosimo would hear about the incident in time to send his guards round to rescue his model for Venus, since I doubted that he would bother to send anyone round merely to rescue us. Instead, it was Angelina herself who saved us, by her smile. Bronzino pushed her up to the window as though she were a plaster statue on a trolley. While Pontormo worked his magic massage on her back, which the crowd below could not see, Bronzino wickedly smiled too.

'There you are!' he cried triumphantly. 'She is happy to be here.'

Angelina, of course, probably had no idea where she was, but the crowd knew nothing of her strange disposition and behaviour. Bronzino continued to beam, with a cheery and jolly expression that I had never seen before, and of which I would not have believed him to be capable.

He even took Angelina's hand in his own, and held up their clasped hands for the mob to see. I expected that in a moment he would go too far and kiss her. He did, and someone in the crowd cheered. Two or three more voices echoed the cheers. Bronzino held Angelina's hand until the crowd began to disperse. Angelina continued to smile, even though Bronzino's grip was so tight that I would have thought that it was hurting her. At last Bronzino released Angelina's hand, and stood back from the window. He wiped the sweat from his face.

'How I hate having to smile and look friendly,' he remarked to me.

'I've never seen you smile before, Master,' I replied.

'Never trust me when I smile,' he warned. 'Ask Pontormo.'

'You smiled on the day that I took you on as my apprentice, Bronzino,' Pontormo answered. 'Were you dissembling then, too?'

'No, Master,' Bronzino replied. 'That was my last honest smile.'

In the silence that followed, we all noticed how hot the afternoon was. Just as sometimes one becomes aware of a sound that has been going on for a long time, so I became aware that I had been sweating so heavily that my clothes were soaked. Bronzino stretched and yawned.

'There's an imbalance in the composition of the day,' he declared.

'We've had too much movement and excitement. Now we need some stillness and quiet.'

'Should I stay?' Pontormo asked.

'Why, yes, Master,' Bronzino told him. 'You know you always have a place in my house.'

While Bronzino and Pontormo retired to Bronzino's room for their siesta, I clumped Angelina down the stairs and around the stifling house to show her where everything was. She showed no sign of having taken in what I had pointed out to her, but I had to try. I was already certain that Angelina was not one of those unfortunates whose minds never develop. She did not speak, and yet there seemed to be no reason for it. She was not deaf. She simply seemed to see us, to hear us and to be aware of all her surroundings, and yet to pass through the life of humanity like a ghost made of flesh. I took her back up to my room, because I could think of nowhere else in the house to take her for the hot afternoon. I did not want to leave her alone in the studio, which was the only possible other place. In spite of all Bronzino's anxiety about the painting that he was going to create, he had not given me orders to continue working on preparing the gesso ground on the panel which was going to receive the picture.

I was always able to fall asleep in the afternoon, in spite of the heat in my room under the roof. I stripped off the old shirt and hose that I had put on in the morning, following the advice of Captain Da Lucca that we might encounter a fight. Angelina went over to the table, where the jug and basin were still lying, and poured herself another mug of water. The sound of the water tumbling into the mug was startlingly loud, so quiet had the room, the house and the whole street become. It was hard to believe that, only a little while earlier, there had been a roaring, angry crowd pushing at our door. I took my clothes and spread them on the floor as a substitute for a mattress. I took my winter blanket out of the chest in which it was slumbering away the spring in the company of some dried herbs which were meant to protect it from the moths. Bronzino had learned that trick in the village of Monticelli where he had been born, and of which he normally never spoke. When I shook out the blanket, it sounded like a thunderstorm. I almost expected our immoral neighbours opposite to come round demanding that I should stop disturbing the city's siesta with my noise. I sat down on my outstretched blankets, and pointed at the bed.

'Angelina, you take my bed,' I told her. 'I'll sleep here.' I wondered whether Bronzino would give her a permanent place to sleep in the house. Angelina smiled at me, and removed her own clothes, folding them carefully and putting them down on my little stool. Sister Benedicta had trained her well and thoroughly, as I had guessed. What I did not expect was that Angelina would remove all her clothes. Well, I had already seen her when Bronzino had rudely stripped her at Sister Benedicta's house, and nobody else could see her through my window.

Angelina lay down, facing away from me, and fell asleep even before I had stretched myself out. She had no fear of assault by me, obviously. It was as if I were not there. It was neither innocence nor ignorance, but that strange indifference with which she lived her odd life.

I contemplated her beauty again for a few moments before I lay down to sleep myself. It is a crime against art that Bronzino's painting would show my posterior and not hers, but then I can think of no painting by any artist that shows Venus from behind. I fell asleep deciding that she should really model for a sculptor rather than for a painter.

I woke up when I felt someone tugging at my hand. As I rose towards wakefulness, the first thing of which I became aware was how uncomfortable I was lying on the floor. I opened my eyes, and realised that it was Angelina who was kneeling beside me. She said nothing, of course, and did not make any sound, but it was clear enough that she wanted me to lie down with her. Angelina would not let go of my fingers, so I had to use my one free hand to balance myself as I got up.

As I bent over to get onto my bed, Angelina slipped off my drawers, and pulled me down with her. I found myself lying face to face with her. She closed her eyes, took my right hand in her own right hand and put her right leg over my left leg. She breathed out and immediately fell asleep. I realised that all she wanted was the touch and closeness of another human being. Perhaps she had shared a bed with another woman at Sister Benedicta's house, probably another strange woman like herself.

It was odd that I felt no more erotic desire for her at that moment than she had felt for me. I remained awake for a long time. I had never experienced the touch of a woman's body, or at least not since the mother whom I cannot remember. The only embrace I had ever known was that of Bronzino. He had a surprisingly muscular body with not a pennyworth of fat, and he did not take me tenderly. Because I had felt only the hardness of a strong man, Angelina's soft and smooth female body was like discovering a new world.

I lay still and silent, listening to her breathing and enjoying the novel feeling of someone touching me other than to hurt me or for their own selfish pleasure. I did not want to wake her, but I risked gently reaching up with my left hand and placing it on her bottom. She did not stir, and I lay motionless and quiet, marvelling at the sensation of a female body, and how different it was to the firm and rough body of Bronzino.

Bronzino's buttocks were square and hairy. I had never wanted to look at those buttocks, and I doubt that anyone else ever did, either, except perhaps for Pontormo. They were not objects of beauty, and they had hurt me hundreds of times with their cruel thrusts. Some men and boys have told me that they had come to enjoy receiving another man in that way, but I never learned to do so.

I expected that my happy waking siesta would be brought to an end by Bronzino calling for me to do some job or other, but instead it was ended by Angelina waking up. She disentangled her limbs from mine, knelt on the bed and then climbed over me as indifferently as if I had been a bolster. She washed herself again and then dressed, while I dressed myself as well. Perhaps we woke Bronzino up by walking around over his head.

'Giuseppe!' he called. 'Bring the woman down to the studio!' Would he ever learn to call Angelina by name, I wondered, as I led her downstairs.

Bronzino had laid out four cups, and was pouring out one of the better wines from the cellar. Pontormo, with his hair pointing in all directions was sitting in his usual place. Bronzino had evidently decided to play the affable host, a role which he usually put on only when he was entertaining other artists, or philosophers, or powerful men whose favour he wanted.

'Giuseppe, please sit down, and make her sit down, too,' he commanded, and Angelina placed herself in the chair which he had indicated to her. Bronzino raised his cup, preparing to propose a toast.

Pontormo, still not quite fully awake, followed with a slight delay. I raised my own cup, and watched Angelina follow my example.

Four different hands hovered in the air. Bronzino's hand was as perfect as the hands of Michelangelo's David. Pontormo's hand was thin and stringy, with prominent tendons, and it trembled.

My own hand, as I was forced to admit to myself, was as square and heavy as the hand of a labourer. Angelina's hand was nearly white, because she had been kept indoors for years. Her long fingers held the cup of wine as though it were weightless.

Bronzino propounded his toast. 'To Venus and Cupid!' he cried.

Two voices joined him in endorsing the toast. Angelina, naturally, ignored it, but when he raised our cups to drink she followed our gesture, only a brief moment behind us. We all sat down again.

Bronzino remained cheery and expansive, always a bad sign to those who were obliged to live close to him. He was boiling over with enthusiasm.

'I'll amaze Duke Cosimo. More than that, I'll amaze King François. My Venus will be even more admired than Botticelli's.'

Pontormo spoke to him severely. 'If you boast like that, Bronzino, I'll expect you to follow through on all these promises.'

'Don't worry, Master,' Bronzino replied. 'I'll tell everyone how much I owe to your training when I was your apprentice.'

'Your style is nothing like mine,' Pontormo said. That was not entirely true. Bronzino's contorted figures were certainly derived from the remarkable postures of the characters in Pontormo's paintings. What Bronzino had developed was a style that did not have Pontormo's disturbing strangeness, but to which Bronzino contributed instead an unusual grace and arrogance.

Pontormo continued to play the role of the critical master. 'You should not praise your painting before it has been created, Bronzino. You haven't even settled on the theme.'

'There's not going to be any theme, Master,' Bronzino declared, with the air that he was finally freeing himself from his apprenticeship to Pontormo, 'except for the faces of love.'

'No theme?' Pontormo exclaimed. 'Then how will you compose it?' Bronzino grinned like a man who knows the answer to a puzzle that is tormenting everyone else in the room. 'King François likes philosophy and art. He considers himself to be a learned man. I'm going to send him a picture full of philosophical and mythological references.'

Pontormo was scandalised, and tried to reassert his former artistic authority as Bronzino's master. 'Beware, Bronzino. It is not seemly to appear to be too clever.'

'It is surely more unseemly to appear stupid and ignorant, Master,' Bronzino replied. 'Any painter in Florence could do a painting showing Venus and Cupid. This city is full of beautiful women and pretty boys. Not every painter would send the king a picture full of allegories and philosophical statements.'

Pontormo shook his head. Where another man might have torn his hair or rent his clothes, Pontormo reacted by poking his fingers into his beard in a futile attempt to tidy it. 'This is a dangerous idea, Bronzino,' he muttered.

'The Duke has placed me in great danger already, by giving me this commission,' Bronzino replied. 'If I displease him, he will find some reason to have me executed. I cannot find safety anywhere now. If I tried to run away, Duke Cosimo would have me pursued throughout his territory. Since I'm in peril of my life anyway, there's no greater risk to me in creating a new and original kind of picture.'

I decided that I had better go down to the cellar and fetch more wine, and, when I got up from the table, Angelina came with me. I led her down to the courtyard, where everything was hot except for the rough stone of the well-head, and left her for a moment while I looked for one of

Bronzino's lower-quality wines to take up to him. I talked to Angelina, because I was still not sure whether she could understand language or not.

'The Duke has placed us all in danger, Angelina. Oh, he'll spare you. You might even come out better off from being sent here.'

Angelina shifted slightly, and idly grasped the rope from which the bucket hung in the sinister depths below. It was odd to see her elegant fingers toying with the rough coarse rope. I became conscious again of the voices of Bronzino and Pontormo, arguing over my head. I could not make out the words. I wondered if life for Angelina was always like that: being aware of other people, but not being able to understand what they were doing. I used one hand to hold the jug of wine, while I held onto Angelina's arm with the other, and urged her back upstairs, step by step.

As we came back into the studio, Pontormo was objecting to some suggestion of Bronzino's. 'It's not right, Bronzino. People will talk, and make a scandal out of it.'

'There won't be a scandal, Master,' Bronzino replied. 'Everyone in Florence knows you.'

'You heard that crowd who came round this afternoon. Someone sent them here. It could happen again.'

'That sorceress Sister Benedicta put them up to it, I'm sure,' Bronzino declared, 'but there's a limit to what she would dare to do. I'll ask the Duke to deal with her if I need to. She doesn't want another visit from Captain Da Lucca and his gang of apes.'

I poured out more wine while Angelina sat down again. I had thought that the conversation was not going to include me, but Bronzino had orders to give to me as his apprentice.

'Giuseppe, make supper early. Buy more food from now on, because the woman will be taking all her meals with us, although she will be staying at my master Pontormo's house.' I nearly dropped the jug of wine.

'Shouldn't she be staying here, Master?' I asked. I had just begun to believe that Angelina was starting to recognise and trust me. I have to admit that I was keen to embrace her again, but Bronzino knew nothing of what had happened in my room during the siesta. If he did, would he have cared?

'Of course she can't stay here,' he snapped. 'We've got no spare room for her. She can take her meals here, as I said, but she'll have to stay at Pontormo's house. He's got plenty of space.'

I was so outraged that I could not speak, but Bronzino took my silence as meaning that I had no further objections to make. I managed to contain myself, but I feared greatly for Angelina's welfare. At least I would be able to make sure that she was fed properly, and I could see that her clothes were washed and aired and put in the press, but what would Pontormo's house be like? I thought seriously about running to Duke Cosimo and asking him to forbid it, but then I decided that as long as Angelina was kept alive and appeared as Venus in the painting, Duke Cosimo would not care whether she was comfortable or not.

Bronzino had made his mind up.

'Giuseppe, after supper you and Pontormo will take the woman to his house. Tomorrow morning you will fetch her from there, and you will do so every day.'

While I had been thinking about Duke Cosimo, Duke Cosimo must have been thinking about us. I suddenly realised that someone was knocking quietly at our door. Bronzino did not move.

'More soldiers?' he asked. 'Or another angry crowd?'

'The knocking is too diffident to be a soldier or a rioter,'

Pontormo commented, 'unless it is an unusually timid soldier or an unusually courteous rioter.'

'Giuseppe, go and look,' Pontormo ordered. Rather than open the door immediately, in case it was more trouble, I went to the studio window and looked down. All I could see was the head of a young boy, with neatly combed long hair.

'It's only a boy, Master,' I reported.

'Find out what he wants, then,' Bronzino responded. I ran down the stairs and opened the door to the tidy young boy.

'Please, sir –' he began.

'My name's Giuseppe,' I told him. 'Nobody has ever called me "sir" before. Do you want to see my master, the painter Il Bronzino?'

'Please, Messer Giuseppe, my name is Clemente Bandinelli. My father has sent me to tell you –'

I interrupted his speech, rather rudely, I admit. 'Come in. I think you ought to speak to my master directly. Your message is for him and not for me.' I showed Clemente upstairs, still wondering who he was and what his message might be. Ever since that afternoon when the Duke had discovered me putting gesso on the panel, messages seemed to bring only unwelcome tasks and obligations. I pushed Clemente into the studio. He stood before Bronzino like a criminal before a tribunal, and Bronzino glared at him severely.

'Well,' Bronzino said, 'I'm ready to hear your message.'

'Messer Bronzino, I am Clemente Bandinelli. My father is –' This time it was Pontormo who interrupted him, with a long sigh.

'– the sculptor Baccio Bandinelli,' Pontormo said. 'I have known him for many years.'

Bronzino tried to be polite. 'Everyone knows the fame of your father as a sculptor,' he said. 'What does he require of me?'

'The Duke has told my father that he must help you to design a painting which you are making for him. My father wants to know what the painting is, and when he should come to help.'

Pontormo interrupted again. 'Your father's skills are as a sculptor rather than as a painter. How can he help Bronzino with a painting?'

'My father is a painter as well, sir,' Clemente replied with unexpected spirit, 'but he is not to do any painting. He is only to advise, so he sends me to ask what the painting is about. Duke Cosimo would not tell him, for fear that someone in the Palazzo would overhear and let out the secret.'

Bronzino smiled. 'If we were pagans here, Clemente,' he said, 'I would tell you to kneel, because you are in the presence of the goddess Venus.' The boy looked round nervously, to find Angelina smiling at him. As I had done when I had first seen her, Clemente assumed that the smile was meant for him alone.

'I am honoured to meet you,' he said to her apparent indifference.

'She will not answer you,' Bronzino said, 'because she speaks to nobody.'

I interrupted my master. 'Her name in Angelina, Clemente. She is to be a model in the painting.'

Bronzino was furious with me. 'Let me speak for myself you insolent – you insolent apprentice. Now, Clemente, this lady is to be the model for Venus. Difficult as it may be to believe, my apprentice Giuseppe is to be the model for Cupid, by special order of the Duke. If it were my own choice, I would have Giuseppe model only as an over-age putto, because he is fit for nothing else.'

Clemente recovered himself surprisingly quickly and recalled his mission. 'Am I to tell my father that the painting is to be of Venus and Cupid?'

'Yes,' Bronzino replied, 'but there are to be other figures in the painting as well, and other symbols, too. I haven't yet decided on what they will be. That is my message to your father. Tell him that my door is open to him in the middle of tomorrow morning.'

Clemente turned to go, but I held out a cup to him. 'Will you not have some wine before you leave?' I asked him, because of my shame that Bronzino had offered him nothing.

'Thank you,' Clemente replied, 'but my father has forbidden me to drink wine for a month. It's one of his punishments.' I showed him down to the door and watched him march smartly away down the street.

After supper that evening, Bronzino made me pack up Angelina's belongings again. I hoped that she would rebel against being put out of our house for the night, but Pontormo once again demonstrated his strange instinctive knowledge of how to calm her. Angelina let him lead her out of the house, with his hand firmly grasping hers.

If it had not been for Pontormo's dishevelled appearance, anyone might have taken them for a prosperous merchant and his newly acquired young wife. Bronzino had ordered me to walk behind them, to maintain the dignity of his household, so that people should not believe that he had no servants (which, of course, he did not). He had to lend me his official night-walking licence. All the way, Pontormo muttered words to Angelina that I could not hear. He kept hold of her hand, and rubbed her back with his other hand. Angelina remained as quiet as usual, which I had expected, but I was not prepared for the silence of the people who watched from their windows.

That afternoon a mob had come to our house to demand liberty for Angelina, but where were they now? They did not even stare in contempt and amusement as they would have stared at a Moor or a Jew or a leper. Since I had nobody to talk to, and nobody spoke to me, I thought about how I could gain Angelina's freedom. I even asked myself what she would do with it. Perhaps she already had more freedom than I had ever known in any other person.

At Pontormo's door, he took Angelina's possessions from me, and I transferred my unlit lantern from my left shoulder to my right.

'Good night, Giuseppe,' he said. 'We'll see you tomorrow morning.'

I had never known the closing of a door to cause me such anguish. There was nothing for me to do but to walk back to Bronzino's house.

Then I thought of one thing I could do. I lit the lantern and held it before me as I made my way home, unnecessarily consuming Bronzino's lamp oil. This time people did look at me, trying to see what grand person I was preceding through the darkening streets. I ignored them, carrying my lantern defiantly in front of me. I even thought of crying, 'Make way for Giuseppe!' as I went.

When I arrived home, I extinguished the lantern and put it away before Bronzino could notice that I had been presumptuously lighting myself through Florence. I found him seated in front of the wooden panel on which he would have to execute his painting. He was making more rough sketches, and as I came in he did not ask whether Pontormo and Angelina had arrived safely. I am sure that he was not thinking of them at all.

'Tomorrow,' he announced, 'we shall start trying out some poses.'

He poured out two cups of wine and pushed one across the table to me. It was the first time that he had ever served me anything.

I had another new experience later that night. With Pontormo having gone back to his own house, Bronzino hauled me to his room and worked his unclean desires upon me instead. I had undergone that degradation many times before, but now that I had touched a woman for the first time, I was newly resentful of the hardness and roughness of Bronzino's body. I had always known that it was a sin in the eyes of God and in the eyes of most people, but now I felt for the first time how wrong it was for two male bodies to be clasped together. I submitted without complaint, as I always did, but as I climbed shakily upstairs with aching bowels, I now felt not only resentment of Bronzino. I felt ashamed of myself.

6

I woke up long before dawn. It was one of those awakenings when you instantly remember what was on your mind before you fell asleep. I was struck by two strong feelings at once: concern for Angelina, and a wish to rebel against Bronzino.

The sellers of groceries were surprised at the size of the orders that I placed with them from the studio window. I spent Bronzino's money freely on the best bread and meat, vegetables and the small soft fruits of the spring. I had not devised much that I could do to help Angelina, but at least I could make sure that she was well fed. Even if she ended up in a shape more associated with the god Bacchus than with Venus, I did not care.

I had only just put away all this profusion of food in the pantry, and hidden the meat in a marinade in the cellar, when Bronzino stalked into the studio.

'Why are you still here?' he demanded. 'You should be on your way to Pontormo's house by now. I expect they're already waiting for you.'

Pontormo might well be waiting impatiently, I thought, but Angelina would be serenely indifferent, expecting nothing at all from the day. In fact, when I did arrive at Pontormo's house, the shutters were closed as firmly as those of the House of Idleness and Immorality opposite Bronzino's.

I knocked several times before Pontormo's voice quavered, 'Go away!' from somewhere deep within.

'It's me, Giuseppe,' I called. 'My master is expecting you.'

'Well, I'm *his* master,' Pontormo retorted, 'so let him wait.'

'I'm waiting, too, out here in the hot sun,' I called back.

'All right, all right,' Pontormo replied. 'Give me a little while.'

I had to wait indeed only a little while before Pontormo came out, wincing at the morning light. He pulled Angelina out behind him. He obviously had no idea how to arrange her hair, so it hung down around her shoulders. Bronzino would probably reprimand me for taking Angelina about publicly with loose hair, but I found the effect pleasing and beautiful.

As we set off, a breeze threaded its way towards us from the banks of the Arno, fondling Angelina's hair. I was reminded of the hair of Simonetta Vespucci, fluttering in the sea winds as she stands in her giant seashell, representing Venus newly created for gods and men.

The door of our house was opened for us when we arrived. It turned out to be the boy Clemente Bandinelli, who must have been watching out for us from the studio window.

'Good morning!' I said. 'Perhaps I'm on the wrong side of this door.'

'Good morning, sir. And Madam. And sir as well,' he replied.

Bronzino came down to meet us, and greeted Pontormo first.

'Welcome, Master. Please will you bring the woman up to Giuseppe's room?'

Pontormo pushed Angelina past me, and he gently urged her up the stairs. Clemente closed the door behind me, while I, who had been given no orders, went into the studio. A man with a long beard was sitting in one of our chairs, with his hands on his splayed knees, contemplating the half-prepared wooden panel. As I entered, the man turned his head towards me, but he kept his hands fixed on his knees.

'So you're the elderly Cupid, are you?' he said, in a voice so loud that it made me start. 'That oaf Bronzino must be on a tight budget for models. He's lucky, though, isn't he? Duke Cosimo provides most of them free.'

'I am an apprentice,' I replied, 'and I must serve and honour my master.'

'So you must!' he agreed. 'That snivelling weed Clemente, cowering behind you now, is my apprentice, and I thrash him when he doesn't serve and honour me as I require.'

'My master has never struck me,' I replied, not mentioning that Bronzino frequently used another instrument of punishment to hurt me.

'Oh, I wasn't being particularly rude to him,' the man said. 'My name is Baccio Bandinelli, and I speak badly of everyone. When I know you better, I will speak badly of you, too, all around Florence.'

'I have heard of you, Messer Bandinelli,' I said.

'I am sure you have heard hostile remarks about me, too? You must have heard them from that mad old rooster Pontormo. Well, ask him what the terrible fate was that befell the Golden Child.'

I did not then know that Bandinelli was actually six years older than the 'mad old rooster' Pontormo. I also knew nothing about the Golden Child, but I was not willing to gratify Bandinelli by revealing my curiosity. I had no memory of ever hearing any Classical legend that featured a Golden Child, although I had heard of the legend of the Golden Man of South America, whom the Spaniards call El Dorado.

We heard Bronzino and Pontormo coming down to the studio.

'Cover your eyes, Clemente,' Bandinelli ordered. 'Don't open them again until I tell you to.'

Clemente put both his hands over his eyes in a childish way. To my horror and shame, Bronzino and Pontormo brought Angelina into the studio in a state of complete nudity. Pontormo made her kneel in front of the panel. Bronzino tugged at my doublet.

'You too, Giuseppe. We are going to start planning the painting.'

I was so angry that I was surprised that Bronzino did not perceive how flushed I was all over when I had stripped off as well.

'Kneel beside the woman, Giuseppe,' Bronzino commanded.

'Her name is Angelina, Master,' I reminded him as I obeyed.

'I doubt that she knows she has a name,' Bronzino replied.

Bandinelli finally took his hands off his knees, linked them behind his head, and rocked back on the chair.

'Yes, indeed, very Classical, I admit,' he remarked. 'We can do something with this if you take my advice. Clemente! You can look now.'

Clemente took his hands down from his eyes, stared at Angelina and myself in shock, and then started to lift his hands again to hide the sight.

'Clemente!' Bandinelli roared. 'I ordered you to look. You'll pay for this disobedience when we get home.'

Clemente looked at us miserably, and Bandinelli began to laugh, so loudly that the four legs of the chair danced agitatedly on the planks of the floor.

Even Bronzino seemed to be made uncomfortable by this, and he started another topic of conversation. 'What are your thoughts on how we can represent Venus with a grown-up Cupid?'

Bandinelli forced himself to stop laughing. 'Ah, well, we must make up our own legend. I don't know of any tradition of a grown Cupid.'

Unexpectedly, Clemente made a contribution. 'There's the story of Cupid and Psyche, Father,' he remarked.

Bandinelli glowered at his son. It was not merely fatherly anger, of which I had seen plenty in my own boyhood. There was an evil rage in Bandinelli's eyes. Many accused Bandinelli of madness, but I am convinced that he was not mad: I believe that he consciously chose to hurt people for his amusement. It was brave of Clemente to assure himself of an even more cruel beating by pointing out a story that his father had failed to think of.

Bronzino considered, and dismissed, the suggestion. 'Venus does not appear in the story of Cupid and Psyche,' he said. 'We would also have to find a Psyche, and God knows it took enough trouble to find a Venus. Anyway, it would make the story unbalanced.'

'You couldn't make a sculptural group out of it,' Bandinelli agreed.

'You would have to work out a relationship between Venus and her daughter-in-law, and Cupid might prove too strong for Venus to control.'

'That's it!' Bronzino exclaimed, making both Angelina

and myself jump. 'Cupid has grown up, and Venus is trying to keep control over his activities.'

Pontormo added his own thoughts. 'It wouldn't be a subject for me,' he admitted, 'but if it were, I would ask how the viewer will know that the two central figures are Venus and Cupid? You will have to give them attributes by which they will be recognised.'

'Bronzino could do it with the title,' Bandinelli suggested. 'Venus Restraining Cupid, or something like that. Not many people would be able to tell that Botticelli's painting of Simonetta Vespucci – God preserve her beauty even in Heaven – was representing the birth of Venus if he hadn't given the painting that title.'

'I'll give Cupid wings and a bow, and a quiver and an arrow,' Bronzino declared. 'Even the uneducated would recognise him as Cupid, and King François will not need any more clues.'

'What about Venus?' Pontormo asked. 'She could be just a beautiful mortal woman, or be mistaken for a different goddess.'

'We'll work on that,' Bronzino said. 'Let's look at our models.' He clasped his hands behind his back and walked around us as though we were a pair of statues that he had just removed from their crate and straw. 'Bandinelli,' he said, 'come and give us the sculptor's point of view.'

'Is that what the Duke sent me here for?' Bandinelli remarked as he, too, came to inspect us. 'I'm also a painter, you know.'

Pontormo crossed his arms and cast an angry look at the floor.

Bandinelli studied Angelina and myself at all angles.

'The bodies are good,' he conceded. 'They suit your light, Bronzino. You always paint your people in a soft light.'

'No, I don't,' Bronzino objected. 'I paint only what I see, as I see it.'

'That is your style,' Bandinelli said. 'I carve and chisel only what I see, as I see it, and yet people recognise my sculptures as being by me.'

That was a bold claim by Bandinelli. Not many scholars and artists in Florence considered that Bandinelli had a recognisable style of sculpture, and his few paintings were so dull that they had no merit at all. On the other hand, Bandinelli did have a manner of behaviour that was distinctive. It was also probably, and fortunately, inimitable, although in later years the blustering sculptor Benvenuto Cellini did try, but that was after I had left Florence and knew that I would never be allowed to return.

Bandinelli stalked back to his chair and sat down again. 'There's no point in wondering about poses until we've decided on how the two figures are to be represented. Will they be touching each other, or apart? Are they to be alone, or with other figures?'

Angelina seemed to have become tired of kneeling painfully on the bare boards of the floor. She lay down upon her belly and giggled to herself.

'What is she laughing at?' Bronzino asked suspiciously.

Nobody else seemed to want to answer him, so I did. 'What does it matter, Master, if she's in a happy mood? Perhaps she's just laughing at us. Perhaps it's we who seem strange and odd to her.'

Pontormo ran his fingers through his beard until they collided with a tangle of whiskers. He pulled his fingers out. 'Yes,' he remarked, 'she is not an idiot. She is lively, and aware of us and of herself. I would like to know her thoughts.'

'Well, I know my thoughts,' Bronzino said. 'I'm getting

hungry. Giuseppe, dress yourself and make some lunch.'

'Clemente, you help Bronzino's apprentice,' Bandinelli ordered his son.

'What about Angelina?' I asked.

'I'll take her back to your room and get her dressed,' Pontormo reassured me.

Clemente followed me obediently into the kitchen, where I set him to chopping vegetables and washing strawberries.

'Giuseppe, I envy you,' he said to my surprise.

'Why?' I asked. 'How is my life better than yours?'

'You are an artist's apprentice, and you do not have to live with your father.'

'I couldn't live with my father even if I wanted to,' I replied, and I told him the story of how my father had handed me over to Bronzino like an unwanted puppy.

'I wish my father would apprentice me to a sculptor,' Clemente said. 'He could abandon me as your father did if he wanted to, just as long as I could be apprenticed to a good master.'

'Why do you need a master?' I asked. 'Isn't your father a good enough master and teacher? All Florence knows him as a sculptor.'

'He can't see any talent in me,' Clemente said quietly, looking away from me. 'He teaches me a little, but he always loses his temper. He never takes on an apprentice. Who would bind themselves to him, with his rages? He offends the rich people who give him commissions. He even quarrels with the foundrymen who cast his bronze statues.'

'Have you asked him to apprentice you to someone else?' I asked.

'He says he won't shame himself by inflicting a useless dolt on another sculptor,' Clemente replied. 'Anyway, he's the best sculptor practising in Florence today. I couldn't find a more expert master.'

When we served lunch, we found that Pontormo had once more somehow got Angelina dressed. She was sitting quietly in her place at the table. I realised that I was going to have to learn how to arrange and fix up her hair. That was an art in which Bronzino had not instructed me, and I did not expect that he would be willing to learn it himself.

Both Bandinelli and his son showed extraordinarily elegant table manners, handling their cutlery like swords in the hands of fencing masters. When we rose from the table, Angelina remained seated, and Bandinelli once more walked round behind her. 'Most beautiful,' he said.

'More than beautiful,' Bronzino commented. 'I chose her because she is so special and unusual.'

'Why don't you paint her with her hair down like that?' Bandinelli suggested.

'Because that is not my style,' Bronzino said.

'This morning you claimed not to have a style,' Bandinelli reminded him.

'I don't mean my style of painting,' Bronzino replied. 'I mean the type of subject that I paint. I make representations of order and calm and restraint.'

'Botticelli painted Simonetta Vespucci as Venus with loose and blowing hair,' Bandinelli said.

'Everyone would say that I was trying to imitate Botticelli,' Bronzino replied. 'In any case, I want the painting to be an interior scene.'

Even then, when the painting had not even been begun, I had to admit that Bronzino was right. Botticelli's world of ocean winds, flowing hair and light, joyous figures dancing through flowers in forest groves, was not one that Bronzino could ever enter. He was a man of interiors and soft light from curtained windows. Indeed, he might have been better as an architect, dealing only with shapes and patterns rather than people. I wondered whether his bent for austerity and coolness came from the Moorish ancestors that I suspected him to have. If Bronzino had dressed in robes and a turban he would have been stoned in the streets.

Some of Bronzino's words had stuck in Bandinelli's mind as he prepared to go home with Clemente. 'An interior scene,' he repeated. 'Venus and Cupid at home, somewhere on Mount Olympus. That's original. I'll think about it.'

I was thinking about something else. I was looking forward to another afternoon with Angelina, up in my room. Bronzino might have been reading my thoughts, because he disappointed me.

'My master Pontormo will take the woman home with him,' he told me. 'They'll be back with us for supper.'

I looked desperately at the unsuspecting Angelina. 'Master, she cannot keep going out with unbound hair.'

'Bind it, then.'

'I don't know how to, Master,' I replied.

'Well, find out. The knowledge must be available somewhere in Florence. You're right. I don't want to have to keep bringing in a hairdresser when we start work on the painting.'

'May I go out this afternoon?' I asked him.

'Yes,' he replied, 'after I've finished with you.'

The price of my few hours of liberty was, of course, a sweaty and uncomfortable session to satisfy Bronzino's immoral desires, which I did well enough that he fell asleep immediately afterwards. When I crept out of his room, I washed myself all over, more thoroughly than I had ever done before. The innocent perfection of Angelina's body had taught me that men's bodies were coarse and ugly. I had never felt such a sense of shame and pollution.

I went out into the silent city, hurrying towards Sister Benedicta's house. With nearly everyone asleep, it was like walking through a city that had been magically stilled in a brilliantly sunlit night. Eventually I found myself in front of that door with its intimidating grille. I looked up for a moment at the window where I had first seen Angelina, hoping that by a miracle she would be there again, and that the events of the past few days would have been struck away so that she could live on in peace in what was her only home.

There was no miracle, and no face at all was in the window, so I knocked upon the door. When I had waited a polite length of time without an answer, I knocked again. This time I could just overhear an exchange of voices within. I tried to compose my courage to confront the basilisk eyes of Sister Benedicta, but when the grille was opened I found myself looking into the face of an old man.

'What do you want?' he demanded, in a foreign accent that I could not identify.

'I would like to speak to Sister Benedicta,' I told the old man. 'My name is Giuseppe, and I am an apprentice to the painter Bronzino. Sister Benedicta knows me. I want to speak to her about the welfare of her ward Angelina.'

'Angelina!' the old man exclaimed. 'Come in, come in.'

He swung the door open to admit me once more to the dark hall.

When I stepped inside, I noticed a strange smell in the house, not unlike the smell of gunpowder, which I knew from the smell of the smoke when Duke Cosimo's cannons were fired at the climax of public ceremonies. Now that I could see the old man completely, I was struck by two aspects of his appearance. The first was that he was underdressed almost to the point of indecency. He was wearing nothing above the waist, but he had on a heavy blue apron decorated with white and green stains of irregular shape, like the meaningless dark patches on the moon.

The second striking aspect of the old man was his bald cranium. Like only a small minority of bald men, the falling away of his hair had revealed a skull that was perfectly shaped, with a dome that the great architect Bramante would have admired. We stood staring at each other, so I felt obliged to speak.

'Is Sister Benedicta in?' I asked.

'She is in the laboratory,' he replied. 'We are in the middle of a chemical process that must not be interrupted. She will come up when the next state of the matter is stable.'

Sister Benedicta's voice called up from below like a soul begging for an early release from purgatory. She must have opened a door, because thin smoke came drifting into the hall, together with a smell like that of house paint, and the sound of some liquid somewhere giving off bubbles. Sister Benedicta came up, wiping her hands on a cloth. Instead of being dressed in her nun's habit, she was wearing the coarse smock of a peasant woman, and an apron like the one the old man was wearing.

For the first time I noticed his strong bare arms and his bulging shoulder muscles. Was he, I wondered, some sort of household servant or guard?

Yet this was supposed to be a house only of women.

'Well, Giuseppe?' Sister Benedicta snapped at me. I noticed the coppery brown of her hair. It must once have been deep red. What an artist's model she would have made then.

I explained my unusual errand, while I still wondered who the old man was. When he heard that I had come in order to be instructed in how to bind up a woman's hair, the old man laughed, showing a surprisingly good and complete set of teeth. Sister Benedicta was less amused.

'You've come here, not because you care for Angelina, but so that you can keep her groomed for your own convenience. Do you think that she is an animal, to be brushed and washed?'

'I'm sorry,' I said, 'but I do want to help her. I don't know how to do women's things, and Bronzino will not have any other woman in his house.' I explained how I had been brought up in an all-male family with neither a mother nor sisters around me, and had then passed on to the house of Bronzino, where only he and his master Pontormo ever resided.

'You little devil!' Sister Benedicta cried. 'You just want to solve your own problems. You care nothing for Angelina's happiness.'

Living with Bronzino had taught me many skills, and one of them was how to feign patience.

'If I do not do these things for her,' I said, 'nobody else will, and Duke Cosimo will not allow her to come back to you. Pontormo cannot even look after himself properly, and I fear very much for Angelina if she is left to him. Sister Benedicta, I am not asking you to help me. I am asking you to help Angelina.'

The old man intervened at this point.

'Listen to him, Benedicta, please. I would help him myself if I could, but I probably know even less of women than he does.'

'What, even after more than forty years as a priest?' Sister Benedicta retorted. 'You must know a vast amount about women after hearing their confessions for all that time.'

'I know how to care for their souls, but not for their bodies,' the old man replied. Obviously he was the priest who said Mass for the inmates of that odd house, but I had never seen a priest half-naked in a stained and smelly apron before. I decided to throw a provocative firework into the conversation, since the two of them seemed to have forgotten about me.

'Bronzino says that Angelina has no soul,' I remarked.

'The brute!' Sister Benedicta replied. 'Tell him that she is a baptised Christian. Is he, I wonder? He looks like a Moor to me,' she continued, making me wonder in horror whether her alchemical activities had given her the ability to read my thoughts and inspect my shameful memories.

'Bronzino is certainly a Christian,' I said. I was more familiar with his body than any man ought to be, and so I knew that he had not suffered religious mutilation.

'Then let him behave like a Christian,' Sister Benedicta declared, and at that point I lost the ability to pretend to be patient with her.

'Why don't you behave like a Christian, and give me the help that I need to help Angelina?' I asked. 'I could have ignored her, and let her become dirty and ill, and nobody would have punished me for it, as long as she still looked beautiful in the painting. Instead, I came to you because I thought you cared about her.'

'I do care about Angelina!' Sister Benedicta protested.

A puff of grey and green smoke vented up from below, and Sister Benedicta's eyes flickered towards it. I could not make out whether the sight of the smoke was causing her anxiety, or excitement. I took it as an opportunity to attack her again.

'You care more about your devilish magical practices

than you do about Angelina!' I cried. 'I should report you to the bishop.'

The old priest answered on Sister Benedicta's behalf. 'The bishop knows, and has given us special approval,' he informed me. 'We are alchemists, not sorcerers. The Church forbids magic. She does not forbid seeking after knowledge.'

'I thought the Church also told you to feed Christ's sheep,' I replied. 'Angelina needs help. I want to give it to her, but I need help as well.'

Sister Benedicta's eyes turned back to the smoke, which was now slowly dispersing around the ceiling, and sending filaments into the corridors, as though it were setting off to explore the house. The old priest offered a suggestion.

'Sister Benedicta, why don't you call for Maria to advise Giuseppe, while you attend to the Athenor?'

'Maria!' Sister Benedicta called. 'Come down here!'

With no further words to me, Sister Benedicta scuttled off down the steps to attend to whatever the mysterious Athenor might be, holding up her skirts with both hands like a woman farm worker running through the fields.

Maria came down shyly, and for the first time I noticed that she was as dark as Bronzino.

The old priest spoke to her gently in his strange accent. 'Maria, please take Giuseppe up to the solar and give him some refreshments. I'll join you both in a moment.'

Maria showed me up to the solar on the next floor. I was surprised at how luxurious it was. The room was furnished with sumptuous chairs, and the walls were decorated with tapestries and paintings that were at least a century old, to judge by their primitive style. When Maria brought in a jug and three cups, the old priest was already coming up behind her. I was grateful for the open window, even though it admitted the sun as well as the air. I wished that the rules of politeness that Bronzino had taught me did not forbid me to look out on what might be below, to see whether it was a paved courtyard or a garden. The old priest sat down opposite me. I began by saying, 'Father, you must forgive my curiosity.'

'It is my trade to administer forgiveness, even if I do not actually give it myself,' the old man replied. 'In any case, honest curiosity is not a sin. What is your question?'

'Well, Father, Sister Benedicta has forgotten to give me your name.'

'Ha! Well, I'm as guilty as she is, because I should have introduced myself. Would you like my name in the original English version, or in the Italian garb in which I have dressed it?'

'I'll try the English version first, Father,' I replied, glad to learn that not all his nation had joined their king Enrico the Eighth in turning away from the Church.

The English priest emitted a sound that sounded like someone who was having a sneezing fit while simultaneously spitting out a plum stone.

'Now,' he continued, 'perhaps you would rather call me Radulfo Fleccia?'

'Yes, if you please, Father Fleccia,' I replied.

I don't know how he spelt his name in Italian, and I certainly have no idea how the English version could possibly be spelt at all. Perhaps the Moors or the Jews could spell it in their frighteningly alien letters. Father Fleccia turned his face to the window, so that his bald head was illuminated, and his whiskers shone like silver. 'I do enjoy your sunlight and heat in Italy,' he remarked. 'I have been in some gloomy and cold places in my long life.'

'You speak Italian very well,' I said, and it was true.

'I had a good grounding in Latin and French,' he said, 'and I get plenty of practice. Nobody who is not English knows our language, and the only other Englishmen in Florence are heretical merchants who would like to see me executed by our king.'

'So you have nobody to talk to,' I said in commiseration.

'Not in my own language, no, but I have plenty of people to talk to in Italian, and in Latin, and sometimes in French. Sometimes I'm allowed to read books at the university, although they're suspicious of me because it's a secular university and I'm a priest.'

'You must miss English books,' I said.

'English books! The only books we write are account books. Our best writers write only in French or Latin,' Father Fleccia explained. 'We have no literature, no painters and no sculptors. I blame the grey and damp climate.'

At that point Sister Benedicta came up and joined us. She had clearly spent part of the time tidying herself.

'The Athenor is in no danger of exploding,' she announced cryptically, as she poured herself some wine. 'Giuseppe, has Father Fleccia introduced himself to you? I should have done it myself.'

'Yes, he has, thank you, Sister,' I replied.

'Father Fleccia is very good with the girls and women here in the house,' Sister Benedicta said. 'They all trust him.'

'I had a sister who could not speak,' Father Fleccia remarked. 'Some of the women remind me of her.'

I wanted to ask what an Athenor was, but I remembered why I had come to disturb the peace of the house that afternoon, if indeed there was peace there at all, with all this smoke and bubbling and threatening smells.

'I would like Angelina to trust me,' I said. Of course, I said nothing about our long embrace in my room the day before.

'Yes,' Sister Benedicta said, 'I can see now what it is that you need from us. Maria!'

Maria came forward, and bent down to listen to a long, whispered set of instructions from Sister Benedicta.

'Maria will bring you what you need,' Sister Benedicta said. 'I will tell you what to do, if Father Fleccia will permit me to mention such matters in his presence.'

'Nobody can shock a priest,' Father Fleccia replied. 'Everything is mentioned in our presence. It's the nature of our life to know all about matters in which we never participate ourselves.'

He sat back and gazed out of the window at the blue sky and hot roofs of Florence. He must have known a great deal of cold, if he took such delight in the heat from which we native Florentines were always trying to shelter. While Father Fleccia contemplated the burning May sky, Sister Benedicta explained to me what Angelina would need. She even demonstrated on Maria how I was to comb and brush and bind up Angelina's hair. She even apologised to Maria for using her as the model.

'Giuseppe's own hair is too curly, and Father Fleccia no longer has any hair at all, ha, ha, ha!'

'My hair was never bound up anyway,' Father Fleccia replied.

Maria prepared a bag of necessary articles, and gave it to me.

'Now I must ask something of you,' Sister Benedicta said. 'What is this painting to be like?'

'My master has not decided the details yet,' I answered, 'but I am to be Cupid and Angelina is to be Venus.'

'I knew that already,' Sister Benedicta replied.

'You know as much as I do,' I said. 'Bronzino is planning

the composition with the help of the sculptor Bandinelli.'

'Why are all these men coming to your house, and no women?' Sister Benedicta asked.

'Because it has always been a house of men,' I said, 'and because Duke Cosimo will not allow Angelina to go out of our care.'

'How is she to go to Mass, then?' Father Fleccia demanded.

'That hasn't occurred to Bronzino,' I replied, 'and indeed it had not occurred to me.

'Well, then,' Father Fleccia replied, 'I shall bring the Eucharist to Angelina myself next Sunday afternoon. Your master cannot prevent that. Let me be the next man to be admitted to your house.'

7

By the time the following Sunday came, our peculiar household had settled into a kind of eccentric but organised routine. Every morning, I bought the best food that the vendors were offering.

Bronzino had noticed the extra expense, but when I told him that the additional (and better) food was for Angelina, he did not object. He must have realised that he would have to answer to Duke Cosimo if our Venus were to start looking hollow-cheeked and bony.

Before breakfast, Pontormo would bring Angelina over from his house, and after breakfast I would tidy her up and see to her hair as Sister Benedicta and Maria had taught me. This ritual was as tricky as applying gesso. I had to brush Angelina's hair back as tightly as I could, and then draw it through a ring of horsehair. While I was doing this, I had to remember not to swallow any of the pins that filled my mouth, making me look like a ladies' dressmaker. I then had to bind every lock of Angelina's hair and pin it to the horsehair ring.

I would still rather have seen Bronzino paint Angelina with her hair flowing freely, as Sandro Botticelli painted Simonetta Vespucci when she had posed as Venus. If I had been born in that time, perhaps I would have been happier as Botticelli's apprentice than I was as Bronzino's – but of course I would never have known Angelina. I discovered by accident that if I set Angelina in a particular posture she would hold it for an unnaturally long time while I washed her face and brushed her hair. Bronzino would find that useful when we had to begin posing for the painting.

We would spend the rest of the morning waiting around while Bronzino and Bandinelli discussed the elements of the composition. Bronzino had already made a decision about Angelina's hair.

'I'll have her hair up, bound with a fillet of pearls,' he declared early on in the week. 'Giuseppe knows how to do it.'

'What about Cupid?' Bandinelli asked. 'How will you decorate him?'

'His quiver and arrow will be enough,' Bronzino replied. 'What more does Cupid need?'

Clemente offered a contribution to the discussion. 'Will you give Cupid wings, Signor Bronzino?'

Bandinelli reached over and clouted Clemente around the ear so hard that Clemente fell off his stool onto the floor.

'Keep silent and stay out of this!' Bandinelli roared. 'This is a conversation between master artists, about art. You're nobody and you know nothing, so say nothing.'

Clemente said no more, but Bronzino did reply to him indirectly.

'Yes, Cupid must have wings, but I'll try to keep them inconspicuous. An adult Cupid would need wings so large that they would dominate the whole painting, if I follow convention and make them snow-white and prominent.'

'What will Venus do with her hands?' Bandinelli asked. 'Will she cover herself modestly, as Simonetta Vespucci did?'

'We'll think of something for her to hold. We'll decide

that when we've worked out what objects and other figures are going to be in the painting.'

Clemente had set himself back on his stool, and was slowly rubbing his face. His father ignored him, and so did Bronzino, so I moved my own stool over and sat next to him, on the side which had not been struck by the blow. Angelina showed that she could still surprise me by picking up her own stool and sitting next to Clemente on the other side. She was really far too tall to sit on the stool, so her splayed posture was less than graceful. She was much taller than Clemente, who had always seemed frightened by her. He stopped rubbing his face, and looked up nervously into her baffling eyes.

While Bronzino and Bandinelli carried on their self-important conversation, I watched as Angelina reached out to Clemente and gently caressed the hurt and swollen part of his face. Clemente sat still. It reminded me at first of a man sitting obediently but apprehensively while the tooth-extracting pliers of a barber loom ever closer to his eyes.

'Clemente,' I murmured, 'is Angelina making you uncomfortable? I can try to stop her.'

'No,' Clemente replied out of the near side of his mouth, 'I like it. She has a perfect touch.'

It was a strange phrase, but in my secret guilt I knew what he meant.

At that moment, Bronzino happened to notice us talking quietly together. He held up his hand and silenced Bandinelli, a feat that few men had ever achieved, and then addressed me.

'Why aren't you listening to us? You're both appren-tices.' (Clemente was not even an apprentice, but Bronzino may not have known that.) 'You should be trying to learn from us.'

'Master,' I replied, trying to protect Clemente from another blow from his father, 'Angelina was trying to comfort Clemente.'

'Damn you for a useless fool!' Bronzino shouted. For an instant, I had the unbearable thought that perhaps he only kept me in his house so that he could misuse my body. Pontormo, who had been wedged sideways into the window in a boy's posture which hardly suited his age, sprang up and glared at his former apprentice. Bronzino ignored him, and continued to address me.

'If you have no time to listen to your betters talking about art, then you might as well not be here. Go out and look at the art of the streets, and take the woman with you so she can get some air.'

He reached into his shirt and took out two coins, which he flung at me. I caught the coins in mid-air. They were still as hot as his body.

'Buy the woman a hat, a wide-brimmed hat!' he shouted. 'To keep the sun off her face.'

'Her name is Angelina,' I said defiantly, as I put away the coins. I was determined that I would spend all of Bronzino's money while we were out.

'My son's name is Clemente,' Bandinelli added sarcastically. 'Take him out with you as well, although showing him art is as much use as holding up a prayer book before the eyes of a donkey.'

Clemente scrambled up and held the door open for us, while I led Angelina by the hand. When we came out into the sunny street, we could still hear the voices of Bronzino and Bandinelli coming from the upper window. I wanted to get away from that sound as quickly as I could, so I took Angelina and Clemente off in the direction of the river Arno. People stared at Angelina, but only, I think, because of her unusual height. I wondered whether they thought she was my wife, or my older sister.

I expected Clemente to know his way around Florence, but he was quite lost. 'My father has never let me out on my own,' he explained. 'He thinks that I might run away.'

I would not have blamed Clemente if he had deserted Bandinelli, but he continued his explanation. 'I would never run away from my father. He represents the only chance I've got of becoming a sculptor myself.'

Angelina, whose parents had run away from her and entrusted her to the care of Sister Benedicta, seemed as always not to have heard any of this. We stopped at a stall that sold hats, which were piled and hanging down all over it like round white fungi. I placed Angelina in front of the stall, while the tough-nosed woman who owned it glared at her suspiciously. I pointed to all the hats. 'Which one do you want, Angelina?' I asked, but Angelina took no notice of them, or of me. 'I'll have to choose one for her myself,' I told the stallholder. 'Can you help me? What size do you think she takes?'

The woman picked one of the hats out of her stock, and tilted her head at Angelina. 'Is that tall girl an idiot, then?' she asked.

'No, she isn't,' I replied, 'and she isn't deaf. She just never speaks or behaves normally with people. We don't know why.'

I reached up and put the hat onto Angelina's head. She did not even bend down a little to help me do it. I tied the strings under her chin. Now she would be safe from turning brown in the sun, as Bronzino wished to prevent, although she would have had to spend a long time in the sun before she would have turned as brown as he was. The woman examined Angelina more carefully.

'She isn't the girl who was carried off to that artist's house, is she?' she asked. 'There was a lot of anger about that, the other day.'

Both Clemente and I realised that we were uncomfortably alone in the middle of a large number of people who might turn upon us at any moment. Angelina remained serene and silent and smiling.

'Somebody was telling lies,' I said. 'Does she look like a prisoner to you, free here, in the public streets?'

'They say she was taken by force,' the woman persisted.

'Yes,' I said loudly so that all the bystanders could hear me, 'she was taken by force from the house where she lived. The force was a squad of Duke Cosimo's guards under the command of Captain Da Lucca.'

The woman grunted at the name of the stern dark captain.

'I am looking after her as best I can,' I said. 'Her name is Angelina.' I hoped that her parents, whoever and wherever they were, would hear about it, and perhaps feel shame. 'If anyone judges that Angelina has been badly treated,' I continued, even more loudly, 'let them go and make their complaint to Duke Cosimo de' Medici, or to Captain Da Lucca who carried out the Duke's order.' I hoped that would guarantee safety for Angelina, if not for myself and Clemente. 'Now,' I finished off, 'how much do you want for her hat?'

I was disappointed when the stallholder actually named a fair price at the first time of asking. The mention of the Duke must have frightened her as effectively as I had hoped. I had been expecting her to follow ancient Florentine tradition and ask for an outrageous price, which I would have paid without dispute – in Bronzino's money, of course.

We left the hat stall and its now-silenced owner, and walked to the bank of the river Arno. I watched Angelina to see if I could detect any sign of interest from her in anything that she saw. I still feared that inwardly she suffered from boredom, because she never did or said anything, but most of the time she did not even look where she was going. Clemente enjoyed all the sights: the buildings, the shops, the statues, the little shrines built into the walls of the houses of those who wished to be thought pious and the brightly dressed people of Florence performing noble or shameful activities in the street.

The heat of the May sun bounced off the idle surface of the river and offered up the smells of everything that was alive and dead in the water. The surface showed a broken, reflected Florence, and for the first time it struck me how the public buildings of the city were all equipped with defences. Even the merchants' houses often had towers with crenellations from which archers could fire. I drew Clemente's attention to the reflections.

'I wish I could paint that,' I said.

'Why not?' he replied. 'You're a painter's apprentice.'

'I haven't got the money to buy the materials,' I told him, 'and even if I did, Bronzino would dismiss me as his apprentice, for daring to go beyond my limits.'

For the time being, my job was still to grind powders, to mix size and to apply layer after layer of stinking gesso. I wondered when Bronzino would allow me to do more than paint small unimportant figures in the margins of his uninspired religious paintings, or do the boring job of colouring in the dark green or brownish backgrounds of which he was so fond. At least it was less-hard work than being a sculptor, and I wondered what Clemente's dreams were.

'Who would you like to sculpt, Clemente?' I asked. 'Do you ever see anyone in the street and think to yourself that you would like to turn them into a work in marble or bronze? Would you like to make a statue of Angelina?'

Clemente answered so immediately that I knew he must already have thought about it. 'Angelina is made for marble, not bronze,' he said, 'but if a sculptor did manage to catch her stillness, all the humanists, and the common people too, would say that it was unnatural.'

'Who else, then, would you carve in marble?' I asked him.

'Very few real people are suited for marble,' Clemente replied. 'I would not carve Duke Cosimo in marble. I would represent him in bronze.'

'Would you do Bronzino in bronze?' I asked. 'He even calls himself the little bronze man.'

Clemente surprised me by his answer. 'No, I would paint Bronzino as a portrait. There is something flat about him which would not suit a sculpture.'

I stopped conversing with Clemente about art and culture, because I noticed that a crowd was beginning to follow us. I was holding Angelina by her soft obedient hand, and she was walking along in quite a graceful movement, for her. The wide-brimmed white hat made her appear even taller than she was. She looked like a windmill sailing through the heads of the shoppers, beggars and thieves of Florence. Although I thought she was safe, I felt nervous and I hoped that my own hand was not communicating my apprehension to her. Although Angelina did not seem to understand words, she could certainly feel emotions.

When we came to the riverbank, I knew that there could be no escape from the curious crowd if they were to reveal themselves as hostile. I leaned against the wall, and hung over it, looking down into the slow waters sliding by. Clemente did the same, so that we had both turned our backs to the crowd. It was one way to find out quickly whether we were in danger or not. I prepared myself to let go of Angelina's hand at once if I felt my legs being whipped out from under me, so that I would not drag her with me if I took an involuntary dive into the river.

At first nothing happened. I could hear the people chatting and murmuring, but all they were talking about was Angelina's unusual height. Because both Clemente and I were looking down into the indifferent river, Angelina bent over the wall and did the same. She breathed in the ugly smell of the Arno, and then she began to laugh – not wildly, not madly, but a long natural laugh of happiness and joy. That turned the attitude of the spectators more effectively than anything that I could have said would have done. I feared that they would laugh, too, at Angelina, spoiling the mood, but instead they cheered her.

Angelina laughed on, while Clemente and I gazed ruefully at each other across her long back. I gestured to Clemente that we should move on, and this time we were not followed, although I did wonder whether the Duke had made arrangements for us to be kept observed. Probably not; he was so confident of his own power that he had little need of professional spies and paid informers, because his position was based on the people's acceptance of his strong and orderly rule.

'Clemente, where shall we go?' I asked.

'I don't know, Giuseppe,' he replied. 'You're a lot more familiar with the streets of Florence than I am.'

'Well, I can't ask Angelina,' I said. 'Look, she's stopped laughing now.

I wonder what caused her such delight?'

'It must have been the smell,' Clemente suggested. 'She liked the smell of the Arno.'

At first I wondered how anyone, even someone as unique as Angelina, could revel in the smell of fouled and sick waters, and then I remembered how the threatening smells of the alchemical laboratory had curled through the enclosed house in which she had lived. Was that why she had embraced me on my bed: because I was stinking of the unpleasant ingredients of the gesso? It was a humbling but risible thought, and now it was my turn to laugh, to Clemente's puzzlement.

'Now it's you who's laughing without a reason,' he said.

'No, I've just realised how we can keep Angelina happy in our house,' I told him. 'We must use lots of gesso, and let her stand close when I'm grinding and mixing the paint. What a good thing that the Duke didn't commission a sculpture instead!'

'Why?' Clemente asked, offended.

'Because sculptures don't smell,' I replied.

'You've obviously never been in a sculptor's studio and smelled the dust and the clay and the freshly cut stone,' Clemente said. He wiped the sweat off his face. 'Should we go in for a drink somewhere?'

It was a good suggestion, but I was nervous at the idea of taking Angelina into a public tavern. What might she do, and what might be done to her? 'No,' I said, 'let's go home instead.'

Angelina's new hat was so wide that I had to take it off her so that she could get in through our door. I doubt that Bronzino and Bandinelli had noticed how long we had been gone. While Clemente stayed downstairs to draw us some fresh cool water from the well, I took Angelina up to the studio. We found my master and Bandinelli gesticulating at each other in front of the panel that was to receive the painting. Bronzino was holding a sheet of paper with rough sketches on it.

'Cupid and Venus here in the centre,' he was saying. 'All the other figures and symbols can go around them.'

'You need to decide the rest, or you can't decide on the poses for Venus and Cupid,' Bandinelli objected.

Clemente came up with a jug of water, but his father ignored him.

We poured out the water, sat Angelina down, and then sat on the floor next to her, to enjoy the argument. After all, we had been told that we should listen to, and learn from, our betters.

'No,' Bronzino said, 'I'll set Venus and Cupid, who must dominate the composition in any case, in the centre. The other elements can be set with respect to the two central figures.'

I realised that Pontormo was not in the studio, and wondered where he had gone.

I forgot about Pontormo when Bronzino seemed to remember suddenly that he had an apprentice.

'Giuseppe! This afternoon you will mix some *gesso sottile*, the very best quality. When it's dry, you must prepare and apply a surface of *imprimatura*. I want the surface of the panel to be ready in the next few days, so that I can start the painting.'

Bandinelli rose from his chair. 'Then I'll go home. When should I come again?' he asked.

'Come on Friday,' Bronzino told him. 'We can talk about the composition before I actually start it. My master Pontormo will, I hope, be in a better and more courteous mood by then.'

'You might have had a worse boyhood,' Bandinelli

replied. 'You might have had me as your master.' Bandinelli laughed, but nobody else did. Clemente hurriedly finished off his mug of water before leaping up to hold the door open for his father.

When they had gone, I asked Bronzino whether Pontormo would be back for supper.

'Oh, yes. He simply wanted to get away from Bandinelli. You see, Bandinelli was taunting him about the business of the Golden Child.'

'Master,' I asked, 'what was the Golden Child? It sounds like something out of alchemy.'

'Sadly, it was not alchemy, but real life,' Bronzino said. 'Many years ago, there was a great triumphal procession here in Florence. We still have them, of course, but this was the greatest Triumph ever seen. You've certainly never seen anything like it.'

He continued, 'Pontormo was commissioned to help with designing the cars in the Triumph. He did splendid decorative paintings, and Bandinelli carved many figures, which Pontormo coloured.

'The first car had giant wooden painted statues of the Roman gods Saturn and Janus. It represented the ancient Age of Saturn. After the Age of Saturn there was the car of King Numa of the Romans, and – well, I'll tell you all about it another day, perhaps, but you must never ask Pontormo to talk about it.

'Anyway, after four more magnificent vehicles, when all the citizens thought that there could not possibly be anything more marvellous to see, there came the car representing the Golden Age, on which Pontormo and Bandinelli had done their best work.

'The car of the Golden Age was covered with Bandinelli's carvings and Pontormo's paintings. The centrepiece was a vast globe. On the globe, Bandinelli had put a statue of a dead man lying on his belly, sprawled across it. The man's arms were painted reddish-brown to look like rust, because the corpse represented the brutal Age of Iron, which was passing away. The back of the rusting Man of the Iron Age was split open, and from the opening there stood out a boy who seemed to be made out of gold.'

'What could that have cost?' I wondered aloud, imagining the stately procession of allegorical figures, and the colours and the paintings, and the carvings and the statues.

'It cost more than anyone had imagined!' Bronzino replied. 'You see, the golden naked boy was not a statue at all, but a live boy, who had been gilded all over. I was only young myself, then, but I can still remember how he smiled and waved to the crowed as he passed by slowly on the great car, which was pulled by six heifers.

'The Golden Child was Pontormo's idea, not Bandinelli's. It doesn't sound like the Pontormo you know, does it? Well, he has never tried an idea like that again.

'Of course, as soon as the parade was over, the boy was taken down to his father's baker's shop, and the gilding was peeled away to be used again. Even while they were doing it, the boy began to complain that he felt ill, and two days later he died, poisoned by gold.'

'What did the father say?' I asked in horror.

'He came to Pontormo and demanded the payment of ten crowns that he had been promised for the services of his son, and Pontormo paid him.'

'Is that why Pontormo will not allow anyone to speak of death in his presence?' I asked.

'No, he already had a terror of death,' Bronzino replied. 'It's not the idea of dying: it's the presence of the dead, and being close to corpses.'

'Surely nobody could have blamed him for the child's death?' I said. 'If anyone had foreseen the danger, the idea of gilding the boy would never have been carried out. The family wouldn't have allowed it.'

'Oh, the baker would still have allowed it,' Bronzino said, 'in order to get the ten crowns. Many men have sold their sons for less.' Bronzino looked down at his own fine hands, as though he were seeing them for the first time. 'I remember the baker's hands,' he said. 'When he came to Pontormo to demand his money, he held his hands out in front of him, with the huge fingers opening and closing on air. The fingers only stopped moving when they closed down on the coins after Pontormo had counted them into the baker's palms. If I were a sculptor, I would put those hands on a demon seizing a sinner and dragging him down to hell.'

Bronzino stared through the wall beyond our heads, obviously still seeing the memory of the evil hands which had belonged to the father of the Golden Child. I wondered whether the baker was still alive, and whether I had unknowingly met him. I did not ask Bronzino, because I did not want to know. I made him a promise. 'I'll certainly never mention the Golden Child again,' I said.

'You'd better not dare to,' Bronzino replied. 'At least I can be sure that the woman will never repeat the story to anyone.'

'Her name is Angelina, Master,' I said for the hundredth time. He seemed to see her only as an object to be painted, with no more feelings than a plaster bust or a bowl of fruit in a still life.

Bronzino poured himself a mug of water and drank it.

'I'm going to have a rest. Arguing with Bandinelli has reduced stronger men than me to exhaustion.'

'Do you want me to work on the gesso now?' I asked.

'Yes, but do it quietly. The woman will have to stay here, because Pontormo has gone home without her.' With that, Bronzino stretched himself as though it were late on a dark night instead of in the middle of a hot searing afternoon, and stalked off into his bedroom. He slammed the door shut behind him, which was an uncharacteristic thing for him to do. He usually only displayed passion when he was performing the unnatural act upon a lover (such as Pontormo) or a victim (such as myself).

I was left alone with Angelina, with no other instructions than to mix and apply gesso. While Angelina sat at the table, pouring and drinking water because of the heat, I assembled the unpleasant ingredients of the gesso. I took off my shirt and as much else as I could, partly so as not to have to wring out the sweat afterwards, and partly to avoid fouling them with the gesso. I could see that Angelina was as hot as I was. Awkwardly, I tugged her dress off, while she offered neither resistance nor cooperation. I removed her shoes as well, which was easier, and left her in her chemise.

When I began stirring together the ingredients of the gesso in the bucket which was never used for any other purpose, Angelina began to show interest. She left her chair, came over to me, and knelt beside the stinking bucket. I reached down and stroked her hair, in case she wanted contact, but Angelina showed no reaction.

I had been stirring the gesso mixture with a wooden spatula, which, in its youth, had once stirred food in some nobler household than ours. It would certainly never see itself be allowed to touch food again. I passed the spatula over to Angelina and put it into her fingers. I grasped her hand and guided it to make the rotary movements that were needed.

Angelina laughed softly, and I feared that she would go into one of her fits of noisy merriment. Bronzino would be infuriated if she woke him up, but all I heard from him was the sharp resentful grunt that sleepers make when a sound disturbs them but does not awaken them. To my relief, Angelina remained quiet. There are many tales told of idle apprentices who avoid doing their work. I was letting Angelina carry out my task for me, but I felt no shame, because she was completely fascinated by it. I allowed her to keep stirring the gesso even when it was ready, but I was not willing to risk letting her apply it to the panel. After all, this was the *gesso sottile*, the final layers, which must provide a perfectly even and unblemished surface for the artist.

When Bronzino woke up late in the afternoon and came back into the studio, he showed no interest either in Angelina's state of undress or in mine. He marched straight to the panel and examined the new gesso closely.

'Quite good, Giuseppe,' he commented, 'and it had better be, or the Duke will have something to say to us. Why is that woman stirring the bucket?'

'She finds the activity soothing and agreeable, Master,' I explained.

'Well, the smell doesn't amuse me,' Bronzino replied. 'Get rid of the stuff before Pontormo comes back, and turn the panel to the window so that the sunlight catches it and dries it more quickly.'

I took the bucket out and emptied it into the common drain, so that the smell spread itself throughout our whole quarter of the city, as quickly and thoroughly as a scandalous rumour. I took Angelina up to my room to help her wash and dress, and arranged her hair in an informal way, once again profiting from Sister Benedicta's and Maria's instruction.

When I brought Angelina down again, Pontormo was arriving, so I pulled out the dining table and sat Angelina down in her place, even though it would be more than an hour before I could serve our supper.

I hoped that the meal would not smell of gesso, or taste like it. Of course, I do not know what gesso tastes like; but knowing the smell, and what the ingredients are, I can construct an unpleasantly vivid and convincing idea of its flavour.

Over the next three days, I applied more *gesso sottile*, and Bandinelli came to argue with Bronzino over the composition, while Pontormo sat frowning in the window, and Clemente sat silent on the floor, and Angelina smiled sweetly at all of us.

By now Bronzino and Bandinelli had settled on some of the details of the painting. Venus, who was aware of Cupid's greater strength and wilfulness now that he had grown up, would be shown trying to take away some of the power with which she had invested him when he was the chubby small boy that we usually see him as.

First of all, Cupid had to be equipped with a bow and arrow, and a quiver to be slung across his back. I expected Bronzino to send me out to buy them, but I should have known him better. He despatched me to the Duke's palazzo to ask to borrow them from the military stores.

Bronzino gave me precise instructions.

'You remember that old battering ram we took to the house of that mad witch? I want a bow and arrow, or at least a quiver, that are slightly antique, like that.'

When I reached the guardroom of the palazzo, I wondered whether I dared to ask for Captain Da Lucca, but it was unnecessary. The guards all knew who I was, which I found worrying rather than flattering. I was at once conducted to the stores, where I picked out an old cavalry bow, four short arrows and a quiver with a green strap which was decorated with a brass buckle and a polished stone cut like a jewel. The armourer made me sign for the items in a register book, and I still wonder whether Bronzino ever returned them to the stores, and, if he did not, whether he was ever charged for their cost. I carried the bow and arrows back in one hand, and carried the quiver with the other, ignoring all the shouts of 'You're supposed to sling it across your back!' and 'You'll hurt yourself playing with those, sonny!'.

One wit even called out, 'So who are you? Cupid?' I would have been quite justified in answering, 'Yes, I am.'

8

Late on Sunday morning, while I was clearing away breakfast, there was a firm knock on the door downstairs. Bronzino surprised me by telling me to carry on, as he went down himself to answer the door. He must have been expecting Bandinelli, or perhaps Pontormo and Angelina. Instead, I heard a few words from a male voice that I could not quite recognise, and Bronzino replying in his most purringly courteous manner. This must be someone upon whom he wanted to make a good impression. I was just brushing the last crumbs off the table when Bronzino showed Father Fleccia into the room.

'Welcome, Father Fleccia!' I said.

'Evidently you'd forgotten that I would be coming,' Father Fleccia replied, correctly. 'I see that you haven't been fasting, either. Well, let's not start our reunion with a rebuke.'

'Giuseppe,' Bronzino said, 'bring out the best chair for Father –'

'– Fleccia,' the good Father replied. I could not quite get the name right myself. There seemed to be a faint 't' in it as well, and an equally faint 'r' on the end.

Father Fleccia settled himself into the chair while I brought up some wine from the cellar. 'Half and half with water, if you please,' he asked. 'I like to drink my wine diluted, in the manner of the Ancients.'

'Are you a Classicist, then, Father?' Bronzino asked.

'No, only a priest who has studied his Latin and Greek,' Father Fleccia replied. 'Or were you perhaps taking your turn to rebuke me, Messer Bronzino? I am told that you are a humanist.'

'To celebrate the beauty of what is human is not to deny the beauty of the divine, Father,' Bronzino said. He was clearly pleased at meeting the elderly priest, and I wondered why. Bronzino must have been seeing some advantage to himself from establishing an acquaintance with Father Fleccia, but I could not imagine what it might be.

Father Fleccia looked round the room. He was seated in the chair in as magnificent and assured a pose as if he had been a king sitting on his throne.

'I don't see Angelina about,' he remarked.

'She doesn't spend the night here,' I explained. 'She stays at the house of the painter Pontormo.'

'Ah, Pontormo,' Father Fleccia said. 'I've seen some of his paintings. What strange, contorted figures. The postures are rather unnatural.'

Bronzino obviously felt that he ought to defend his old master and teacher. 'Pontormo is an exponent of the style called *maniera*,' he told Father Fleccia. 'The aim is to create a beautiful picture, even if it is necessary to distort the image of the body to do so.'

'Oh, I wasn't criticising Pontormo,' Father Fleccia replied. 'What would be the point of art if it was completely realistic?'

Neither Bronzino nor I ever got a chance to give an unsolicited answer to Father Fleccia's rhetorical question, because just then Pontormo and Angelina arrived. I should have been ashamed when she came in with her hair unbound and flowing freely, but it was so beautiful that I was proud, as though it were an effect that I had planned and created myself. Father Fleccia turned in his chair with an expression of concern. He and Sister Benedicta must have worried greatly over what state they would find Angelina in.

I was amazed when Angelina squealed with joy and rushed to embrace Father Fleccia. She flung herself across the arm of the chair, and I heard Bronzino cluck with anxiety at the possible damage to his furniture. Father Fleccia gently sorted out Angelina's long limbs and manoeuvred her so that she was kneeling on the floor facing him, with her long delicate hands clasped in his strong square ones.

'Father Fleccia, she recognises you!' I exclaimed. 'We've never known her to recognise anyone before.'

I must confess that I was feeling jealous. I wished that Angelina would show such a reaction to me.

'She has known me for years,' Father Fleccia said, 'and perhaps we have something in common in our lives.'

'You have nothing of her strangeness and silence, Father,' I said.

'No, but she and I are both living in a world that was not really made for our characters,' he replied, stroking Angelina's liberated hair like a grandfather might do. 'I chose to be in Florence, but Angelina did not; and then again, in what place does she belong?'

'At Sister Benedicta's house?' I suggested.

Bronzino glared at me, but he did not dare to say anything in front of Father Fleccia, so I voiced yet another thought, which was even more provocative. 'I hope she will return there soon.'

Bronzino intervened at that point. 'As soon as we have no further need of her,' he said. 'Father, will you be celebrating

Mass in my home? It would be an honour.'

'I mean no dishonour to you,' Father Fleccia replied, 'but I've come here only to pray with Angelina, and for her.'

He slid himself off the chair and into a kneeling position on the floor, with surprising grace and suppleness for a man of his age and build. Father Fleccia began quietly murmuring prayers, so I stood back on the other side of the studio, not wanting to seem to be listening to his private words. Angelina of course made no reply, but she was clearly paying close attention. Once again, I wondered how much language she understood.

When Father Fleccia stood up, I poured him more wine, remembering to cut it half-and-half with water, and put the question to him. 'Does she understand you, Father?' I asked. 'How do you communicate with her?'

'I'm not sure that I do,' he replied. 'It reminds me of a situation when I was a young priest. I was sent to minister to the English fishermen on the island of Terra Nuova, on the other side of the Atlantic Ocean. While I was there, I found myself faced with converting a pagan woman of the native people. I knew nothing of her language, and she knew nothing of mine. At first we simply stood staring at each other. We were both baffled.'

'And did you convert her, Father?' I asked.

'No, I didn't,' he replied. 'God did that.'

I realised that Bronzino had left the studio, and that he and Pontormo were having a muted but lively conversation behind the now-closed door of Bronzino's bedroom. I could not make out the words. The rhythm of their voices was like that of a quarrel, but I could tell that in fact they were vehemently agreeing with each other about some proposed course of action.

Father Fleccia bent down, and drew Angelina up to

stand beside him. 'Where is your master?' he asked me. 'I need to speak to him.'

I had to knock quite loudly before Bronzino came out. The conversation within had been so forceful that behind Bronzino I could see that Pontormo was actually having to get his breath back.

'Father Fleccia wants a word with you, Master,' I said.

Bronzino instantly assumed the charming manner that he always presented to anyone who might be in a position to do something for him. 'Yes, Father?' he said. 'We are all at your service.'

'I'm pleased that Angelina is so well,' Father Fleccia replied. 'I shall assure Sister Benedicta that she is being cared for properly.'

I could imagine what desperate anxiety Sister Benedicta must have been feeling, and would go on feeling, until Angelina was delivered safely back to her. I was certain, though, that Bronzino would not allow any harm to come to Angelina. She was a vital asset.

'We know our duty towards her, Father,' Bronzino said. I wondered if he would ever bring himself to be able to speak Angelina's name.

'If I may,' Father Fleccia continued, 'I will return next Sunday morning, and celebrate Mass for Angelina in this house. I'll come early, so that you won't have trouble making her fast.'

This was bad news for the late-rising Bronzino, but he could only agree.

'That would be a privilege for us,' he told Father Fleccia, and, with much bowing and flourishing, and, stepping aside, he conducted Father Fleccia downstairs again.

Bronzino bounced back up the stairs like a boy. He

planted himself in front of Pontormo and declared his triumph. 'There you are, Master!' he crowed. 'Isn't he the very image of Time, the god Saturn himself. I must ask the Duke to order him to sit as the model for Time.'

'He would indeed do very well as the figure of Time,' Pontormo agreed, 'but how will you construct a mythological scene with Venus, Cupid and Time? There is no such story in the Classical sources.'

'We'll get around that,' Bronzino assured him. 'I wish Bandinelli had been here to see him.'

I wondered how Father Fleccia would feel about being ordered to pose by Duke Cosimo. He would have to obey, or run away from Florence, and I did not think he would do that. He had fled so far already to reach Italy. I offered a suggestion.

'Master,' I said to Bronzino, 'when Father Fleccia comes again next week, could you not ask him then, instead of having him put under compulsion by the Duke?'

'He might refuse,' Bronzino replied.

'I don't believe so, Master,' I said. 'You saw how much he wants to care for Angelina. I'm sure he would consider it an opportunity to see her more often.'

'Well, I could always have the Duke compel him anyway, if he were to refuse,' Bronzino decided. 'I won't need him soon. We'll begin with the figures of Venus and Cupid.'

Before any painting could begin, the final preparation of the panel had to be completed, and, needless to say, it was I who did the work, starting the next morning.

It may be that Bronzino's name will be remembered for decades, perhaps even for centuries, as the painter, but who will ever know the name of Giuseppe who applied the gesso, sprinkled charcoal dust all over the final layer and swung away at it with a little plane until it was perfectly smooth? Who will ever know that it was I who applied the final layer of size over the gesso, and then mixed and applied the golden-brown layer of *imprimatura* to finish off all the preparation?

That was the end of my own work on the panel. From then on, it was the hand of my master Bronzino that took over. He would not even let me apply the wash. The first thing the painter does upon the surface of this painting is to apply a coloured or grey wash to it. The gesso is to prevent the paint from being contaminated by the materials of the surface underneath. The painted image must float above the vulgar wood or canvas, and never come into contact with it. Most painters in Florence applied a grey wash to prevent the white gesso making its influence visible through the painting. The gesso was to remain as unseen, but as necessary, as the apprentices. I asked Bronzino whether he would be using grey.

'Yes, I will,' he said, 'even though Michelangelo in his prime used green. This was because we use green in frescos, but I will underpaint the flesh tones in green, of course.'

I marvel that only in our time have artists come to notice the green in the colouring of human bodies, and yet it is truly there, if only you have been taught to look for it.

While Bronzino busied himself with applying the grey wash, he chatted and argued with Bandinelli. Because Bronzino had to face the panel while he worked, he could not see Bandinelli sitting behind him, so Bronzino's voice bounced back off the panel like an echo. He questioned Bronzino's mythology.

'How will you drag Time into this composition?' he asked.

'Who can evade Time?' Bronzino replied. 'That is how I'll

bring him in. He will be at the top of the picture, drawing back a veil to reveal the scene. It will be a blue veil.'

'Blue?' Bandinelli said. 'I thought you didn't like to use blue. You said it belonged to the old-fashioned way of painting. You said that the painters only used blue so that their patrons could show off how much money they had spent on azurite and ultramarine.'

'I stand by that, Bandinelli,' Bronzino said. 'This is to be a diplomatic gift to the king of France, after all. Duke Cosimo will want to display the wealth of Florence, and there's no better way than to use azurite and ultramarine.'

'There is a better way,' Bandinelli replied. 'You could use gold leaf.'

'Now that would be vulgar and old-fashioned,' Bronzino said. 'Besides, you are maliciously trying to embarrass my poor master Pontormo. He suffers to this day from the memory of that dead gilded child.'

'Everyone associates me with malice,' Bandinelli boasted. 'It is my attribute, like the attributes of the figures of Classical mythology. Cupid must always have his bow, Neptune must always have his trident and poor unloved Bandinelli must always show his malice to all.'

'Perhaps you should consider why you are universally unloved,' Bronzino responded. 'In any case, we are discussing a technical question about my painting. We are not discussing you, although I'm sure you would prefer it if we did.'

I interrupted, because their petty bickering had become very boring to both Clemente and myself. Angelina seemed incapable of boredom, or perhaps, I imagined, it might be all that she knew. Just as fish must have no idea that water exists, I supposed that Angelina had no notion that her life consisted almost entirely of boredom.

'Master,' I said to Bronzino, 'I believe that we should take Angelina out for a while. May we?'

'Certainly,' Bronzino replied. 'I expect she needs a walk,' he added, as though we were speaking of a house-bound dog. 'Make sure that she puts her hat on, though. I don't want a suntanned Venus. I know they call me the little bronze man, but I can't help my colour. It's not the fault of the sun, it's the fault of my ancestry.'

Bandinelli, unseen behind Bronzino's back, grinned at him. 'Tell me, Bronzino,' he said, 'are you a Moor, or are you a Jew?'

The rhythm of Bronzino's hand as he applied the wash did not show any disturbance as he received this insult, and he did not even bother to turn round to answer Bandinelli's taunt.

'Neither, Bandinelli,' he replied. 'I am a proper Catholic Christian.'

I judged that this was an astonishingly impudent claim to come from a man who spent so much of his time putting my hindquarters to a purpose that God never intended and had expressly forbidden.

When we got outside, I made a suggestion to Clemente. 'Now that we know Angelina is interested in smells,' I said to him, 'let's take her to places with strong characteristic smells.'

'That's a strange way to entertain a lady!' Clemente remarked.

'Well, she's a strange lady,' I replied. Angelina showed no reaction at all. 'Is she even a lady? I suppose she must be.'

Clemente looked alarmed.

'Hey, she's not really a man, is she?' he asked. 'I mean, she is so tall –'

'No, Clemente,' I reassured him, 'I can definitely assure you that she's a woman.'

'But there are men who –'

'Yes, Clemente, I know all about that sort of man,' I said, 'but Angelina is not one of them. I have seen her in her nudity, so you can take my word for it. Come to think of it, you've seen that too.'

I wasn't really looking,' Clemente confessed. 'I only pretended to because my father was so insistent.'

'I expect he's afraid that you'll grow up to be one of those men who like to dress up as women,' I joked.

'Or one of those men who do for other men what women are supposed to do for them,' Clemente retorted.

In my stupidity and arrogance, I had always imagined that Bronzino's behaviour towards me was a guilty secret. It was guilty, indeed, but for the first time I realised that everyone knew what was going on.

As I led Angelina by her limp submissive hand through the crowds in the hot streets, I wondered how many of the faces I was passing knew who I was and what I was. My own face began to burn when I realised that Bandinelli must know, too, and I could not stop myself from imagining what kinds of remarks he must be making about me all over Florence.

We took Angelina around all the smelliest places I knew in our part of the city. We went back to the river Arno, of course, and let her lean out over the fouled waters. We led her through the fish market, past the tannery, and by every stable and dairy. Poor Clemente, whose nature was clearly more sensitive than Angelina's or mine, was suffering all this as an ordeal.

'Do we have to explore every stink in Florence,' he asked, 'and in this heat, too?'

'I can't help the heat,' I told him, 'but I promise you some pleasant smells as well.'

First of all, we went to the flower market. I myself have always hated the smell of flowers. To me, it is a thick unpleasant odour that makes my throat tighten, but it seems that everyone else in the world loves the smell of flowers. In spite of her oddness, Angelina proved to have the same love of floral scents as the rest of humanity (except me). As we went by the stalls stuffed with flowers, she broke into that bright beaming smile that we so rarely saw. It was not just that little soft smile that she bestowed on everyone when she seemed to be in a happy mood: it was a broad smile that made even the habitually surly stallholders smile in response, one of the greatest miracles ever seen in Florence.

Clemente was nearly as delighted as Angelina was. 'Look, Giuseppe,' he cried, 'she likes that! Perhaps we should buy her some flowers.'

'They wouldn't last long in this weather,' I said. 'She might not understand why the flowers decayed, and why we would have to throw them away. Hey, I know. Let's go to the street with all the perfumers.'

It was quite close by, so close that its own smells invaded the margins of the area held by the florists. Because Angelina had already detected the perfumes, she did not resist when I tugged on her hand to pull her away from the flower stalls. First of all, we strolled from one end of the street to the other. The perfumers, who count themselves rather grander than the flower-sellers, have permanent shops instead of stalls. Like all shops, the counter was on the front of the house at ground level, while the proprietors, their families and their domestic animals lived in the rest of the house. I wondered what it was like on the upper floors where the high smells of perfume intertwined with the stink of beasts.

As I had hoped, Angelina was delighted by the perfumes. We went by all the shops, right up to the end of the street, and as we turned round to go back Angelina pulled on my hand to urge me to let her stay in the street of perfumes. It was the first time that she had made any gesture to me that I could understand. I determined to spend Bronzino's money on a gift for Angelina from a perfumer's. Clemente could not see the slight but eager tightening of her hand that was the beginning, I prayed, of the exchange of meaningful information between Angelina and myself.

'Clemente,' I said, 'Angelina likes it here. She just pulled at my hand. She wants to go down the street again.'

Clemente understood at once. 'So she does think, like other people!' he exclaimed. 'Perhaps we could teach her to talk.'

'I doubt that we could ever do that, if Sister Benedicta has failed,' I said, 'but now we know that she does take in what's going on around her in the world.'

We took her to all the shops, and let her sniff at all the vials which were presented to her little nose, so small on such a tall woman. At every shop I explained that she could not talk, and did not seem to understand language, but that she was somehow capable of appreciating the beauty of scent. (I did not tell the perfumers about Angelina's love of foul smells as well; it was the strength of the smell, rather than its character, that seemed to attract her.) I had no doubt that the perfumers all knew who she was. She must have been hidden away all her life, first in the house of her parents (whoever they may have been) and then with Sister Benedicta. Now that Angelina had begun to appear in public, a wonderfully tall woman in a peasant's white hat, all Florence seemed to know of her. Half the city asked who she was, and the other half answered that she had been abducted on the Duke's orders for some mysterious purpose.

Every perfumer sold little cloths which could be soaked with diluted or full-strength perfume. Ladies, and many men, would hold these cloths to their faces to mask the smells of the city, many of which were highly obnoxious to everyone except Angelina, who loved smells for their power rather than for their beauty. At the shop of the perfumer Lodovico Corsilli, I asked to be sold one of the little cloths.

'I can keep it perfumed for Angelina,' I explained to Clemente, 'and so she can enjoy the scent for a long time.'

'Make sure she doesn't blow her nose on it,' he advised. 'That is not only an ill-bred thing to do, but it would spoil the scent.'

'I know nothing of her breeding,' I replied, 'and I don't think it would ever occur to her to use the cloth in that way.'

Corsilli was already sprinkling some perfume onto the cloth. He held it up to Angelina's nose, and gently guided her hand up to hold the cloth in place. Angelina laughed until her breath ran out.

'That means she likes it,' I told Corsilli. 'You've made a sale. I don't expect you to give away your trade secrets, but can you tell me something about what you've put in it?'

Corsilli graciously told me some of the ingredients, and I wished that I had not asked him. There is such a thing as being told more than you want to know. It is just as with the ingredients of gesso and of some kinds of paint colours. The bright beauty of art hides a secret origin in sources that come from foulness and death, and so does the ghostly, invisible beauty of perfume.

All the way back to Bronzino's house, Angelina held the cloth to her face, laughing from time to time, although the laughter came muffled through the cloth. Her eyes sparkled and blinked in the shade of her huge wide-brimmed hat. As we approached the house, I was worried to see a troop of the Duke's guards marching towards us. I pointed them out to Clemente.

'Look, Clemente,' I said. 'I fear we're in for another visit.'

'They won't arrest us, will they?' Clemente asked.

'I hope not,' I said, 'but I never know what they'll do, and they've seen us. They know me. We can't turn back now.'

'Perhaps they'll only arrest my father for offending everybody in Florence,' Clemente suggested hopefully.

'They'd have to arrest Bronzino as well on that charge,' I replied, 'and then I'd be out of work.'

I examined the faces of the guards. I was relieved to see that Captain Da Lucca was not leading them, so I relaxed for a moment, until I saw that Duke Cosimo himself was marching in the middle of his guards, once again having disguised himself. As it happened, both our parties arrived outside Bronzino's house at the same time, although of course it was I and Clemente who stepped aside, drawing Angelina with us. Duke Cosimo recognised me, which did not flatter or reassure me in the least.

'Ah, it's Bronzino's naked apprentice in all the arts that he practises!' the Duke boomed to my discomfiture. 'Go in and tell your master that I'm here. Wait, no. First tell me who that woman is.'

'If you please, my lord,' I replied, 'her name is Angelina, and she is to be the –'

'Shut up, boy!' the Duke snapped. 'If you ever again come close to bawling one of my secrets to the public streets, I'll make sure that you can never tell a secret again.' He looked Angelina over, and seemed to like what he saw. 'Well, go in,' he said. 'I'll be following right behind you with my men, so you'd better announce me quickly.'

I reached the top of the stairs two paces before the first of Duke Cosimo's guards, and I think that I must have been only a perilously short distance in front of the point of the guard's halberd.

'His Grace the Duke of Florence!' I managed to bellow with the last of my breath.

Bronzino and Bandinelli took in the news just fast enough for them to be standing up when Duke Cosimo strode in. I doubt that he would have noticed whether they were standing or sitting, because as he entered the room he found himself facing the wooden panel, which was half-covered with the dull grey wash, but otherwise blank.

'Bronzino!' he roared, so that even my statuesque master jumped. 'Where is my painting, Bronzino?'

The studio was crowded with all the guards. Clemente had brought Angelina up behind them, and he was trying to manoeuvre her up to my bedroom to get her out of the way. Bronzino scuttled across the room. With what would normally be considered flagrant rudeness, he even passed in front of the Duke himself. Bronzino grabbed at Angelina as though he were drowning in the sea and Angelina were a passing boat.

'Your Grace,' he gabbled, 'we are ready to start painting the figures. Look, I've even begun applying the grey wash which is to receive the paint, and here is your Venus.'

'I know,' the Duke replied. 'I've already met her down in the street. Did you say that she was picked out by that underdressed apprentice of yours? I must commend his taste, if not his manners and morals.'

All this time Bandinelli had been silent, probably for the longest time since his infancy. He had lowered his face into the tawny expanse of his beard, and was for once trying not to be noticed.

Clemente had halted Angelina, who raised the perfumed cloth to her face again, and smiled a hidden smile. I feared that Duke Cosimo would lunge forward and snatch the cloth away, but with surprising restraint he addressed Clemente instead. I was even more surprised that he knew who Clemente was.

'Clemente, please take that cloth away from Angelina and uncover her face,' he ordered. Clemente took the cloth away gently, so Angelina did not protest. I wished that Pontormo had been there, with his knack of handling Angelina so that she always did what she wanted.

Duke Cosimo considered Angelina like a newly delivered sculpture.

'It's true,' he pronounced. 'She does have an unusual look in her face. She's not like a mortal woman at all. She might be a real goddess.'

Bronzino actually simpered, for the first time since I had known him. He must have been badly frightened. 'Her body is just as divine, Your Grace,' he said.

'Can she be graceful, even though she's so tall?' Duke Cosimo replied. 'I'll see for myself.'

He turned to his guards. 'Out!' he commanded. 'Wait on the staircase until I call for you. I don't need guarding in here. I'm in no danger from a painter, a sculptor, two boys, and a silent goddess.' The guards filed out, apparently reluctantly. 'Right,' Duke Cosimo said when they had all gone. 'Let me see now. Get her clothes off.'

I was hotly angry on Angelina's behalf, but I could not show it.

Clemente nervously helped me. I was resentful that poor Angelina had been stripped off more times than the lowest prostitute in Florence. The fact that she seemed not to care made no difference to me. Clemente and I pushed her forward to stand in front of the Duke, but he stepped back.

'No, no, I want to see her in the pose that you intend for her.'

Bronzino and Bandinelli glanced at each other, apparently each wanting the other to speak first. Bronzino was forced to act.

'Giuseppe, bring the woman over here,' he ordered.

I brought Angelina to where we would be posing when Bronzino would finally start painting the picture.

'First, make her sit down on the floor,' he instructed me, but Duke Cosimo interrupted him.

'She is in my service, Bronzino,' he told my master, 'so do her the courtesy of addressing her directly.'

'Please sit down, Angelina,' Bronzino said, as though her name were an over-hot piece of food in his mouth.

Angelina sat down quite obediently when I pressed down on her shoulders, and Bronzino started giving instructions to me.

'Giuseppe, kneel down next to her,' he said, but once again the Duke stepped in.

'Strip off as well, Giuseppe,' he said. 'I want to get the best possible idea of what the finished painting will be like.'

By now I was so worried about Angelina that I was thinking of nothing else, so I undressed quickly and knelt on the floor.

'Now,' Bronzino said, 'perhaps Clemente will be good enough to fetch the quiver and arrow from over there.'

Clemente brought the quiver and I put it on. Bronzino took the arrow himself.

'Giuseppe,' he said, 'see if you can make her sit up straight. Here, take this cushion – no, two cushions. Get her to sit on the cushions with her legs drawn to this side.'

I pushed Angelina into the posture that Bronzino wanted, and then, to my surprise, he came over and placed the arrow in her hand. Bronzino lifted her arm so that her hand was poised in the air, lightly grasping the arrow by its shaft, with the point downwards.

'Now, Giuseppe, sit behind her, with your right leg coming forward. Put your left hand behind her head, and tilt her chin up with your right hand.'

When I had put Angelina into this pose, which she held even though it must have been most uncomfortable, Bronzino had one last instruction for me.

'Bring your face down to hers and kiss her,' he commanded me.

With both my master and, more importantly, the Duke watching me, I had to obey. Angelina's expression did not change.

Bandinelli could not suppress his sculptor's instincts. 'Where is Cupid's right hand to go?' he asked.

'On her left breast,' Bronzino replied. I reached down and made the astonishing discovery that a woman's breast was much softer than I had imagined. Bronzino crossed his arms over his chest in triumph. 'There, Your Grace. There are to be other figures, such as Time, for whom I have already found a model.'

'Father Fleccia the English priest,' Duke Cosimo replied, and I enjoyed witnessing Bronzino's discomfort at how much the Duke knew.

Duke Cosimo did not play any further games with Bronzino. 'The poses please me well,' he declared. 'Start painting, but first get Giuseppe and Angelina out of the way before I call my guards back in. They wouldn't know which of the two to assault first.'

9

The next morning, the outlines of Angelina and myself began to take form on the honey-coloured *imprimatura* which now covered the surface of the panel, after I had worked so hard and so long to make it perfectly white. At first, Bronzino worked from his rough sketches, so Angelina and I did not have to pose. Unlike many painters and sculptors, Bronzino did not mind other people seeing his work in progress, so I was able to see my own outline beginning to appear on the cartoon from which the outlines of the figures would be transferred.

Bronzino surprised me by telling me to hold out my hands. He examined them as though he had never seen them before, in spite of the fact that he knew my body far better than he had any right to. Evidently Bronzino did not like what he saw.

'These hands will not do for Cupid, Giuseppe,' he said. 'These are like the hands of a workman. Well, not as rough as that – after all, you've never really worked. They're the hands of a painter, not the hands of a young god.'

'They're the only hands I've got, Master,' I protested.

'That's no problem for modern painters such as myself,' Bronzino replied, waving away my hands as if they had been an unpleasing dish that a servant had offered to him at the table. 'I have studied the techniques of *maniera*, and I believe that I have the solution very readily available. We'll see, when you and my master Pontormo bring the woman back here.'

As soon we arrived with Angelina, Bronzino asked Pontormo to bring her over and hold out her hands. Bronzino looked closely at Angelina's hands, but he did not touch them. I cannot remember ever seeing him physically touch a woman, except for the time when he had kissed Angelina at the studio window.

'Yes,' he declared, 'I'll use her hands for Cupid as well.'

Pontormo smiled at his former pupil's initiative, but he brought up what he saw as a problem. 'The hands will be perfect,' he said, 'but surely the Duke and King François, and indeed everyone who sees the painting, will notice that Venus and Cupid have the same hands.'

'So what if they do?' Bronzino replied. 'The cultivated people will know that it is a technique of *maniera* to place parts of other models' bodies onto a single figure in order to increase its beauty. As for the uneducated people, they will never see the painting anyway.'

The common people, as I knew, would bear the expense of the painting through their taxes, but Bronzino was right in saying that they would never be able to see what they had paid for.

He was making minor changes to the poses. When he was already quite advanced in painting me sitting behind Angelina, he changed my pose completely, so that I was now kneeling beside her. I wondered what the Duke might say, although he was used to Bronzino's habit of making changes to what had been agreed when a painting was commissioned. Bronzino also decided that he would show my own left hand supporting the back of Angelina's head, because only my fingertips would be visible. The light would be coming from the left, so my foreshortened left arm and hand would be in shadow.

It was Bandinelli who had thought up the awkward posture in which I would have to pose. I am truly sorry for the plight of Bandinelli's own models, if he treated them with the same indifference to their discomfort. Anyone who wants to know how much human suffering is involved in producing art should place themselves in the posture of my Cupid, and see how long they can hold it before their back and limbs and joints begin to ache unbearably.

Those who try it will also discover that with their bottom thrust up and out, it is impossible to suppress the release of noxious vapours. My memories of posing for Cupid are made up of sweat, aching and the sound of flatulence. Fortunately we posed in the shade in the interior of the studio, because Bronzino always liked a soft, pearly light, and did not want direct sunlight falling upon his subjects.

Bandinelli came less often, so I did not see so much of Clemente either. Now that Bandinelli had made all his suggestions for the composition, I suspected that he would now appear only to make caustic criticisms of the developing painting, and of Bronzino's methods, and of me. On the other hand, we saw more of Pontormo. He had to bring Angelina from his house every morning, with my help, and take her back at night, but he seemed not to be doing any artistic work of his own all the time that Bronzino's painting of Venus and Cupid was in progress.

Pontormo had surprisingly few words to say about the painting, because it was so unlike his own style, except for the distorted figures.

Anyone who ever sees me as Cupid should be reassured that I do not, in fact, have a broken neck, and that my neck is not actually as long as my forearm. Pontormo's criticism was that the figures were not distorted enough.

'Look, Bronzino,' he objected, 'you have Venus vertical, but with her legs sideways, and Cupid is all at square angles. You could have made graceful curves out of them.'

'I will fill the spaces around them with other figures and objects,' Bronzino replied. 'In any case, Master, I would never presume to imitate your own style.'

Although anyone can see the influence of Pontormo's poses in the painting, none of the faces could have been painted by Pontormo, whose own people always have one of two facial expressions: tortured anguish or pop-eyed astonishment. Now that I think about it, those were Pontormo's own characteristic looks.

I was honestly grateful for his presence in our house, because Bronzino shared his siesta with Pontormo rather than with me. That meant that not only was I spared Bronzino's indecent assaults upon me, but I was able to spend the afternoon with Angelina.

Bronzino was quite aware of it. 'Take her upstairs to your room, Giuseppe,' he told me.

Although Angelina took time to become accustomed to new experiences, she did understand the idea of a routine. As soon as we were in my room together, she would undress while I did, and then we would lie down and fall asleep together in the gentlest, sweetest and most chaste of embraces. Did Bronzino guess? I am sure that he did, but that he did not care what happened to Angelina as long as she remained a beautiful Venus to decorate his painting – not a suntanned Venus, or a thin Venus. Perhaps Bronzino believed that he had enrolled me irrevocably in the Guild of Sodomites, that ancient and dishonourable brotherhood to which so many artists belong. Oddly, that was one charge that I cannot lay against Baccio Bandinelli. He had so many character defects and sins to keep up, that perhaps he had used the entire supply of wickedness with which Satan had furnished him. I am not sure, even, that it was a sin for me to lie with the sleeping Angelina in the hot quiet of the Florentine afternoons. I told my confessor, who bluntly accused me of fornication.

'I haven't, Father,' I protested. 'I have never touched her lewdly.'

'Yet you say she is beautiful,' said the weary and experienced voice on the other side of the grille. 'I believe it. I have heard her beauty spoken of all around the parish, but all I have seen of her myself is a white hat floating down the street on a tall figure.'

'Yes, that's Angelina, Father,' I said. 'I've come to you before and confessed to sodomy with my master. Surely I would have been willing to confess to fornication with a woman? It must be a lesser sin.'

He gave me a penance after I had undertaken to try to avoid the sin in future, but I could not keep my virtue in the face of the temptation to spend hours clasped in Angelina's soft embrace. I wondered what she thought we were doing. It was as far from passion as is the eager embrace of a child, not that any child has ever wanted to climb into my lap. Sister Benedicta had seemed to trust me with Angelina. She knew that neither Bronzino nor Pontormo would be a threat, because their adherence to unnatural vice was well known, but she might have feared a young man like me.

Of course I was curious to experience woman, because I had no wish to lead a life filled only with men, such as that which Bronzino and Pontormo led. I could not imagine forcing myself upon Angelina, and even if she had accepted me, I would have been uncertain whether she knew what I was doing. Sister Benedicta might have been able to tell me, but I was not foolish and shameless enough to ask her. Often I would bring a bucket of water up from the well and wash both Angelina and myself. She used to laugh quietly, enjoying the brief coolness and relief from the sweat before it began to flow again in the heat. As I lay in peace with the sleeping Angelina, I would try not to think about Bronzino and Pontormo's obscene wrestling which I knew was going on in the bedroom below. Sometimes I would hear their voices murmuring, and I was glad that I could never make out the words.

Sooner than I had expected, the outlines of Angelina and myself on the panel began to take on roundness and weight. Bronzino had even sketched in the right wing which would be attached to my back. After all my effort in borrowing the antique quiver from the armoury, Bronzino had decided not to show it at all. All he would show would be a small part of the carrying strap across my back. The fingers of Angelina's right hand were oddly splayed out in the air above our heads.

'She will be holding an arrow, Giuseppe,' Bronzino explained to me as he worked. 'It's Cupid's arrow. Venus is trying to take Cupid's arrow away from him to stop him causing so much trouble by shooting poor mortals with it.'

'But isn't that against her nature and attributes, Master?' I said. 'Venus is the Goddess of Love. Surely she would approve of Cupid causing as much love as possible.'

'Yes, she's the Goddess of Love,' Bronzino agreed, 'and she wants to keep control of all the love on the Earth. This grown-up Cupid has become worryingly strong and wilful. Venus fears that she may lose control of Cupid's activities. The loves of the world would be ruled by a wild young boy instead of by a wise goddess.'

'Should I fetch the arrow for you, Master?' I asked.

'No, I don't need it yet,' Bronzino replied. 'I'll soon be sending you out to buy all the properties I need.'

Bronzino was not joking. He was making up a list, based upon the sketches he had made and the ideas that he had discussed with Bandinelli. I had already obtained the quiver and arrow and bow, of course. Two days later Bronzino showed me the list of properties that he had come up with.

1 snakeskin
1 honeycomb
1 red silken cushion
1 white dove (live)
3 masks, as used by actors, or characters in tableaux
1 large hourglass
1 ornamental wax apple

Bronzino reassured me that he would not need all these items at once, or even at the same time. 'The apple wouldn't last long, anyway,' he said, 'although perhaps the paint will preserve it. Perhaps I'll use gold leaf on it instead.'

'Gold leaf on an apple, Master?' I asked.

'Well, it has to be golden, doesn't it?' he snapped. 'It's the golden apple that Paris presented to Venus when he judged her to be the most beautiful of the goddesses. In Classical mythology, the presentation of the golden apple was the beginning of sin in the world.'

'Why,' I said, 'we Christians know that original sin was created when Eve took the apple from the Tree of Knowledge. Our story is the same as theirs.'

'Don't let any Dominican friar hear you say that,' Bronzino cautioned me, 'or you'll be up for blasphemy.

There's a difference between old Greek stories and the account of Genesis.'

As it happened, I had no need to procure the apple before Father Fleccia came to see us again on the following Sunday. After he had said Mass and completed his prayers while Angelina knelt with her head in his lap, I asked him about the apple.

'Well, there was not really an actual apple,' he said. 'It's a symbol, of course.'

'Do you know about the golden apple that Paris presented to Venus?' I asked him.

'I have studied the Classics, you know,' he replied.

'I am surprised that priests study pagan literature, Father,' I said.

'The Church has never been opposed to poetry and beauty,' Father Fleccia replied. 'What's more, many stories of ancient mythology foreshadow the truths we teach. The golden apple of Paris was the indirect cause of the Trojan War, and so it corresponds to the fruit of the Tree of Knowledge that led to the Fall of Man. There are other examples. For instance, there are plenty of stories about heroes with twelve companions, and young gods who are sacrificed and then resurrected in the spring.'

'You don't think that this painting of Venus and Cupid is immoral, then?' I asked him.

'If I thought it immoral, I hope that I would not have agreed to model for Time,' he replied. 'After your master proposed the idea to me, I must confess that I looked at myself in the mirror, and I must further confess that I really do look like Time, or Saturn, or Cronos, to give that god his other names.'

I wondered which god I would resemble if I ever grew as old as Father Fleccia. I feared that I would end up as a cross between Bacchus the obese god of wine and Pan the hairy god of debauchery. Father Fleccia continued, while he stroked Angelina's unbound and flowing hair.

'In a way it is right that Angelina should be holding the golden apple,' he said, 'because she would be an innocent if it were not for the original sin that we all bear. I wonder whether your master's painting may not bear deeper meanings than he knows.'

'The painting is to be an allegory filled with strange symbols, Father,' I said, 'so that King François may show off his learning and intelligence by working out what they mean.'

'If he is so adept at interpreting symbols,' Father Fleccia replied, 'then perhaps the king should have been a theologian or an alchemist.'

'I thought that alchemy was all about creating magical substances to work spells and miracles,' I said.

'How badly we are misrepresented,' Father Fleccia replied. 'The world believes that we are all conjurers and charlatans.'

'Well, Father,' I said daringly, 'if alchemists hide their activities, they must expect the world to make dramatic and inaccurate interpretations of what they do.'

'You should visit us again,' Father Fleccia replied. 'I'll speak to Benedicta about it.'

I experienced a curious combination of excitement and indifference. I did want to know more about what went on in that subterranean laboratory, and yet I did not want to become involved in alchemy myself. I did not want to be drawn involuntarily into becoming an alchemist in the same way that Bronzino had drawn me involuntarily into becoming a sodomite.

In the week that followed Father Fleccia's visit, the painting progressed faster. On the Monday morning a stern and silent pair of the Duke's guards brought Bronzino a letter from the Duke, which had been rolled into a cylinder, tied with the Ducal ribbon, and sealed with a lead seal. As I carried the letter upstairs to my master, I was surprised by the weight of the lead seal swinging on its ribbon. An ordinary letter would have been roughly sealed with wax, into which the sender would have perfunctorily pressed his ring to make a blurred impression. I handed the heavy letter to my master. Bronzino examined the seal, and then carefully untied and unwound the ribbon.

He scanned the letter, quickly, and then released it so that it snapped back in his hand into a tight cylinder. Bronzino then carried the letter into his bedroom and shut the door behind him. He came out a few moments later, obviously having shut the door so that I would not see where he had placed the letter. Bronzino stood in front of the painting for a few moments, contemplating the two figures that were beginning to emerge out of the rough outlines and dull green and grey wash.

'The Duke wants his painting to be completed more quickly, Giuseppe,' he told me. 'You and the woman will have to spend more time posing from now on. I will ask my master Pontormo to bring her earlier in the mornings.'

I knew that he did not want me to know what was in the letter, but I had no doubt that it was a threat, explicit or implied, that Bronzino would suffer if the painting were not delivered to the Duke when he wanted it. Now that we had to spend longer in our poses, Angelina started to become difficult. It was hardly surprising, because we were so uncomfortable. Although Angelina's pose was not as awkward as mine, it was awkward enough, as I discovered when I tried it for myself. Her legs were turned to the left, her back was twisted to the right and her head was pulled back as far to the left as it would go. Bronzino had not yet made her hold up her right arm and rotate her hand inwards, and that would be even more tiring and painful.

I knew there would be trouble when we set to work on the third day after Bronzino received the letter from the Duke. Pontormo had gone home immediately after we had brought Angelina over. This was soon to prove unfortunate. Angelina did not resist being undressed, or having her hair combed and tightly bound with the ivory pins. When I sat her down on the floor and assumed my own strained pose, and tried to turn her towards me, Angelina let out a wail of protest and betrayal. I let her squirm away, and murmured, 'Angelina, it's all right, Angelina,' in the hope that she would calm down.

Bronzino did not share my patience with her. 'What's the matter with that woman?' he demanded. 'I've got work to do. I've got no time to waste on her tantrums.'

'Master,' I replied, 'if she does not cooperate, your painting will take even more time.'

'The Duke will send men to make her cooperate,' he replied.

I knew that Bronzino would not hesitate to call for that sort of help, so I appealed to him on the basis of his own interests, not on those of Angelina. 'Master,' I said, 'if she is forced to adopt and hold the pose, she will be hurt. She will become unhappy and unwell.'

'Better her than me,' Bronzino replied.

'Would you be able to disguise her distress when you come to paint her, Master?' I asked. 'Please, if you will not listen to me, fetch your own former master Pontormo. I'm sure that he will advise gentleness.'

'In spite of the respect that I owe to Pontormo, he is no longer my master,' Bronzino said. 'I have no wish to hurt the woman, but she will pose as I have decided, and I am willing to use any means to make her do so.'

'If you will not bring Pontormo, at least let me try, Master,' I begged. Bronzino waved his hand away in his habitual gesture of dismissal or consent.

All this time I had been holding my own pose, but now I broke it and knelt before Angelina. She softened enough for me to hold her head against my cheek. I had to stretch to do it, because she was so tall. I murmured quietly into her ear, trying to persuade her to sit as we wanted. As always, I did not speak merely nonsense to her in soothing tones. I spoke to her as a rational human being, because I still had hope that she could understand language even though she never used it. Again I tried to twist her into the pose that Bronzino required, but she cried out and struggled away again.

Bronzino lost his temper. 'I haven't got time to waste!' he shouted. 'That creature will do as I want.'

He strode across the room and raised his arm. I jumped up and confronted him. For the first time, I noticed that I was now taller than he was.

'Master,' I said, 'if you strike Angelina, you will never use my body again.' It was the only threat that I could think of in the rage and terror of the moment, and it stopped Bronzino.

'Don't presume to give me orders, Giuseppe,' he said. 'Remember that you were apprenticed to me.'

'I was apprenticed to you to learn the arts of painting, Master,' I replied, 'and not to learn the other arts that you were taught by Pontormo.'

'Pontormo!' Bronzino replied with a surprising lack of anger. He appeared to be remembering something. 'It was I who taught him. He had never known love before.'

'Love?' I repeated in amazement, but Bronzino seemed

suddenly to have forgotten me. He paced back and forth.

'I must have that painting,' he muttered.

'I want the painting to succeed, too,' I told him. 'If Angelina could speak, I'm sure that she would say the same.'

'Her?' Bronzino snapped, clicking his fingers in Angelina's direction.

'She doesn't know what I'm doing, or even what she's doing.'

At that moment, Angelina relaxed into my arms so completely that I had to hold her up to prevent her sliding down onto the floor. I drew Bronzino's attention to her change of mood.

'Look, Master,' I said. 'She's not frightened any more.'

'She isn't in her pose,' Bronzino pointed out. 'It would be better if she were frightened. The problem is that she has no fear of you, or of my master Pontormo. Who can I call upon to frighten her?'

I did not have time to protest in response to this monstrous question when Bronzino found an answer for himself.

'I know! That officer who brought her over from the witch's house. What was his name? It was the name of a town.'

'Captain Da Lucca,' I replied, because Bronzino would have thought of the name in the end anyway.

'Yes, Captain Da Lucca! I'll send you to the palazzo later to ask him to come tomorrow. In fact, why don't you go today? There's no point in trying to get on with the painting. Neither of you looks right.'

I led Angelina upstairs and helped her to dress, and then dressed myself. When I brought her down to the studio again, I asked when he wanted me to go to the palazzo.

'Now. Why not?' he replied.

'Where will Angelina stay while I'm away? Should I take her with me?'

'Don't be ridiculous!' Bronzino snapped. 'The Duke doesn't want her paraded around the palazzo. She's his secret.'

'A secret, Master?' I replied. 'Everyone in Florence seems to know that she's here.'

'Only the kind of people who come out in the street,' Bronzino answered. 'The aristocracy haven't seen her, and nor have the artistic community, except for Bandinelli. It doesn't matter that the common people have seen her.'

I might have retorted that Bronzino himself came from a much more lowly family than he cared to remember, but I was suddenly weary of trying to score points off him with words in the way that a fencer scores points with swords.

'Well, then, Master,' I said, 'where am I to take Angelina?'

'Put her in your room,' Bronzino replied.

'What, on her own?' I said.

'Yes, of course, do you think that I'm going to stay in there with her?' Bronzino replied. 'Sit her down on the bed, or on the floor, or anywhere. She seems a tractable creature most of the time, so I don't think she'll wander around. Don't worry, she won't disturb me.'

Disturbance to Bronzino was the least possibility that concerned me, but I took Angelina up as he had instructed. I pulled the bed round, and sat her upon it, propping her up so that she could see the patch of blue sky through my window. I hoped that it would distract her, especially as the smells of the city were drifting in through it while the smells of Bronzino's studio were drifting up from below. I dressed in my best clothes so as to look presentable at the palazzo, while Angelina sat obediently where I had placed her. She did not even look at me when I left and closed the door behind me. I hurried down the stairs, and Bronzino, too, did not even bother to acknowledge me as I passed the studio on the way.

This time I attracted no attention from anyone as I walked to the Palazzo della Signoria. The bored guards were not expecting me, but when I asked to see Captain Da Lucca, they showed interest. I expected them to conduct me inside the palazzo, but instead they told me to wait, while one of them carried the message inside. I looked for something to sit down on, but there was no bench or chair nearby. I could have sat down on the wall across the street, but I did not want to look undignified in my going-to-the-palazzo clothes. I stood stiffly where I had been left, hoping that I looked like someone who was not accustomed to being kept waiting. I heard shouts approaching, and I tensed up. Was there some kind of disturbance going on in the palazzo?

I then realised that the shouts were in fact commands, and that one set of guards after another was coming to attention as Captain Da Lucca made his way towards me. He stepped all the way out of the palazzo and scrutinised me as though he were inspecting the turnout of one of his own men before a parade.

'Well,' he demanded, 'what do you want? Another massed assault on Sister Benedicta's house?'

'It is my master Bronzino who wants you, Captain,' I replied. I did not know how he would respond, and I was certainly not expecting what he did, which was to bark at the sentries on the outer door of the palazzo.

'I'm off to the painter Bronzino's house,' he told them, and then he turned his attention back to me. 'Bronzino wants me?' he asked. 'Then let's go to him. I haven't got a lot of time to waste on unexpected and unexplained errands.'

He must have memorised the way to our house, because he marched away in the right direction, and he set off so quickly that I was nearly left behind. I had to scuttle after him to catch up. Captain Da Lucca said not a word to me on the way, and I was afraid to speak to him. The fact that he could abandon his post and leave the palazzo at once, without asking anyone's permission, had made me realise just how powerful he must be. I wondered whether Bronzino understood that. When I opened the door of our house, Captain Da Lucca strode up the stairs, so I had to break all the rules of courtly manners and announce him from behind as he entered the studio.

'Captain Da Lucca of the Duke's guard!' I piped.

I heard Bronzino say 'Welcome, Captain,' before I came in.

'What do you want?' was Captain Da Lucca's blunt, and entirely justifiable, reply.

'I want you to frighten somebody for me,' Bronzino answered.

'You should be ashamed to ask me to intimidate a man because you can't frighten him yourself,' Captain Da Lucca replied.

'Ah, but it's not a man,' Bronzino told him. 'It's a woman.'

'A woman!' Captain Da Lucca repeated. 'This gets even worse. You can't frighten a woman? Well, you probably can't do anything with a woman.'

'I've never wanted to try,' Bronzino replied equably. 'I'm talking about an unusual woman, that woman whom you brought over from Sister Benedicta's house. I need her to do what I want in order to complete my painting. My apprentice Giuseppe has tried kindness, but there's not enough time. I want to use fear instead.'

'I don't like the sound of this,' Captain Da Lucca said. 'There's not much that I wouldn't do to a man – except what you're reputed to do, that is – but I've never struck a blow upon a woman.'

Bronzino was already moving towards the stairs, and he beckoned to us both to follow. I pushed ahead of him so that I could go first, and when I did, I was puzzled to see a chair placed across the stairs in front of the door of my room.

'Master,' I began, 'why –' I stopped my question when I heard Angelina sobbing inside my room. Captain Da Lucca flung Bronzino's chair over his shoulder and down the stairs, which would have given me great satisfaction if I had not been preoccupied with getting to Angelina. We pushed in and found her sitting on the floor, with the binding ribbons torn out of her hair. Angelina sat weeping with her hair wrapped in disorder around her head and shoulders as though someone had dropped a net over her from above. I knelt and embraced her while Captain Da Lucca roared down at Bronzino.

'Bronzino! It's not this woman who should fear me, it's you! This is the Duke's valuable model, and she's under his protection and mine.' I heard no reply from Bronzino, but Captain Da Lucca strode heavily down the stairs and into the studio. While I comforted Angelina, I heard Captain Da Lucca say 'I shall be spending more time here in future.'

10

I was glad that Angelina now had another protector, with more power than either Father Fleccia or myself. True to his threat, Captain Da Lucca did spend more time in Bronzino's studio, and Bronzino took a silent, evil and subtle revenge upon him, which will endure for as long as the painting does. Bronzino began by asking Captain Da Lucca if he would not be bored hanging around a painter's studio, with nothing to do.

'I'm not here with nothing to do,' Captain Da Lucca replied. 'I'm here to check on the welfare of Angelina.'

'Perhaps you would like to have something to occupy your time,' Bronzino suggested. 'Perhaps you would like to have your image presented to the king of France.'

'What?' Captain Da Lucca exclaimed.

'I need a figure in my composition to represent Rage,' Bronzino told him. 'I am going to include various figures to represent the emotions of love. Who was not felt rage against a loved one?'

Bronzino had expressed rage against me when I had threatened to withhold the use of my body from him. He had never referred to the incident, but he treated me less cruelly in the shameful act, or so it seemed to me. The shame would also of course be mine for continuing to submit to him.

'Do I look to you like a man who is prone to rage?'

Captain Da Lucca replied. 'My anger is disciplined. I use it when I need to, and it is always under my control.'

'You have the ability to inspire fear in men who are strong and brutal,' Bronzino said. 'Your rage would be like that of a demi-god, like that of Hercules.'

'All right, I'll think about it,' Captain Da Lucca said.

Part of the irony was that Angelina was not in fact afraid of Captain Da Lucca at all. She ignored him, and she neither showed signs of fear nor the signs of what I hoped were affection that she showed to me.

As the summer achieved its full strength, seeming to be boastfully triumphant in showing off how it could make the city sweat and gasp and suffer, Captain Da Lucca came to visit our house even more often than Father Fleccia did. I was disappointed that he and Father Fleccia never met, at least before I left Florence and heard no more of them, because I should have liked to see them together in Angelina's presence. The low actors who perform comedy in the streets would never accept a scenario which did not allow for two such interesting characters to meet. It is certainly a pity, because the experienced old Father Fleccia would have been able to tell Captain Da Lucca that Bronzino was playing a malicious practical joke on him.

Bronzino gave Captain Da Lucca many fussy instructions in setting up the pose. 'I want to show off your muscles,' Bronzino said. 'Clasp your hands above your head, like this, so that they seem to be about to grasp your own hair. That will twist your hands so that the muscles which work your fingers will stand out.'

Captain Da Lucca obligingly pulled his hands into a static gesture of extreme tension. It was of course extremely painful. Even Baccio Bandinelli himself could not have devised a more tormenting pose, although of course no sculptor would place a figure in such a position anyway. Neither bronze nor marble could take that shape without collapsing into fragments.

'Now look down,' Bronzino further instructed his unpaid model, 'and open your mouth as though you were roaring with anger at an enemy or a foolish subordinate.'

Captain Da Lucca obeyed with alacrity. If any of his soldiers had seen it, they would have howled with laughter. Only Bronzino would have had a mind so cunning and wicked as to see that Captain Da Lucca would be charmed to appear in a picture that was painted for his Duke to present to a king. He did not chance his luck by prolonging Captain Da Lucca's sitting, in case the mistreated captain realised what was going on, or someone with a less-honest and direct mind told him that he was being played with. The result was that Captain Da Lucca's figure was the first to be completed in the whole composition. This gave a misleading impression of what the finished painting would be like.

Angelina and myself appeared only as ghosts of ourselves, like statues seen through a thick fog, but Captain Da Lucca, or at any rate his upper right torso, his head, and his twisted hands and forearm muscles, stood in full detail halfway up the left-hand side of the composition, just behind where my feathery wing would be.

Angelina seemed to have forgotten that Bronzino had imprisoned her in my room, or perhaps she did not associate the distress with Bronzino at all. She had once again become calm and apparently contented. After Captain Da Lucca had become convinced (wrongly) that Bronzino had a proper solicitude for Angelina's welfare, he stopped coming to our house. Like many practical men who consider themselves to be wise in the ways of the world, he made a naïve victim for malice such as Bronzino's. Captain Da Lucca was a tough and knowing man, but he was upright and bluff in his toughness, and he had no insight into the feline malevolence of a decadent character like Bronzino.

One morning when Angelina and I were posing, I tried to distract myself from the aches in my back and thighs by asking Bronzino why he had painted Captain Da Lucca as Rage.

'That's what I told him he is,' Bronzino replied. 'Actually, his figure represents quite a different aspect of the effects of love. His pose is intended to demonstrate pain and madness, because what he is representing is not Rage, but The Ultimate Symptoms of Venereal Disease.'

'That is a cruel trick to play upon an honest man, Master,' I said.

Angelina squeaked because I was so indignant that I had unconsciously gripped her breast too hard. Bronzino shrugged. He was not even human enough to laugh over his underhanded triumph.

'He insulted me, and in my own house,' he said. 'If I were a soldier I would kill him in a duel. If I were an aristocrat I would pay ruffians to kill him in a back alley. I am a painter, so I take my revenge in the best way that is available to me.'

I hoped that King François would not be able to interpret the meaning of the middle figure on the left of the picture, lurking behind my out-thrust bottom, but I fear that the king did understand what it represented. At least the painting will never go on public display for everyone to see the trick that Bronzino played upon Captain Da Lucca.

The only agreeable part of our routine was the quiet

afternoons that I spent in Angelina's embrace, while Bronzino slept quietly below or performed the unnatural act with Pontormo.

On the Tuesday after Captain Da Lucca's scurrilous portrait was finished, Bronzino let me go out for the morning because he planned to start painting the three masks that I had finally found for him.

He had originally planned to place them on the left-hand side of the painting, but now he prepared a new cartoon, with the masks on the right, two of them lying upon the third.

It had taken me a long while to obtain the masks, because summer in Florence is the wrong time of year for masquerades. That turned out to be an advantage, because the proprietor of the costume shop, who sold means of disguise for both festive and criminal purposes, was partly delighted at the chance to sell three masks out of season, and partly irritated at having to search for them in the back of his shop.

While Bronzino began painting the masks that I had found for him, two of them being of a pale young woman, and the other of a rufous sparse-bearded old man, I made my escape from the house and set off for Sister Benedicta's.

The solemn Maria opened the grille in the door to inspect me, and then admitted me at once.

'It's the young man who took Angelina!' she called out to announce me, making my conscience squirm like a fear-inducing thing found under a damp rock.

Sister Benedicta bustled down the stairs as though she had been awaiting me all morning. 'Giuseppe!' she cried. 'How are you? How is Angelina?'

'I'm well, and I think Angelina is, too,' I replied. 'I expect that Father Fleccia has been reporting back to you.'

'You make me sound like an informer,' said Father Fleccia's voice from the shadows to one side. His voice seemed to arrive in the hall before he did.

'I am sure you carry only truthful tales, Father,' I said.

'Well, I am pleased to see you,' Father Fleccia said.

'So am I,' said Sister Benedicta, 'but what brings you here today?'

'Angelina has sometimes been difficult lately,' I said. 'Yes, I know that she's been asked to carry out a task that she never chose to do, but she's not been behaving as I've come to know her.'

It was quite unexpected that Maria, whom I had already forgotten about, should speak at that point.

'Sister, should I bring a drink for the boy?'

'Why, of course,' Sister Benedicta told her. 'I am ashamed of myself for not offering him one already. Bring it up to the solar.'

'It's too hot up there,' Father Fleccia said. 'Why not bring him down to the laboratory?'

Sister Benedicta gave him a cautioning look, but Father Fleccia took me by the elbow and guided me towards the stairs.

'You go first,' he told me, and I found myself facing a heavy wooden door, much too solid and grand for an ordinary cellar.

'It's unlocked,' Father Fleccia informed me, and I reached out and turned the ring of the door handle. I would not have been surprised if it had been hot. The door swung open without the eerie creaking and groaning that I had fearfully expected.

I had braced myself for strange and terrible sights, but instead there was only gloom, because the cellar's skylight windows to the street had been blanked off. Whether this was to help with the experiments, or to prevent spying from outside, I do not know. Father Fleccia had come down behind me, and for a moment I was nervous at realising that this old but strong man was blocking my way back. I heard the clank of something metallic being handled behind me, and then Father Fleccia said, 'Let me light the lantern.'

I then heard the familiar sound of stone being struck repeatedly against stone, and then the lantern lit up. Because Father Fleccia was holding the lantern behind me, the light which burst out in the cellar seemed to come from the very walls themselves. I managed to curb the instinct to make the sign of the cross upon myself. I cannot imagine that Father Fleccia would have been pleased by the gesture. I jumped when his voice spoke directly into my ear from behind me.

'I expect this all looks like a sorcerer's cell to you,' he said.

It was stranger than that, not that I have ever seen a sorcerer's cell. I had expected unusual sights and smells, but what struck me first was the disorder of the laboratory. My eyes struggled to find a point at which to start looking. It was like trying to find a vanishing point for the perspective in a badly composed painting. The first thing I said to Father Fleccia was 'But there's no fire.'

'Yes, there is, but it isn't lit at present,' he replied. 'Let me get past you, and then I can show you where it is.' I stood aside and let him carry the lantern into the laboratory. 'Now,' he said, 'this construction of stones that looks like an oven is what we call the Athanor. It is simply a kind of stove for heating substances in the various vessels that we use.'

He pointed to a collection of vessels in odd shapes, as if a family of glass bottles had bred in the darkness, and had produced a range of hereditary deformities which had become worse with every generation. 'This, for instance, is a Pelican. We use it for distillation.'

I glanced up at the ceiling, and around at the bare walls.

'I expected magical symbols to be everywhere, Father,' I said.

'We are not magicians,' Father Fleccia replied, as if he had been able to read my earlier thoughts.

Sister Benedicta came down behind him, and she added her own comments. 'There are those who believe themselves to be magicians, or who want others to believe that they are,' she said. 'If you were to walk into one of their laboratories, you would find a pentacle drawn on the floor to keep out evil spirits, with a candle burning at each of its five points.'

'They mix their compounds in a mortar which is placed like an altar in the centre of the pentacle,' Father Fleccia added, 'and they perform a Banishing Ritual with an old sword to expel all sinister influences from the laboratory.'

'You are taking all the romance out of alchemy, Father,' I told him. 'I had always believed that was what alchemy was all about.'

'That's what your master Bronzino thinks, isn't it?' Father Fleccia replied. 'He accuses us all of promising miracles, such as turning base metals into gold, miracles that we never deliver.'

'That's what the practitioners with the pentacles and the altars and the swords do, and we are all blamed for it,' Sister Benedicta added.

'Nevertheless,' I said, looking around at all the equipment and inhaling the smells of all the substances which lay about in the laboratory, 'there is something of the atmosphere of magic in here.'

'Yes, we're sorry for the smell,' Father Fleccia responded. 'Substances are not really what alchemy is all about, any more than Christianity is about bread and wine and relics and statues of the saints.'

I heard Maria call out to Father Fleccia from the top of the cellar stairs. He went up and brought down a tray with three cups of wine. I wondered whether Maria was forbidden to enter the laboratory, or whether she was simply afraid of it. I could not blame her, because I was far from comfortable in that eerie place myself.

Father Fleccia's big hand moved some vessels on a bench to one side so that he had room to set down the tray.

'Sit down,' he said, pulling out a stool from under the bench.

While he handed me a cup of wine, Sister Benedicta sat down on another stool next to me. I noticed a broom leaning against the wall next to me. I examined the floor and was relieved to see that the broom was obviously used for its proper purpose, to sweep the floor, and that Sister Benedicta had not been flying on it.

I was ashamed to realise that I had forgotten about Angelina while I had been awed by the sights and smells of the alchemical laboratory.

'The painting is going quickly,' I said, 'because Duke Cosimo has ordered Bronzino to hurry up with it, so I hope that we can bring Angelina home before long.'

'I hope so, too,' Sister Benedicta said. 'She brings a lot of joy to this house. I believe I know now what it feels like to lose a daughter to a husband.'

'Well, Bronzino is unlikely ever to be a husband,' I said, a prediction which came true, but which hardly qualifies me as a seer and prophet. It occurred to me that two other people had lost Angelina as a daughter once before, and I dared to broach the subject to Sister Benedicta. I could not restrain my curiosity.

'Sister,' I asked, 'I cannot help wondering where Angelina came from. Her parents lost a daughter when they put her into your care.'

Sister Benedicta and Father Fleccia looked at each other in conspiratorial sadness.

'I understand why you want to know,' Sister Benedicta said, 'but we are both sworn to secrecy for ever. When Angelina's parents brought her here, they promised to provide for her – very generously, and they still do – but in exchange I had to undertake never to reveal the name of the family. I have told the truth only to Father Fleccia, so that he knows where she was baptised.'

'Her parents still send money?' I replied. 'They are alive, then.'

'Oh, yes, they are alive,' Father Fleccia replied, 'in body if not in spirit. They are not one of the great families of Florence, but neither are they poor.'

'A merchant's family, then?' I asked.

'I can say no more about it,' Father Fleccia replied. 'I cannot reveal anything which might help you to identify the family. I will say only this: yes, her parents are still alive, and you will certainly have seen them in the streets of Florence.'

That was all I ever came to know about Angelina's origins. Every time I saw a middle-aged couple of the merchant class, where the wife was tall, I peered at them for evidence of a resemblance to Angelina. More than once I saw such a resemblance, but then it was like arranging to meet someone in the crowds at a market or a city gate: you see your friend approaching in the distance, but when he comes closer you see that it is an unknown person who hardly looks like him at all. I knew that Sister Benedicta and Father Fleccia would never break their silence, and I guessed that Duke Cosimo also possessed the secret, because he knew everything about everyone in Florence, or so we believed. Thus did he keep us cowed and obedient, perhaps a fair price to pay in exchange for peace. Thirty years previously nobody would have believed that you would have to look in a locked collection of obsolete weapons to find a battering ram that could break down a door.

Although the truth about Angelina's parentage was an iron secret, the details of alchemy proved to be quite open to discussion. For a couple of hours, Father Fleccia tried to instruct me in the basics of the mystery, while Sister Benedicta put in occasional words, and from time to time Maria fluttered at the head of the stairs with more wine. It was all a waste of effort on their part, because neither then nor later did they succeed in making me interested in the subject, and yet something of it remained with me. I failed to grasp the central meaning of alchemy, which is that the nature of the substances and processes that are used reflect great philosophical and spiritual truths. That may be so, if I understand it correctly, but it was all beyond me. What did remain with me was the wonderful music of the terms that the alchemists use, as obscure and delightful as the terms used by carpenters and masons: Powder of Algaroth, Glass of Antimony, Mercurius Praecipitatus, Mosaic Gold, Flowers of Sulphur.

Then there are the strange processes: colliquation, ascension, impastation, quinta essentia, comminution, albification. Although I cannot tell you what they mean, these words and phrases have clung on in my mind as ineradicably as do painful memories, and in hours of sleepless darkness they tumble through my tired meditations, still challenging me by their majesty and inscrutability. Perhaps they are, after all, only pretentious names for ways to create bad smells. Common and uneducated people can make stinks and smoke by simpler methods which have plain names.

Eventually I decided that it was time that I returned to my master's house. I resolved not to tell him that Angelina's parents were still paying for her maintenance; knowing Bronzino as I did, I was sure that he would immediately demand a share of it for his own expenses, which consisted only of her share of the house's food.

Now that Bronzino had finished with the first completed figure, the libellous representation of Captain Da Lucca as The Effects of Venereal Disease, I was able to reassure Sister Benedicta and Father Fleccia that Angelina would soon no longer be needed as the model for Venus.

'We shall be glad to welcome her home,' Sister Benedicta said.

I knew that this was best for Angelina, but I wondered how easy it would be for me to conduct her back to that great closed house, with its silent rooms upstairs and its eerie laboratory in the cellar. I was certain of one thing: that when the front door closed behind Angelina on her return, I would never be admitted to the house again. All I would ever be able to see would be Sister Benedicta's grey eyes bobbing up and down behind the grille. I grieved in advance, not for Angelina, for whom life in the care of Sister Benedicta was as happy as she might ever know, but for myself, because I would never see her again, unless I spent my whole life looking upwards from the street, hoping for another glimpse of divine beauty such as had been my first sight of her.

When I said goodbye, Sister Benedicta surprised me by asking 'Does Angelina remember us? Does she think of us?'

'Father Fleccia can tell you that Angelina remembers him, because she is always delighted when he comes to see us,' I replied, and Father Fleccia nodded his head.

'Does she remember me?' Sister Benedicta asked.

'I am sure she does,' I reassured her, and indeed I was certain that Angelina would have known her at once, just as she had been elated to see Father Fleccia again.

When I returned to our house, Bronzino greeted me with only three words. 'Get the masks.'

All the time that I had spent at Sister Benedicta's, when I thought he would be studying the masks, he had been waiting for me to bring them to him. He obviously could not be bothered to search for them himself, or he would have found them at once. His house was not that big, but he liked to behave as though it were a vast warren of rooms like the Palazzo della Signoria.

I fetched the masks, and held them up for Bronzino's inspection, one in front of each of my fists, so that I looked like a puppeteer. I restrained myself from inventing squeaky voices for the masks and having them speak to Bronzino. His sense of humour was of the bitter kind at which nobody but the speaker ever laughs.

'The young woman and the old man,' he remarked. 'How would you use them in a painting, Giuseppe?'

At that moment Pontormo brought Angelina into the room. I moved to offer her a drink, but Pontormo gestured to me to sit down with Bronzino, while he fetched her some water himself. Angelina sat down on the floor next to my chair, with her unbound her falling around her shoulders in a manner so perfect that an artist would have had to work and think for hours to achieve the same effect. I returned to considering Bronzino's question about the masks.

'I don't know how I would present them, Master,' I told him. 'It would depend upon what the theme of the painting was.'

'I told you, long ago, that this painting will have no theme!' Bronzino replied. 'It's a good thing that you weren't apprenticed to Bandinelli instead. He would have beaten you into dwarfism by now.'

On the other hand, I thought to myself, Bandinelli would not have committed the unnatural act upon me.

'I remember that the painting has no theme, Master,' I said, 'and that it represents the emotions and passions of love. I suppose the mask of the young woman is a symbol of first love, and the mask of the old man represents memories of love.'

Bronzino sat in silence for a moment. 'Totally wrong, of course, but that's what I expected. Still, an artist training an apprentice can't do more than what is possible with the material that he's given.'

Angelina moved over and rested her head against my thigh. I reached my hand down and placed it upon her hair, which was hot. She must have been sitting where the sunlight could fall on her. Pontormo had been exposing her to the risk of a suntan, or worse.

Bronzino went on with his explanation. 'The masks illustrate the idea of deception. Deception by others and deception of oneself, for these are part of love. The young woman deceives the old man into believing that she loves him. The old man deceives himself into believing the young woman whom he desires.'

I thought that Bronzino was certainly deceiving himself if he believed that I loved him. I did not even desire him, although there was no doubt at all of his desire for me, or for my body, at any rate. My hand was still wandering in Angelina's flowing hair when suddenly an unwelcome, terrifying thought came to me. Angelina squealed, and I realised that I had unconsciously grasped a handful of her hair and tugged on it. I released my grip, and put my hand on the table in front of me, where I stared at it as though it were guilty of something and I were going to punish it. Bronzino was still rattling on about how the masks were going to symbolise deception and self-deception, but I was not listening to him. I examined my hand, and contemplated the idea that had occurred to me. Was I deceiving myself into believing that Angelina had any feeling for me? Was Bronzino right in his belief that Angelina had only the feelings of a beast, with no mind at all?

I turned away from Bronzino and looked down at Angelina. She was gazing at the planks of the floor. I reached down and put my hand on her hair again, and she smiled up at me. Bronzino noticed that I was not listening to him any more.

'By God, I should copy Bandinelli's methods!' he said. 'Apprentice: your master is instructing you.'

'I'm listening, Master,' I replied. 'You were telling me about the masks representing the deceptions of love.'

'I had also asked you where you would put them in the composition.'

I had missed that part of Bronzino's monologue.

'At the top of the picture,' I suggested, 'so that they seem to be hovering, like the masks of comedy and tragedy over actors' stages?'

'No,' Bronzino replied. 'This painting is formal and artificial enough. There is no need to draw attention to its artificiality by having two or three masks with different expressions hovering over it. In any case, there is tragedy in love, but there is never any comedy.'

'Is there never any comedy in deception?' I asked. 'Surely it's one of the most common themes of the rough comedies that are played in the streets.'

'No!' Bronzino replied instantly. 'There is no comedy in being deceived in love.'

I wondered who had ever deceived him in love; certainly not Pontormo. Then, with a stroke as hard as my realisation that Angelina might really feel nothing for me, I realised that Bronzino might be speaking of me. I had not taken him seriously when he had spoken of loving me, but now I thought about it again.

If Bronzino's feelings for me were truly love, rather than coarse lust for my young body, then I could never return them. I could not even return his lust, because his hard hirsute body inspired no desire in me.

Bronzino said no more, but he set masks on the table in a position that satisfied him, and he showed me where on the painting they were to appear, just behind Angelina's heel.

'But, Master,' I said, 'that will leave an empty expanse between the masks and the figure of Father Fleccia – I mean the figure of Time – at the top of the composition.'

'I know how I will fill that space,' Bronzino replied. 'You will appear in part of it, and one of my enemies will fill the rest.'

'Myself, Master?' I said. 'But I am already in the painting as Cupid. How can I appear twice? You told me that was an old-fashioned device that modern painters shouldn't use any more.'

'Ah, but that applies only when the two images are recognisably of the same person,' Bronzino said. 'You will not look the same.'

'I don't understand, Master,' I said. 'How can I change my appearance to model for you?'

'You've already changed it,' Bronzino said. 'I know your body very well.' I could not dispute that, but I let him continue. 'I shall paint you looking like a boy Cupid, as we usually see him, but without wings. You will represent Pleasure. Oh, there's no need to model. I shall simply paint you as you must have been.'

'Why am I to be the model for Pleasure, Master?' I asked, fearing that I knew the answer already.

'Because,' Bronzino replied, 'you cannot represent Love to me, and probably never to anyone else.'

'How will you fill the rest of the space, Master?' I asked. 'Which enemy will you choose?' There were so many whose names I could have guessed, and after seeing him fool Captain Da Lucca into modelling as The Effects of Venereal Disease I could believe that he would be able to fool anyone into exposing themselves to perpetual humiliation in the painting. 'Will it be Bandinelli, Master?' I asked.

'Bandinelli? No, he would never agree,' Bronzino replied. 'I have someone else in mind. When I'm ready, I'll send you to the house of that witch Sister Benedicta to ask her to come here. She won't refuse.'

11

Bronzino refused me permission to leave the house for the next few days, and Father Fleccia was not due to return until Sunday, so I had no chance to warn Sister Benedicta. Bronzino had made fast progress on the figures of myself and Angelina, and he had made a rough outline of the pose in which Father Fleccia was to appear as Time. The three masks were now lying in their place next to Angelina, set off against the blue cloth upon which Angelina and I had been posing.

I now found out how Bronzino was going to represent me as Pleasure. You may well imagine how I had worried over that. As I might have guessed instead, he had devised a humiliation for me which was inspired by a wicked malice, his nearest approach to a sense of humour.

'I'm going to show you as a dancing boy,' he announced, 'nude, of course, and that reminds me –'

As Bronzino paused, I readied myself for whatever my nudity might remind Bronzino to do. Perhaps he was losing his memory if he needed to be reminded to perform the act of sodomy.

'That reminds me,' Bronzino continued, 'go out and find me a large thorn. Find one in a garden.'

I wondered how he knew that I was an expert in sneaking into the private gardens of the aristocracy and the merchants. Every great house in Florence had an enclosed garden, and I used to enjoy wandering uninvited into them, putting my hot hands into the cool fountains and letting my eyes recover from the glaring sunlight by slouching in the shaded colonnades. I was always quick enough to escape back over the wall when I heard someone coming, which was more dangerous than it may sound, because some householders kept crossbows ready to shoot at any intruder.

I welcomed the chance to escape from Bronzino's house for a little while. 'May I take Angelina?' I asked.

'Yes,' Bronzino replied absently.

I bound Angelina's hair up roughly so that it did not look too disorderly. I realised that I certainly could not take her over any walls with me, and nor could I leave her alone on the other side of the wall, so illegal entry was not an option this time.

When we left the house, Angelina squeezed my hand and pressed herself against me as we walked along. I could easily have found a flower, but where could I seek a thorn which was publicly available? We lived in the middle of the city, and there was no time to go through one of the city gates and out into the countryside that comes right up to the walls of Florence like water around an island.

'Help me, Angelina,' I beseeched her. 'Give me an idea.' She squeezed my hand again and then tilted her head up to enjoy some smell which was being carried by the hot wind. Of course! The flower sellers!

We walked to the street where the flower sellers congregated, and I asked at one stall after another for a thorn. They all thought I was baiting them, and they would have responded with impolite invitations to leave their pitch if they had not been transfixed by the sight of Angelina.

'Buy your lady a flower, Sir,' one of the aggressive women suggested.

'She's not my lady,' I replied at once without thinking.

'That's no business of ours,' the woman replied, and I immediately regretted what I had said.

'She's an artist's model, and I'm the artist's apprentice,' I told the vendor. 'I'm not looking for a flower, because my master has sent me out to buy a thorn instead.'

'A thorn?' the woman replied, possibly taken aback for the first time in her no-doubt colourful and wicked life. 'What kind of an artist wants a thorn instead of a flower?'

'The kind of artist which my master is,' I said. 'Anyone in this street could sell me a flower. Are you the special one who can sell me a thorn?'

'You'd better not be wasting my time,' the woman growled, disappearing under the cloth that covered her stall. She came up again like a diver surfacing from the Arno, triumphantly holding up a stalk of some plant bearing a thorn.

'Here you are,' she cried, 'a thorn, a wonderfully sharp thorn, fit to appear in any artist's painting.'

'What do you want for it?' I asked, willing as ever to spend Bronzino's money generously. I paid the outrageous price for the thorn, and the woman slightly mitigated her greed by offering Angelina the chance to choose a free flower.

'She can't talk,' I explained.

'Oh, yes,' the woman replied, her face darkening, 'I've heard of her. Can she point to the one she wants?'

'Give her the flower that smells most strongly,' I said. 'That's what she likes.'

'Those are the lowest of the flowers!' the woman replied. 'Here, take these roses.' She handed Angelina four pink flowers. They looked as if they ought to be red, but were ill. Angelina took them and held them up to her face. Her eyes sparkled, the only sign of a hidden smile.

'How much for those?' I asked the woman.

'You paid for them when you bought the thorn,' the flower-vendor told me. 'I think that poor girl has had more thorns than roses in her life.'

'You're right about that,' I replied, leading Angelina away, and wondering whether I was one of the roses or one of the thorns.

When I led Angelina back into Bronzino's studio, she was still holding the flowers under her nose. They were so tightly bunched together that they looked like a pink cushion of petals. I held out the thorn to Bronzino.

'There, Master, a thorn for you, worthy to crown Christ Himself,' I said.

Bronzino snatched the thorn away without replying or even looking at me. He flung it on the table, and then jumped up and sprang at Angelina. For the first time since we had known her, Angelina acknowledged his presence in her life. She stumbled backwards, and would have fallen if I had not leapt behind her to support her.

Bronzino's face was alight with joy.

'Those flowers, Giuseppe!' he exclaimed. 'They're just what I need for you to hold!'

He snatched the flowers out of Angelina's hands and bore them off to the table, where he set them down cautiously beside the thorn that I had found for him. Angelina crumpled in my arms, and I was lowering her to the floor, because I thought that she wanted to sit on it. Somehow it seemed a privilege even to support her weight. I had misread her, because she lifted herself up again, pushing at my limbs as though I were a tree. With a wail she ran across the room to Bronzino, and lunged at the flowers on the table. Bronzino snatched them away and shouted at her.

'Get away, creature! You'll bruise them.'

Angelina jumped at him and clawed at his arms, trying to make him release the posy of flowers that he was clutching in his arms as tenderly as if it were his child, or perhaps as tenderly as though it were himself.

Angelina cried out again, and now tears were running down her face.

She reached for the flowers a second time, but Bronzino turned away, and so her fingernails clawed across his face. Spots of blood appeared on his cheek as suddenly as bursts of fireworks and then ran into his beard. Bronzino got up from the table and ran to the other side of the room.

'Giuseppe!' he roared. 'Control her, damn you!'

I took Angelina by the shoulders, trying to calm her, but she ignored me and continued to wail. She pursued Bronzino across the room. Her loosely bound hair had escaped from its ribbon and flowed out behind her. It flooded my face, and I brushed it aside.

'Master,' I begged, 'give her back the flowers. She loves the smell.'

'The smell?' Bronzino repeated. 'She loves flowers for the smell? I told you, Giuseppe, I've told you over and over. The woman is simply a mindless beast. Get her out of here. Take her to Pontormo's – no, he hates being disturbed when he's working. Take her up to your room and leave her there when she's calmed down.'

'She's not a beast, Master!' I cried.

'Whether she's a brute beast or a tiresome woman, get her out of here,' Bronzino ordered. 'I've lived my life without animals or women, and I intend to live on without them.'

He was clutching the flowers to his chest like a girl. Although there was nothing feminine about Bronzino, somehow he never seemed completely male. Perhaps it was his vice that made me perceive him so.

I placed myself between Bronzino and Angelina so that she could not see the flowers that he had stolen. I hoped that she would forget them at once. Angelina stopped struggling and began crying, weeping as any other person might weep. Apart from her laughter, it was the first ordinary human sound that I had ever heard her make.

I managed to turn Angelina away from Bronzino. It was as if we were performing a grotesque dance together. I led her up the stairs to my room, where she fell upon my bed, still weeping, with her face in the pillow. I watched for a little while, until she fell asleep, quite suddenly, reminding me uncomfortably of Bronzino's gift of being able to do the same thing.

When I came down to the studio again, after closing the door quietly to my room, I found Bronzino in a happy mood, because he had achieved some advantage for himself. He held up the flowers in his clenched fist.

'This is how you will hold the flowers, Giuseppe,' he told me.

'But I have no free hand, Master,' I objected. I said nothing about his treatment of Angelina. It would have been of no use, and I was afraid that he would dismiss me as his apprentice and drive me out of his house. Not even Father Fleccia and Pontormo could do as much to protect her as I could.

'No, your hands are full when you are Cupid,' Bronzino replied. 'I'm thinking of your pose as Pleasure. Here, let me show you.'

He stood up and adopted a posture like a dancing girl,

with one leg forward and the flowers clasped in a bunch by his left ear. The pose would have been pleasing in a beautiful young girl, but it was ugly and disturbing when demonstrated by a forty-two-year-old sodomite. More from a wish to stop having to look at him in that frozen prance than from willing compliance with his orders, I reached out for the flowers.

Bronzino handed the flowers over to me with a tenderness that he never showed to people.

'Now,' he told me, 'stand in the pose that I was demonstrating. Yes, like that. Don't move.' He sketched me quickly.

'That will do,' he said. 'You can do the formal posing later. That leaves with me with the two other human figures to deal with. I know how I'm going to show the old priest as Time. Beneath him, and behind you in your pose as Pleasure, I'm going to show a female figure as Deception.'

'Is that what you want Sister Benedicta for?' I asked. 'To play Deception? She is the most honest person I've ever met.'

'It's the eyes,' Bronzino told me. 'Those eyes that I first saw behind the grille of her door. Do you remember how I rejected so many beautiful women as the model for Venus because their eyes were too knowing and malicious? That witch of a nun has eyes that were made to deceive men. Let us be grateful to God that He made her swear to perpetual chastity. What daughters she would have bred!'

I interrupted Bronzino's soliloquy of praise upon his own cleverness.

'Sister Benedicta is hardly likely to rush here in order to be insulted by you, Master,' I said. 'Why should she agree to do it?'

'To see the woman again, of course,' Bronzino replied.

'Anyway, I'm only going to paint her face, and you won't tell her how I'm going to use it. If you do, I shall make both you and that mindless animal of a woman pay for it.'

I wanted to ask 'How?', but I knew that I would help neither myself nor Angelina if I were to arouse Bronzino's anger any further. Instead, I asked: 'Shall I bring Angelina down again, Master?' and Bronzino nodded.

When I went up to my room, I hoped to find that Angelina had fallen asleep, but she was sitting upright on my bed with an expression on her face that I had never seen before. At first, I thought it was alertness, and then I realised that it was rage. I approached her cautiously, and laid my hand on her shoulder.

'Will you come down, now, Angelina?' I said, taking her hand in mine, but she snatched her hand away.

This would be great trouble, if she were to see me no longer as a friend, but as an instrument of Bronzino's mistreatment of her. I feared that I would have to ask for Pontormo's help to calm her. That would be a humiliation for me, but my humiliation was of no importance in comparison with Angelina's safety. I left her where she was, and came back down to Bronzino.

'I think it would be better if we kept away from her for a little while, Master,' I suggested. 'When Pontormo comes, he may be able to settle her. You know that he has a knack for doing that.'

'Does he?' Bronzino replied absently. 'I never noticed.'

I suppose that Angelina slept all through the afternoon, while Bronzino began painting me as the figure of Pleasure. I could not help myself from remarking upon this departure from his usual routine.

'Master,' I said, 'you told me that you always paint from

a model. I can't model for you as a young boy. How can you use my body as your model?'

'I'm not,' Bronzino said. 'I do have a model, but in my mind. I'm doing it from memory.'

'But you never knew me as a young boy!' I said.

'I'm not using you,' Bronzino replied. 'I'm recalling my memories of the Golden Child. The figure of Pleasure will have his body. God knows that I remember it perfectly.'

So there it is: the figure of Pleasure, dancing joyfully with a handful of flower petals that he is about to throw over Venus and Cupid, is really a portrait of the doomed Golden Child whom Pontormo accidentally killed. Perhaps Bronzino meant something by the fact that the boy is holding the petals ready to throw, but he will hold them in readiness for ever, for as long as the painting lasts. He will never fling them over the Goddess of Love and her son, never fulfil his ambition to express joy.

I was glad that the bereaved baker would never see his son in the painting. I suppose that if he did, he would demand a posthumous modelling fee from Bronzino.

I did not go up to Angelina again until Pontormo arrived at our house for supper. I took him aside when I showed him into the studio (as manners required, and as if he had never been there before), and told him that Angelina had been distressed during the afternoon and that he might have to calm her.

'I'll do my best,' he said, and then he surprised me by adding: 'Bronzino has distressed me, too, on occasion.'

I washed Angelina's face and combed out as many tangles from her hair as I could. I tied it back with a simple ribbon so that it would not fall into her food, and then brought her down to the table. Bronzino was showing Pontormo how he was going to complete the painting of the boy representing Pleasure. I was afraid that he would devastate Pontormo by saying that the boy was based on the ill-fated Golden Child, but to my relief even Bronzino was not that insensitive.

'Is that the last of your human figures,' Pontormo asked him, 'except for the old man representing Time?'

'No, there is still a woman to add. Well, she won't be entirely human. She'll represent Deception.'

What, I wondered, did Bronzino mean by saying that Deception would be 'not entirely human'? I concluded wearily that I would soon find out, and that I would be better off enjoying my ignorance for as long as I could until the truth was revealed.

Angelina showed no emotion throughout dinner. Her table manners were as elegant and dainty as ever. I wondered how Sister Benedicta had trained her. Pontormo sat opposite her. He spoke to her kindly, although he shared everyone else's opinion that she did not really understand speech.

Bronzino made a request to his former master. 'Could you stay with us tomorrow morning, Master, after you bring the woman?'

'You mean Angelina,' Pontormo responded briskly, in the tone that I hope he used frequently to Bronzino in the days of my master's apprenticeship.

'Yes, Master,' Bronzino replied, obviously determined not to lose a point in the game by being made to speak Angelina's name. 'Your presence will help to calm her, because I want to send Giuseppe to Sister Benedicta's house.'

'Why?' Pontormo demanded. 'I thought you disliked her.'

'I have had little acquaintance with her so far,' Bronzino

said, 'but I must admit that I have not conceived a deep and poetic love for her. I want her to pose as a model.'

'What?' cried Pontormo.

Bronzino explained his plan for Sister Benedicta.

'This is underhanded, Bronzino,' Pontormo declared, and I realised that he had no idea of the trick that had been played upon Captain Da Lucca.

'I admit that it is a petty revenge, Master,' Bronzino agreed, 'but it is revenge nevertheless. Do you not agree that revenge is one of the emotions of love?'

'You don't love Sister Benedicta,' Pontormo objected.

'Ah, but if she had not been a nun, what a tempestuous and famous pair of lovers we would have made!' Bronzino crowed. 'Great poems would have been written about us.'

I flexed my imagination to its utmost strain to try to imagine such a relationship. If Bronzino's taste had been for women instead of for men, I can see that he and Sister Benedicta might well have been ideal candidates for a stormy but passionate relationship. I certainly hope that no misguided poet will ever write about Bronzino's relationship with me. If there was any love involved, which I doubt, it was all on his part and not on mine.

That night, when I carried my staff and lantern in front of Pontormo and Angelina all the way to Pontormo's house, I wished that I could have explained to Angelina the good news that she would be seeing Sister Benedicta again soon. I hoped that she would not take it to mean that Sister Benedicta would be taking her home immediately. The disappointment would be hard for her to bear.

The next morning, when I arrived back at Pontormo's house, he brought Angelina out in such a disorderly state that I begged him to allow me to go in and tidy up her clothes and hair before we carried on to Bronzino's.

Pontormo rebuffed me decisively. 'Absolutely not! Nobody enters my house. I do not allow even Bronzino in any more. I don't want anybody to know what I'm working on at present.'

I had to give in and lead Angelina through the streets just as she was. I was becoming more and more worried over how Pontormo was treating her when she was behind his famously closed door. I knew that he meant well and would do his best, but Pontormo's best, as far as taking care of himself and others was concerned, was rather inferior to most people's worst.

Bronzino shook his head when we presented Angelina to him, but he confined himself to telling me to tidy her up a little after we had finished breakfast. 'Then you can carry my message to that sorceress Sister Benedicta,' he told me.

'When do you want her to come and model for you?' I asked him. 'She'll certainly put many questions to me, Master. You know what she's like. Father Fleccia may be there, too, and he'll certainly have something to say.'

'Tell them that they can come here together, if they want,' Bronzino replied. 'They can both pose on the same day, if they choose. That old priest seems not to have many duties, so he must have plenty of time.'

'When can they come, though, Master?' I asked.

'Today, if they want,' Bronzino said. 'I won't shame you by offering them poor hospitality. I wouldn't want to be seen as not honouring the representatives of the Church.'

I wished that I could have taken Angelina with me, but it would have taken Captain Da Lucca's entire squad of bullies to get her back again. I consigned her to the kindly but muddled care of Pontormo, and walked away, feeling more than ever that I was guilty of being an accomplice in

Bronzino's wickedness. At least his sodomy hurt only me. Now he was using Angelina as a lever to make me help him hurt Sister Benedicta, who had done him no harm.

When I hammered upon the door of Sister Benedicta's house, I heard a window open above me on one of the upper floors, and then immediately slam shut again. I had to wait what seemed a long time, with my face against the grille, preparing myself for the confrontation with Sister Benedicta's knowing and implacable eyes. The result was that I nearly fell into her arms when the door was flung open, without the preliminary scrutiny through the grille that I had been expecting.

'Come in, Giuseppe, come in,' she said with unusual cheeriness. 'I'm afraid that Father Radulfo isn't here today.'

Radulfo? Oh, yes, that was the Italian translation of Father Fleccia's unpronounceable English Christian name.

'That's a pity, but my master Bronzino sent me with a message only for you,' I replied.

Sister Benedicta closed the street door behind us with the air that she and I were going to exchange valuable secrets.

I decided to give the message bluntly. 'Bronzino wants you to come to his house, and to model for the face of one of the figures in his painting.'

'What?' Sister Benedicta replied, with an unconscious rudeness of which I would not previously have believed her to be capable. Before I could repeat myself, she took me by the elbow in a startlingly strong grip, and steered me towards the staircase. She practically flung me down into one of the chairs in the solar while calling to Maria to bring us some wine. I sat breathless in the chair while Maria served us, and, after she had left, Sister Benedicta looked me directly in the eyes. The sun was shining in her face from the window behind me, but Sister Benedicta seemed not to be affected by it. She did not even blink.

'What game is your master playing?' she asked.

'It is simple,' I told her, 'and I am giving away none of his secrets by telling you that he wants you to appear in his painting.'

'What would I have to do?'

'Come to Bronzino's house two or three times. He works fast when he is under pressure, and Duke Cosimo is demanding that the painting be finished soon.'

'I'm not supposed to leave this house,' Sister Benedicta said. 'My work with the women here is the reason that I am exempt from living in the convent for the time being. One day, when I'm too frail to look after the women, I'll have to return there. In any case, it would be a scandal if I went alone through the streets to your master's house.'

'I'll come here and walk with you,' I said. 'My master would insist upon it.'

'That might create an even greater scandal,' Sister Benedicta replied.

I thought of a solution. 'Father Fleccia is going to model for the figure of Time, as I'm sure he's told you. Bronzino says that you can both come together. Surely you could leave your house if you were accompanied by a priest?'

Sister Benedicta broke into a smile that was as brilliant and unexpected as the wonderful, unpredictable smiles of Angelina.

'I must admit that I am tempted, Giuseppe. Would I see Angelina again?'

'Of course,' I said. 'My master will make sure that she's there when you visit.'

'I have another selfish reason to feel temptation,' Sister Benedicta said. 'I have literally not stepped out of this house for thirteen years.'

'Thirteen years?' I echoed, as automatically and thoughtlessly as I give the responses in the Mass at the bidding of the priest, who can hardly be surprised at what the congregation say to him.

'Yes, it was the year 1531,' Sister Benedicta said. 'It was the year after Florence surrendered to the armies of the Pope and the Holy Roman Emperor. How many cities have ever achieved the feat of making enemies of them both?'

'Was Alessandro the Duke then?' I asked, because this was the time of my early childhood, and I could only remember the shocked silence of the streets of Florence, without understanding that the people were recovering from the siege.

'No, the Emperor had appointed him to rule Florence, but he had not yet been created Duke,' Sister Benedicta replied. Cosimo de' Medici had been appointed as Alessandro's successor six years later, because the aristocracy of Florence believed that he would be a passive and weak Duke. Never has a man's character been so misjudged.

'Have you really never been out of this house since then?' I asked.

'I've been out in the courtyard, for the sun and the air and the wind, and to see the birds and the flowers,' Sister Benedicta replied, 'and I've been down in the darkness of the laboratory. I've travelled very far in the paths of the mind and the spirit down there.'

I became interested in the confined life that she led.

'How many women live in this house, Sister?' I asked.

'Up to four,' she answered. 'Often they're quite old, and we lose them only when they die. Their families don't know what to do with them.'

I saw how it would happen to Angelina. She would spend the rest of her life in this house, ending up as an old woman, and I hoped that whoever took over the task of looking after her was as kindly and good as Sister Benedicta.

'How much do you know about what goes on in the world?' I asked her. 'Do you rely only on Father Fleccia?'

'I had only Maria to tell me what was going on in the city before Father Fleccia came,' Sister Benedicta said. 'Father Fleccia was still in England when I first came here. He was a priest in an ordinary parish, because his king was only then starting to turn against the Church.'

'You would have had more freedom in a convent,' I said.

'I didn't enter a convent in search of freedom,' Sister Benedicta replied. 'My father paid as much for the dowry to the Order as he would have had to do to get me a husband. The difference is that a husband would have wanted me. These poor women don't want me. They don't even know who I am. They need me. Do you understand, Giuseppe? It seems to me much better to be needed than simply to be wanted.'

'Nobody has ever needed me,' I said. 'My family have had nothing to do with me since the day I was apprenticed to Bronzino, and he doesn't need me.' No, I thought to myself, and he wants me only for foul and immoral purposes. He could find another apprentice at once, and he could find boys anywhere in Florence, except that he would have to pay more for them.

'Angelina needs you,' Sister Benedicta replied. 'Father Fleccia has told me how you look after her.'

'Pontormo looks after her as well,' I said, out of loyalty to him. Even though he had trained Bronzino and, perhaps, made Bronzino what he was, I never held any grudge against Pontormo. Nobody could feel hostility to Pontormo, except Bandinelli, and his opinion counted for nothing, because he hated everybody.

'Bronzino will want to know when you can come,' I said.

'I'll come the next time Father Fleccia visits,' Sister Benedicta replied.

'He visits us only to see to Angelina's spiritual welfare,' I said, 'not to model.'

'Well, if Radulfo has agreed to model for Time, he will have to start sooner or later, and I may as well be there. I do hope he won't be required to disrobe entirely in order to represent the god.'

'No,' I said, 'I am sure that even Bronzino is not shameless enough to demand that of an elderly priest. He might be shameless enough to demand it of a young priest, but I hope that he is never given that chance.'

'You are not as respectful of your master as an apprentice should be,' Sister Benedicta commented.

'I respect him as a painter, and as a teacher, but I have no respect for his character,' I told her.

12

When I came home, I found that Bronzino was not there. Pontormo was sitting on the floor, an odd posture for an old man (yet he was only fifty-one!), holding Angelina's hand in his own while she sat behind him. I wondered whether they had been playing some sort of game. I felt a foolish pang of jealousy to know that Angelina enjoyed Pontormo's company, but I suppressed it, telling myself angrily that if Pontormo could keep Angelina contented I ought to be glad about it.

'Where has my master gone?' I asked him.

'Ah, the Duke has summoned him to the Palazzo,' Pontormo replied. 'There was no other message, but Bronzino has left in haste.'

'So would I, if I had a summons from the Duke,' I said. 'I assume that the painting is still not proceeding fast enough for the Duke's liking.'

'It must be that,' Pontormo agreed. 'Bronzino is probably having an uncomfortable interview with Duke Cosimo at this very moment.'

Good, I thought to myself. The more uncomfortable the better, and I hoped that the rack and thumbscrews would be brought into use to help the Duke make his point. Pontormo had no such ill will towards Bronzino, but he squeezed Angelina's hand, and she leaned against him. It hurt me to see it.

'Signor Pontormo,' I asked, 'may I put a question to you?'

Pontormo seemed to have read my earlier uncharitable fantasies about Bronzino's reception by Duke Cosimo.

'If you agree to question me more gently than the Duke is questioning Bronzino at this moment,' he said.

'I would like to know what my master Bronzino was like when he was your apprentice. Was he like me?'

'What a strange question!' Pontormo exclaimed. 'I never expected it. Like you? No, he was more passionate, and more impatient at being an apprentice. He was desperate to be recognised as a painter, and I kept having to tell him that he must wait until he was fully trained and educated.'

I remembered the portrait of the young Bronzino sitting on the steps in Pontormo's painting *Joseph in Egypt*. He is looking upwards, yearning for something, or perhaps waiting for someone to say to him: 'Yes, you are now an artist yourself, and you can walk through Florence as a man of consequence.' I persisted with one more question.

'Would you say that I am more advanced at painting than Bronzino was at my age?'

'You are just as advanced as Bronzino was at developing your own talent,' Pontormo said, 'to judge by what I've seen of your efforts, but your talent is smaller than Bronzino's. You will never be as good a painter as he is.'

It must not have occurred to Pontormo, being what he was, how painfully his words would strike me, and more so because I knew that he was right. Pontormo was not being cruel: he was simply stating his judgement, and it was fair, because I had long admitted to myself that while I could become a journeyman painter, I would never become an artist like Bronzino, or like Pontormo himself. If my father had beaten me through an apprenticeship as a carpenter, I would probably have qualified in the trade and been able to do a competent job, but I would never have created those marvels of woodwork that one sees in the furniture and fabric of great men's houses.

Pontormo tried to comfort me, with that skill he had which Angelina had sensed. He would have made a marvellous beloved grandfather for small children if he had married a good woman instead of misbestowing his love upon Bronzino.

'I didn't mean to hurt you by what I said to you, Giuseppe,' he said, 'but you did ask me for my opinion.'

'I know, Signor Pontormo,' I replied. 'May I ask you something else?'

'I hope that I won't have to give you another unwelcome answer,' Pontormo said.

'Then may I ask you why you took Bronzino as your apprentice? Could you see his ability already?'

'Oh, yes,' Pontormo answered, 'but one can see ability in many youths. What I saw in Bronzino was the passion that would develop that ability. I knew that he had already had two bad teachers, and I feared that if he went to another bad master he would give up painting altogether. It nearly happened to me after my short apprenticeship to Andrea del Sarto, God forgive me for my unhappy memories of him.'

I had no more questions. I sat silent on the floor, waiting, as Pontormo was waiting, for the return of Bronzino. I was filled with despair. I knew that Pontormo was right, and that I would never be a first-class painter. For that matter, my father had judged that I would never be a first-class carpenter, and I have never doubted that he was right. I had to face the fact that, living in the artistic community of Florence, I was surrounded by men who were my betters and that I could never match their achievements. If I could not be first class at anything, I wondered, in what could I achieve the second class? I was an acceptable but ordinary apprentice painter, and my master kept me only for unnatural acts that he could purchase from others on every corner in the city.

Sitting on the floor of Bronzino's studio, I looked back at my seventeen years of life, and astonished myself by bursting into tears. I cried without dignity, weeping loudly for shame at what I was and how little I would ever be. Pontormo was nearly as surprised as I was.

'Whatever is the matter, Giuseppe?' he asked. He looked at me with the plain kindness that one sees in the faces of the sort of people who rush to attend to someone who has collapsed in the street, while most others hurry past pretending that they have not noticed. I am sure that Pontormo had never seen any such exhibition when Bronzino was his apprentice.

'I'm sorry, Signor Pontormo. I'm sorry,' I sobbed.

Through the wet blur that was veiling my eyes, I saw Pontormo release Angelina's hand. He leaned towards me as though he were going to say something, but Angelina squirmed away from him and flung herself across the floor towards me. Her weight hit me hard, and her arms gripped me like someone drowning. I almost fell onto my back, wondering desperately why Angelina had attacked me, and then she clutched me to her. She could not have understood why I was so hurt, but she was trying to comfort me.

Pontormo's voice came to me from nowhere. 'Don't push her away, Giuseppe. Let her do what she wants.'

Ever since I had first met Angelina, I had been trying to communicate with her. Now she had taken the initiative in trying to communicate with me. I could not control myself, and I wept upon her bosom while she held me tightly against her. Sobbing upon her bodice, I felt an intimacy with her far deeper than the times when we had lain naked against each other. I realised that she was weeping with me when her hot tears slid across my brow and cheek. In my distress I never noticed that Bronzino had returned to the house and entered the room. I did not know he was there until I heard him shout.

'What is going on here? Giuseppe! Giuseppe! It's no use asking that woman. She's a brainless beast.'

'You could ask me,' Pontormo said. 'Giuseppe had an attack of melancholy, and Angelina is only trying to help him feel better.'

'She's not here for that,' Bronzino replied. 'She's only a beautiful body, and I don't want her eyes to be puffed and swollen like that.' He pulled at Angelina's shoulder, and then let out a howl as she snapped her head round and bit him. 'Get her off me, Master!' he yelled, and even while I was springing forward to try to get her teeth out of Bronzino's hand, I somehow had time to notice that he had called for Pontormo's help and not mine.

I put my hand on hers. 'Let go, Angelina,' I begged her. 'Let go.' I stroked her arm and hand, and Angelina released her bite.

Bronzino snatched away his hand. I was relieved to see that her teeth had not drawn blood, but that was little consolation to him.

'That beast!' he cried, as he studied his hand. 'Thank God it's my left hand. If I were left-handed I would kill her for ruining my career.'

So small a bite would hardly have ended the career even of Bronzino, a man who was always acutely sensitive to his own sufferings even though he cared nothing for the feelings of other people.

Pontormo looked at Bronzino's hand, as though Bronzino were still the small boy who had once been entrusted to his care.

'It's nothing, Bronzino,' Pontormo assured him. 'Just wash it.'

'Get me some water and a clean cloth!' Bronzino shouted at me.

I untangled myself reluctantly from Angelina's embrace, and fetched the water and cloth. I offered them to Bronzino, but it was Pontormo who took them from me and washed Bronzino's hand. There was no blood, only the indentations of Angelina's teeth, but from the fuss Bronzino was making anyone would have thought that he was bleeding to death.

I put my arm around Angelina to try to calm her, and she smiled at me. For the first time, it was not that undirected smile that she gave to everyone in the world. She looked straight into my eyes.

Bronzino finally stopped fussing, and handed the basin of water back to me to dispose of. 'Now that calm has been restored,' he said to Pontormo, with a vicious glance at Angelina, 'I can tell you why the Duke summoned me to the Palazzo.'

'He wants his painting even more quickly,' Pontormo guessed, and although I said nothing, I had assumed the same thing.

'No, although he did demand to know why it wasn't finished yet. I told him that I still had two or three figures to complete first, as well as most of the background. He wants me to bring the woman to the Palazzo tomorrow evening. God grant that she doesn't bite anyone, or my chances of ever being appointed officially as court painter will be bitten off as well.'

'Tomorrow evening, Master?' I cried. 'What will she

wear? I must go to Sister Benedicta's and ask if Angelina has any best clothes.'

'What does it matter what she wears?' Bronzino retorted. 'It's not as if she were a real human being.'

'She is a person, Master, with a soul!' I objected. 'It will look bad for you if she comes to Court wearing ordinary clothes. Please let me go to Sister Benedicta.'

'You've only just come back from there,' Bronzino pointed out. 'I'm not having you running back and forth like that. Are you conducting an illicit love affair with Sister Benedicta?'

Now there was a terrifying idea. It is a mark of the wisdom and compassion of God that He ensures that such women take vows of perpetual virginity.

'Let me go tomorrow morning, then, Master,' I begged.

'I'll think about it tomorrow,' Bronzino replied, but then Pontormo interrupted him.

'Leave the boy to his work, Bronzino,' he said. 'I'll go and ask for some good clothes for Angelina.'

'You?' Bronzino replied, too startled to remember to address Pontormo with the respect due from an apprentice to his master. 'You are not a servant!'

'No, but I have the time to spare. I remember the way,' he declared, surprising me who had thought Pontormo to be completely helpless in all practical matters.

'If you so choose, Master,' Bronzino replied, as he had no choice but to do so.

A little while later Pontormo left us. I watched from the studio window to make sure that he was shuffling away in the right direction, and prayed that he would not be found wandering and starving in the streets of Siena or Pistoia a week later. Bronzino vanished into his bedroom to change out of the formal clothes that he had worn to go to the Palazzo. I was sorry that Angelina had not used her teeth on his expensive garments instead of on his ugly body.

While we were left alone, I embraced her and wiped her tears away. Bronzino was right about one thing: she could not pose as a convincingly serene Venus if she had been crying. Angelina became calm again. I helped her to stand up, and led her to the half-finished painting.

'Do you recognise yourself, Angelina?' I asked her as we stood hand in hand in front of it.

Her image was more substantial than mine at that stage. I was still handless, because Bronzino had not yet painted Angelina's hands on the end of my arms. Angelina's face was turned towards mine, but my body was ghostly and still brownish-yellow where the *imprimatura* was showing through. The panel itself still looked like the piece of wood that it was. I supposed that Angelina was seeing it as a rectangular block with irregular blobs of colour and sinuous lines on it. I was sure that she could recognise neither herself nor me.

Bronzino stalked out of his bedroom. 'Don't be too quick to admire the work, Giuseppe,' he said. 'Admire it when it's finished and the Duke has given his approval.'

'Haven't we the right to admire it before the Duke gives his judgement, Master?' I asked.

'No, because the only criterion by which we can judge it to be successful is if the Duke gives it his approval and pronounces it good enough to be sent to King François,' Bronzino said. 'If he rejects it, that will be the end of me as a painter in Florence, and it will be the end of you as my apprentice.'

'It will also mean that Angelina goes home to Sister Benedicta,' I said, 'so someone would gain from it.'

'If that happens, perhaps the witch will take you in as a house servant,' Bronzino replied, 'and that's the best that you could hope for, because you will certainly never become a professional artist without my help.'

I imagined that at least I would see Angelina every day in this scenario, but I knew that Sister Benedicta would certainly never allow me to spend the siesta with her, and in any case no male servants would ever be employed in that house.

We all became quiet, as though someone had ordered it. Bronzino dabbed and scratched at the painting, but he did not seem to be interested in his work at that moment. The silence was broken when Pontormo came back.

'Sister Benedicta wouldn't let me into the house,' he announced, 'but I spoke to her through the grille. She will arrange for some clothes to be delivered here by noon tomorrow.'

'Noon?' Bronzino echoed. 'That's not giving us much time to prepare the creature to be presented at the Duke's court.'

'I am sure Angelina will not disgrace us,' Pontormo replied. He examined the painting. 'If I have succeeded in anything as your teacher,' he remarked to Bronzino, 'at least I have not prevented you from developing your own style. Nobody could ever make the mistake of believing that this picture had been painted by me.'

'Thank you, Master,' Bronzino replied.

'I must have taught you properly,' Pontormo continued. 'Giuseppe has been asking me about you when you were my apprentice.'

'Has he, indeed!' Bronzino said. 'Who gave him permission to question you?'

'He was entirely respectful,' Pontormo said with an

indulgent glance at me. 'In fact, though, I can't tell him a lot. I wonder whether my memory is not what it was.'

'You are not even an old man, Master,' Bronzino said.

'I should have put more details into my diary,' Pontormo remarked.

'Diary?' Bronzino repeated. 'I didn't know you had ever kept a diary, Master.'

'Nobody has ever known until this moment,' Pontormo said. 'I write it up every night. I started keeping it when I went to stay with the prior of the Certosa. That was when we left Florence to escape the plague. Which year was that, Bronzino?'

'It was in 1522,' Bronzino replied. 'Have you really been keeping a diary for twenty-two years? That pest Vasari will want it.'

Vasari was a minor but capable painter and architect who was planning to write a collection of biographies of artists. He would not be the only man to want to read Pontormo's diary. Now that I knew about it, I wanted to read it myself, but it would be somewhere in Pontormo's house which nobody was allowed to enter.

What, I tried to imagine, could Pontormo be writing about Angelina? What would he be writing about Bronzino, or even perhaps about myself? I guessed that Bronzino would have liked to forbid me to put any more questions to Pontormo, but he could not countermand the permission that Pontormo himself had given me without undermining his own rights of discipline and control over me. He still feared offending Pontormo. I can think of no other example of a qualified painter remaining in the almost daily company of his former master.

Bronzino turned his attention to another matter. 'I won't do any more work on the painting today. Giuseppe, clean up this studio. Bandinelli is coming over later. Tidy up the woman while you're about it, or else keep her out of sight.'

I cleaned up the studio, and put Angelina's clothes and hair in order, and washed her face in cold water, which made her recoil, but she let me do it.

Once again I answered the door to Clemente, who announced his father with all formality even though Bandinelli was standing right behind him. I announced Bandinelli to the studio with equal formality.

'The sculptor and painter Baccio Bandinelli is here, Master,' I said, throwing in the title of painter as well as sculptor in order to annoy Bronzino. Clemente and I stepped out of the way as Bandinelli stalked in. Pontormo looked down and would not face him. Bandinelli stared at Pontormo for a few moments, and then, having failed to elicit a reaction, swallowed the insulting remark that he must have been planning to deliver.

He addressed himself to Bronzino. 'So, Bronzino, the painting is progressing nearly as fast the Duke wants,' he declared, gazing at the half-completed picture rather than speaking to Bronzino directly.

'I have not yet made appointments for two of the models,' Bronzino told him.

'So I guessed,' Bandinelli replied, 'but I am still interested to see how our idea is working out.'

Bronzino did not rise to that particularly foul bait. I believe that he was right to observe the courtesies of polite discourse even to a boor such as Bandinelli. He did not want either myself or Clemente to admire Bandinelli's rudeness, and neither did we.

'I flatter myself that it is working out well,' Bronzino said.

He turned to Pontormo. 'I value no opinion more highly

than that of my master Pontormo. What do you think of it, Master?'

'It will intrigue King François,' Pontormo replied without looking up, 'and so it will please the Duke.'

Clemente moved over to Angelina. 'Hello, Angelina,' he said. 'Are you well? You look as if you've been crying.' He reached his hand out to her, and Angelina took it in her own. Once more I felt a pang of jealousy.

'She was a little melancholy earlier,' I explained, 'but she's better now.'

'I hope so,' Clemente said, lightly squeezing her hand. I feared that Angelina would embrace him, and the most painful aspect of my fear was that I knew I had no right to try to stop her. Angelina did not belong to me any more than she belonged to Bronzino. Indeed, I wondered, what did Bronzino consider her status in his household to be?

Even I, as a mere apprentice, had certain rights under the articles of the Guild of St. Luke. Even models who had been recruited from the streets were paid, but Bronzino had never made any mention of paying Angelina.

Bandinelli ignored us all and examined the painting very closely. I suddenly realised that he was short-sighted, which may explain the bad proportions of his sculptures and the dull vagueness of his painting. He should have chosen to be an engraver instead, but then who would have felt safe around Bandinelli if he had an engraver's sharp burin in his hand?

'Yes,' Bandinelli said to nobody in particular, bestowing his judgement as universally as Angelina bestowed her light smile. 'Yes, it will work as we intended.'

'If it doesn't work,' Bronzino replied, 'that is, if the Duke doesn't like it, will you still claim that you had a share in its design?'

'When did I ever make such a claim in the hearing of the Duke?' Bandinelli replied. 'Everyone who knows me will admit that I'm willing to give any man my opinion, but that I won't risk my own disgrace by defending that opinion if it becomes dangerous.'

Bronzino seemed to notice Clemente for the first time. 'What lessons have you learned from this painting to point out to your son, Bandinelli?'

'Lessons?' Bandinelli said. 'What good are lessons to him? You might as well challenge your mute model to work out the meaning of the allegories in the picture. I keep him to grind paint, clean my house, and precede me through the streets.'

Pontormo put in another quiet word. 'Those are the tasks of an apprentice, Bandinelli. You should either enrol him formally as your apprentice, or send him to another artist who will take him.'

'Then I would have to pay the wages of a servant,' Bandinelli said.

As Bronzino had taught me, I was serving out wine without being asked to. When I filled Bandinelli's cup, he waved it at me and asked Bronzino how he rated me as an apprentice. It seemed to be the question on everyone's mind that day, except for the weary mind of Clemente and the unreadable mind of Angelina. Bronzino refused to give Bandinelli an assessment of me.

'If I tell you he's bad, you'll mock me for keeping him on. If I tell you he's good, you'll poach him for yourself and turn your son out of your house.' That might have been thought a cruelly insensitive thing to say in Clemente's presence, except that Clemente knew that it was probably true.

Bandinelli grinned. 'I hear that you only took Giuseppe

on because his own father turned him out of the house.'

He must have had the story from Clemente, but Bronzino was not taken aback.

'I took Giuseppe on because I was impressed by a drawing that he had executed, and, in any case, Giuseppe's father was not a painter, but a carpenter.'

Pontormo put in another remark while still contemplating the floor.

'It is no disgrace to have a father who is a carpenter.'

'No, indeed,' Bandinelli said, 'but you could not make a great sculpture out of wood. A good sculpture, yes, but not a great one. We sculptors cut into hard materials that fight back, worthy opponents of our talent. We do not use soft oils and egg yolks as you painters do.'

'Why, Father, you are a painter, too,' Clemente said, a timely reminder that Bandinelli was always boasting of his paintings. I hope that Bandinelli did not batter Clemente too brutally for that remark when they got home.

Bandinelli must have realised that he was not succeeding in cowing anybody in the room with his insults, not even his own son. 'Do you know what your next commission will be?' he asked Bronzino.

'I haven't got one,' Bronzino replied. 'I gave out the word that I could not take on any more commissions for the time being. I hope to get some more portraits. That's what I really like doing, and it pays well.'

'Well, only the well-off can afford to have their portraits painted or to have a sculpture made of their features,' Bandinelli said. 'Of course, that's why we work for them. In the old days, there were religious paintings in which poor people appeared. In the future, everyone will think that all the people in the Florence of our day were rich and beautiful.'

'If they're rich enough, I make them beautiful,' Bronzino replied. 'Honesty is for self-portraits.'

Pontormo unexpectedly came to life. He jumped up from his seat in the window, and, still looking down at the floor, he scuttled past me to the door and rushed out like somebody who had just been struck by an attack of nausea and needed to get to a suitable receptacle quickly. We all heard him trip down the stairs and go out of the house.

Bronzino's only comment was to say 'Well, I hope he remembers to come back for supper so that he can take the woman back to his house tonight.'

We all knew that it was not stale food that had forced him to flee from the house, but the equally unbearable and sickening presence of Baccio Bandinelli. As it happened, Bandinelli himself left soon afterwards. Having failed to bait Bronzino, and having been deprived of Pontormo as a target, he seemed to feel that there was no further point in remaining at our house. He promised (or threatened) to return to review the progress of the painting.

Clemente was sitting on the floor with Angelina, and Bandinelli lifted his son up roughly by the shoulder as though Clemente were still a small boy.

'Come on, Clemente, bow to Bronzino. No, don't bow to Giuseppe as well! He's only an apprentice.'

Clemente blushed, but he gave a defiant bow to Angelina. She took no notice, but it was a gesture that pleased me.

Bronzino became worried when Pontormo failed to appear at his usual time to have dinner with us. 'I hope nothing's happened to him. My former master is very much a creature of orderly habits. Well, regular habits, even if he isn't very orderly. This is not like Pontormo at all.'

It was still a bright heat-shocked summer evening.

Bronzino waited for another hour. I offered to go to Pontormo's house to fetch him.

'No,' Bronzino said. 'I expect he's brooding because Bandinelli upset him. We'll have dinner without him, and then you can take the woman to his house.'

'What if he isn't there, Master?' I asked.

'Well, bring her back here then, you fool!'

Pontormo still had not come by the time I finished washing up after dinner. Bronzino was worried. I did not often see him show concern for anyone other than himself.

'Make sure you see Pontormo when you take the woman over there,' he instructed me, 'and make sure he's all right.'

I tidied up Angelina's appearance as best I could. Although it was now evening and the sun was sinking and mellow in the bird-spotted sky, I put her white hat on her head so that she would have it with her when we came back the next morning.

I led her by the hand through the streets. Her appearance attracted little interest from those citizens of Florence who come out illegally on summer evenings to argue and fight and rob and murder each other. Some of the brawls and murders are about art and theology. Let nobody say that the Florentines do not possess the sensitivity of spirit to be moved by the great questions of our age.

By the time we turned into the street where Pontormo lived, Angelina's white hat had turned pink in the expiring sunlight, so that it looked more than ever like a monstrous flower on her head.

I was admiring this effect, and wondering how I might reproduce it in one of my own future paintings, when I saw four of the Duke's guards barring the door to Pontormo's house. They had seen us, and they knew who we were, so there was no point in turning back. I was about to speak to them when Pontormo's door opened and out stepped Captain Da Lucca.

For the first time in my life I felt cold terror. Had Captain Da Lucca found out that Bronzino was going to hold him up to ridicule in the painting? Had he come to arrest Pontormo as an accomplice before going on to arrest Bronzino as the culprit, and myself as part of the furniture and fittings?

Instead, Captain Da Lucca greeted me civilly. 'Hello, Giuseppe. Are you bringing Angelina back?'

'Yes, Captain,' I stammered, 'she always spends the night here, because there's no room at our house.'

'Well, I doubt that any woman will ever spend a night at Bronzino's,' Captain Da Lucca replied.

'Is Pontormo all right?' I asked.

'Oh, yes. We did have a discussion before he agreed to let me into his house. He's even more touchy about admitting guests than Sister Benedicta is, but in the end we didn't have to break the door down after all.'

I wondered how many times in the course of his career Captain Da Lucca had broken down a door in order to gain unwanted entrance. I was still very worried about Pontormo.

'Can I see him?' I asked.

'Of course,' Captain Da Lucca answered, and he turned round to shout over his shoulder.

'Hey, Pontormo! Angelina and Giuseppe are here!'

Pontormo shuffled out of the gloom of his house. I tried to peer past Captain Da Lucca, to glimpse some details of Pontormo's forbidden house, but I could see nothing. Pontormo snatched Angelina away from me as though she were a lost daughter who had come back to him after ten years.

'Giuseppe!' he cried. 'Has Captain Da Lucca told you

why he was sent here?'

'I don't think he's had a chance to yet,' I replied.

Captain Da Lucca intervened. 'The Duke has ordered Bronzino to produce Angelina at the Palazzo tomorrow. I was making sure that she was safe here, but I came a little early.'

'We knew that she was to go to the Palazzo,' I said, 'and we'll make her as presentable as we can.'

'What you don't know,' Pontormo interrupted, 'is that the Duke has also ordered that she can't go home to Sister Benedicta.'

13

'Why can't she –' I began to ask, but both Pontormo and Captain Da Lucca lifted their hands to order me to be silent. They made the same gesture in perfect unison, as though they had rehearsed it.

It took Pontormo half an hour to persuade Captain Da Lucca not to leave a guard outside his house all night. It would have been all right with me: it could only make Pontormo's house a safer place, both for Angelina and for himself. When agreement had been reached, and Pontormo had taken Angelina inside for the night, I was eager to question Captain Da Lucca about what he had seen in the house. I should have foreseen his reply.

'Pontormo has sworn me to secrecy,' he told me, 'and what I swear to do, I do.'

'Can't you tell me anything, Captain?' I persisted.

Captain Da Lucca's face filled with anger, like a blank panel or canvas being filled with a coloured wash.

'I told you I wouldn't tell you anything,' he said, not even bothering to shout.

He did not need to. I was too afraid of his anger, and I realised how he commanded and ruled men who were too hard and brutal for anyone else to control. Captain Da Lucca marched away with his guards, and I slunk back to Bronzino's house, wondering whether I would ever discover Pontormo's secrets.

When I came home, I was able to report to Bronzino that Pontormo was all right. As I expected, he showed no interest in the news about Angelina.

'Why would the Duke send his guards to Pontormo's house?' he asked.

'They were going to come here next,' I told him. 'I think that they had orders to find out where Angelina was.'

'The Duke must be afraid that someone's going to abduct her,' Bronzino said. 'She would make a prize for any city that had a community of artists. No Florentine would try to take her away from Florence, though.'

'Why wouldn't the Duke allow her to go back to Sister Benedicta's house?' I asked.

'Because he would have no control of her there,' Bronzino replied. 'Perhaps he really believes in this alchemy nonsense, and he thinks that Sister Benedicta and the old priest might be able to protect her by magic.'

'It didn't work when we wanted to take her away,' I said guiltily, remembering how I had first seen Angelina as a fascinating unknown face at an upper window.

'Well, I'm going to bed early,' Bronzino announced. 'You may find that you have an escort when you bring the woman back tomorrow.'

In fact, when I reached Pontormo's house, the bored morning squad of guards told me that there had already been a caller. A woman had brought a large parcel for Pontormo. What woman would send a gift to Pontormo, I wondered, but when he answered the door to me he explained it before I could ask him.

'Sister Benedicta has sent round some clothes for Angelina to wear to the Palazzo,' he announced. 'Apparently Sister Benedicta and Maria spent all day and half the night working on them.' He stepped back into the shadows, and then emerged again carrying a parcel which he thrust into my hands.

The guards watched apparently without interest as we left to go to Bronzino's house. To my chagrin, Pontormo reminded me of my status as an apprentice by making me carry the parcel in my arms, while he was the one who led Angelina by the hand. She seemed as happy with Pontormo's hand holding hers as she did when I had that privilege.

It was only after we had walked through three streets that I noticed that the people we met were scattering to the right and left to let us pass unhindered. To the eye of a native Florentine, such deference and politeness on the part of his fellow citizens mean that something is not right, and when I looked round I saw that another detachment of guards was following us at a distance.

'Signor Pontormo,' I called, 'some more of the Duke's guards are following us.'

Pontormo spun round with unexpected speed, making Angelina stumble and nearly fall, and shouted at the guards.

'Go away!' he cried. 'What do you mean by following us?'

The sergeant in charge made no answer, but he gestured with his hand to tell Pontormo to keep walking and keep silent. There were times when even the unworldly Pontormo could take a hint, and we walked on with our escort. I had always suspected that the Duke was having us all watched in secret. Now, I realised, his surveillance would be quite open, as a constant threat. I did not dare to ask Pontormo what he had meant by saying that Angelina could not go home.

When we arrived at Bronzino's house, our escort formed

up as a guard outside the door when we went inside. I was sure that there would be a guard there for a long time. Bronzino greeted Pontormo with what seemed like genuine joy and relief.

'I was worried about you, Master,' he said. 'I'm pleased to see that you're well.'

'I wasn't well last night, Bronzino,' Pontormo replied. 'This painting of yours is causing far more trouble than any other painting I've ever heard of. The Duke is excessively impressed with your model for Venus.'

'Don't blame me for that,' Bronzino said. 'Blame Giuseppe. He was the one who saw her at the window.'

I mutely accepted the blame which Bronzino had justly laid upon me. I was sure that it would lie much more lightly on his conscience, if he had one, than it did upon mine.

Whoever had packed the parcel of clothes from Sister Benedicta had done a good job of tying tight and robust knots. Even with my workman's hands which so displeased Bronzino, I had difficulty undoing them, and I could not cut the cords which bound it because Bronzino always insisted on saving such materials for re-use. I allowed myself to interrupt the conversation.

'May I speak?' I asked. 'It was my fault that Angelina was brought here, but we promised Sister Benedicta that she would be able to go home when the painting was finished.' I wanted an answer from Pontormo, but Bronzino spoke first. 'Well, if the Duke has overruled that promise, you can't blame me.'

'I'm not blaming you, Master,' I said, 'but what is this all about?'

Pontormo waved to Bronzino to be silent, as if he were still the master and Bronzino were still his apprentice.

'What Captain Da Lucca told me,' Pontormo began, 'and

you know that he is not a man who ever lies, is that the Duke is so impressed by Angelina's beauty that he wants her to model for other artists in Florence, and become the face of our time. He wants her to become the face of the sixteenth century in Florence, just as Simonetta Vespucci was the face of the fifteenth century.'

'But Simonetta Vespucci modelled of her own free will, or, at least, with the consent of her family!' I protested. 'She knew what she was doing. I don't think Angelina knows what she is doing, and she can't give her consent.'

Bronzino interrupted again. 'I agree with you there. She's mindless, and she can neither consent nor refuse if she doesn't understand what's happening.'

'We promised Sister Benedicta that Angelina would be able to go home!' I protested.

'Sister Benedicta cannot expect me to disobey the Duke!' Bronzino shouted. 'He would kill me, and you, and perhaps even Pontormo.'

While all this arguing was going on, I had not looked at Angelina, but when I did I saw that she was obviously distressed, and she was starting to cry. I put my arm around her and wiped away her tears in the hope of comforting her. Bronzino snorted and looked away, but Pontormo came over and sat down with us. It was odd to see him sitting on the floor. Pontormo was concerned.

'Is it possible that she understands us?' he asked. 'It would be even worse if she knew that she was being prevented from going home.'

'I don't think so, Signor Pontormo,' I replied. 'She's just upset because she can tell that something's wrong. She trusts you, and I believe she trusts me, too.'

Bronzino was studying the painting, but then he turned his attention back to me. 'Giuseppe, concentrate on getting her washed and properly dressed. What did the witch send over in that parcel, anyway?' I finished unwrapping it. Before I uncovered the contents, I found a note from Sister Benedicta.

To the painter Bronzino and to Giuseppe.

Here is what you need to present Angelina at the Palazzo. It was paid for by Angelina's parents. Maria and I sat up half the night altering the clothes to make them fit. Take care of my Angelina.

Benedicta.

Both Sister Benedicta and myself thought of Angelina as 'my Angelina'. Perhaps Pontormo did too. Perhaps even her parents did as well.

Inside I found a gown, shoes, and a tiara decorated with silver and pearls.

Bronzino now became interested.

'My God!' he exclaimed. 'What can that tiara have cost? How could Sister Benedicta have paid for it?'

'She didn't,' I said, showing him the note. 'Angelina's parents paid for it. She hasn't even said anything about bringing it back after the presentation.'

'I'll keep it here until the Duke tells me to return it,' Bronzino declared. 'It's just what we need for her to wear as Venus, the Queen of Heaven.'

'Juno would not be pleased to hear you say that, Master,' I replied, and Pontormo agreed with me.

'Giuseppe's got you there, Bronzino,' he said. 'Juno is the queen of the gods, but of course Mary is the real Queen of Heaven.'

If Bronzino had been my substitute father these past few years, Pontormo filled the place that should have been filled by my grandfathers, whom I never knew.

'Whatever her title, Venus will wear it,' Bronzino said. He was now recovering from the shock of receiving the tiara and the expensive clothes, and his mind began to work again in its usual manner. 'I wonder who her parents are?' he said. 'They must be extremely rich. Surely they must appear at the Duke's court. Perhaps we'll see them at the Palazzo.'

'Even if we do see them, Master,' I told Bronzino, 'they won't identify themselves to us. Sister Benedicta warned me about that. They pay her to look after Angelina, on condition that her real identity remains a secret. The family consider her to be a matter of shame.'

'I don't blame them,' Bronzino replied. 'A beautiful body is no asset to parents in the marriage market if there is no mind inside. Who wants an idiot daughter-in-law?'

'She's not an idiot, Master!' I cried. 'You can see idiots in the street. Have you ever seen an idiot with the grace and delicacy of Angelina?'

Bronzino waved away my words with a scornful downward flap of both his hands. 'The idiots you see in the street come from poor families who are probably little more intelligent than they are, and who have little more idea how to behave. This particular idiot has simply been well trained by Sister Benedicta, that's all, just as one might train a dog or a horse.'

My eyes filled with tears of indignation on Angelina's behalf, because she understood nothing of this and was smiling as sweetly as ever.

Through the wet film across my vision, I saw Pontormo looking at me with a smile which for a moment looked just like Angelina's. In an instant he gave just the slightest nod of his head in Bronzino's direction, and I understood that what Pontormo meant was that Bronzino himself had come from a poor family. I did not bother to argue any more with Bronzino. He was as cold and immovable as the people who sit serene and emotionless in his portraits. I suppose that future ages will believe that the aristocratic and noble families in the Florence of our day were all bloodless and impassive.

We were not due to go to the Palazzo until the evening, so after Bronzino had done a little half-hearted work on the painting we had the rest of the day to prepare Angelina and ourselves. Bronzino slept through the afternoon in Pontormo's company, which meant that I was free to sleep through it with Angelina. At least, Angelina slept, but while I held her against me and listened to her serene and quiet breathing I was too worried about what was to happen to her. I knew that the Duke would not allow any physical harm to come to her, because he saw her as a valuable asset to the prestige of the Florentine state. He had found his Simonetta Vespucci, and he would not let her go.

I could see it all too well. Angelina would one day be taken into the Palazzo, to be looked after by servant women who would be told to keep her fed and washed and tidy. She would be kept a prisoner until she suffered a fate perhaps more cruel than what had happened to Simonetta Vespucci.

Simonetta Vespucci had died of consumption in her youth. I certainly did not want Angelina to die young, but nobody possesses the gift of eternal youth, as could be confirmed by anyone who were to compare my appearance today with the way I look as Cupid in Bronzino's painting.

By the time the escort of guards sent by the Duke arrived

at our house, Angelina was as elegant as Pontormo and myself could make her. Sister Benedicta and Maria would have done a better job, of course, but we did our best, and I was confident that our best would be good enough. Angelina wore her new gown and shoes as if she had chosen them herself and was proud of them, and I had bound her hair up in the pearl tiara that, Bronzino had decided, she would wear as Venus in the painting.

On Bronzino's instructions, I was keeping watch out of the studio window. I had a fright when I saw, in the middle of the squad of marching guards, an enclosed litter which four burly chambermen from the Palazzo were carrying. Was the Duke himself paying another of his alarming surprise visits?

I called Bronzino to the window, and pointed out the relentlessly approaching enclosed litter. 'Could it be the Duke, Master?' I asked him.

'No,' he replied at once. 'It's empty. Look at the way those men are carrying it. They'll be sweating and bending their backs when they've got someone inside it. Can it be for me? Surely not.'

He was right. When we met the guards downstairs, their sergeant told us that the litter was for Angelina.

I was worried, and I told the sergeant so. 'She may become agitated if she's in there on her own,' I said.

'Well, we're not going to put anyone else in there with her!' the sergeant declared. 'It's carried by four men, not four giants.'

Bronzino was becoming impatient. 'We can't wait for her,' he said. 'Just put her in.'

'Master,' I said, 'if she becomes upset, she'll hardly arrive at the Palazzo in a suitable state to be presented to the Duke.'

Bronzino saw my point. He cared nothing for whether Angelina was comfortable or not, but he did not want to be embarrassed in front of the Duke.

'What do you suggest, then?' he asked. 'We can't walk her through the streets.'

'Let me try something,' I suggested.

I ran back into the house, and snatched up a piece of cloth that I used to clean up spills of gesso. I brought down the stinking rag. Both Bronzino and even the sergeant recoiled from it, but they let me place it in Angelina's hand. She held it to her face, entranced, and made no resistance when Pontormo and I helped her into the litter and settled her on the cushions. We drew the curtains closed, and the sergeant gave the order to pick the litter up.

We started off to the Palazzo, with torches carried both in front of us and at the rear. I kept as close as I could to the litter, but I heard no sound from within, which I hoped was a good sign. Those furtive Florentines who were illegally in the streets scattered when they saw our torches approaching, but few of them could resist a glance at the litter.

They must all have known that nobody can ever see into a litter, because its whole purpose is to carry the occupant through the streets in complete anonymity. I wonder who they thought it was. Not Duke Cosimo, of course. He would never adopt such an unmanly device for concealment. I remembered the time when he had put on the uniform of one of his guards and marched among them all the way to our house.

The litter was an object of curiosity for us all. The passers-by saw a cube of white cloth lumbering through the heavy, late summer evening, and asked themselves who the occupant could be. For myself, I knew who was inside, and

I wondered what Angelina thought was happening to her, and what the Duke's plans for her were.

Pontormo walked grimly beside me, with his hands clasped behind his back. He had the air of a man who is going to see a public execution, but does not want to.

Bronzino was walking in front of the litter, probably to admire the strong young men who were carrying it. I guessed that his own curiosity was only about what advantage he could gain for himself from Angelina's beauty.

When we arrived outside the bluff walls of the Palazzo with its narrow, overhanging battlements and high square tower, the litterbearers performed a clever manoeuvre at the door by whipping off the canopy of the litter and enclosing Angelina in it as Pontormo and I guided her into the Palazzo, after I had gently removed the smelly cloth from her face and flung it away. Nobody watching would have been able to see her.

Our reception had been well-planned. Bronzino knew where to go inside the palace, and wherever we went doors were opened for us, and lanterns were lifted up to light our way through dark places where the light of the lamps and candles did not reach.

I expected that we would find ourselves in the hall where we had been received by Duke Cosimo at the banquet, but instead we were led by Bronzino through rooms that I had never seen before. I was holding Angelina's hand. Bronzino was setting such a fast pace that I had to call out 'Master, please slow down!', because I was afraid that Angelina would stumble and fall. The Duke would not be pleased if we presented her with a black eye and a bleeding nose.

The corridor became so dark that I was having difficulty guiding Angelina, when suddenly another door opened, giving me a glimpse of sparkling brightness beyond. I managed to make out the figure of the man who had opened the door. He was only a human-shaped area of darkness that was slightly darker than the gloom of the interior of the Palazzo, but when he stepped forward into the light I recognised him as Baccio Bandinelli.

Bronzino did not seem surprised to see him. 'Are you a servant now, Bandinelli, opening doors? Do you do laundry and groom horses as well?'

'Is that what you did in Monticelli?' Bandinelli replied, a remark which was lost on anyone who did not know that Bronzino had originally come from the village of Monticelli.

Bronzino swept on through the doors without having broken his step once to answer Bandinelli. 'I became a Court painter,' he said, which was not really true, because he had still not been appointed officially to that office. 'What did you become?'

Bandinelli fell in behind us as we entered a hall which was lit by more candles than I had ever seen in one room before. Before I looked around the room to see who was present, I made Angelina squeak by crushing her hand in mine as I tightened it in my astonishment.

I would not have imagined that it was possible to light a room so brilliantly at night. There were so many candles that there were no shadows anywhere. Our procession stopped, and I halted with it. Now I had to time to notice all the faces, sweating in their formal clothes and the light from the setting sun which cast a pink glow on the lintels of the windows. Who could have believed that one could be made to sweat by the heat from candles?

I saw Duke Cosimo just in time to make my obeisance to him along with Bronzino. I knelt down, which was not necessary for the purposes of Court ceremonial, but which

I needed to do in order to make Angelina kneel down with me.

The Duke's voice boomed over our heads. 'Stand up, stand up!' he shouted. 'No, not all of you, not yet! Giuseppe! You stand up, and make Angelina stand up as well!'

I stood up slowly, being careful not to lose my balance, and Angelina stood up with me. She happened to look straight at Duke Cosimo, and broke into her faint smile.

'There you are!' the Duke bellowed to the ladies and gentlemen who filled the room. 'What did I tell you?'

Bronzino stepped in front of us to say something, but he did not get the chance, because the Duke spoke first.

'Bronzino, get out of the way!' he bellowed, and Bronzino had to obey.

I tugged discreetly on Angelina's hand to make her come forward and stand next to me.

The Duke now spoke to me again. 'Introduce her, Giuseppe.'

I had only a moment to try to calculate, desperately, what I ought to say. Was the painting for King François still a secret? Because the Duke had said nothing about it, I decided that I had better say nothing about Cupid and Venus.

'Your Grace, noble ladies and gentlemen,' I began, 'this is Angelina. She cannot answer you herself, because she cannot speak, but she is neither deaf nor afflicted in her mind. She is an artist's model in the studio of my master, the painter Bronzino.'

Angelina did not look round the room, at the assembled lords, ladies, and great merchants. I was trying to concentrate on what to say, and trying not to examine all the faces to see whether they showed a resemblance to Angelina.

'Angelina comes from a good family,' I dared to say. I paused, and scanned all the faces. They were all looking at Angelina. I waited for a man, or a woman, or a couple, to glance at me instead, because I was sure that if they did it would mean that they were Angelina's parents. 'You can tell that,' I continued, 'from her fine clothes and the tiara that she is wearing.'

Even that produced no reaction. Angelina's parents must have developed great skill in denying knowledge of her, ever since her strange behaviour first appeared in childhood. A middle-aged but beardless man spoke out.

'Even if she came from a family of peasants or labourers, her beauty would make her noble,' he said. The beardless man seemed to be with a woman who was ten or fifteen years younger than he was. Even though the man had no beard, so that it was easy to compare his face to Angelina's, I could see no resemblance to her either in him or in the woman I presumed to be his wife.

Duke Cosimo beckoned to me.

'Bring her forward, Giuseppe. I want her to sit next to me. Make room! Make a place for Angelina and a place for Giuseppe.'

I could not have been the only person in the room to note that he had not ordered anyone to yield their place to Bronzino, who stood flushed and silent. He was not silent from fear of the Duke. I knew him well enough to be aware that silence in him was a sign of rage.

Duke Cosimo sat down, with an empty seat on either side of him. I went to the chair on his left and pushed Angelina towards the chair on his right, but she followed me. The Duke saw it, got up, and moved to his right.

'You two, sit down together,' he commanded, so we sat down with Angelina next to him and myself on her left.

'Now,' the Duke said, beckoning with his hand, 'you come here.'

Bronzino came forward.

'Not you, Bronzino!' Duke Cosimo shouted. 'Stay where you are. I mean Bandinelli.'

Bandinelli, who had remained at the door, walked towards the Duke with the grace of a dancer. I thought that Bandinelli might shoot a glance of triumph at Bronzino, but he ignored my master. Bandinelli stopped directly in front of us.

'Bandinelli,' Duke Cosimo said, 'I grant what you desire.'

A disembodied hand made of ice grasped my heart. Bandinelli bowed with surprising, or perhaps well-rehearsed, elegance. The hand made of ice squeezed my heart and would not let go.

The Duke spoke again. 'You will be the first sculptor in Florence to have Angelina as your model.'

The Duke turned to his guests. 'Well, what do you think of her?' he asked.

'Her image will be an adornment to the city,' said a thin young man who was peering at Angelina so intently that I was convinced he was short-sighted and could not see her clearly at all.

The Duke went further. 'Is she more beautiful than Simonetta Vespucci?' he asked. 'You've all seen the paintings of her by Botticelli and others.'

There was a murmur of 'yes, yes,' around the room.

Duke Cosimo gave a smile as wicked as Angelina's smile was innocent. 'Clear a space in front of me!' he ordered. 'Bandinelli, take two paces to the right!' Bandinelli took two dance steps to the right.

The Duke shouted out another order. 'Bring forth Messer Salviani!'

A door opened at the back of the room, and two of the Duke's guards led out a very old man. He was holding two sticks, but the guards were supporting him by his elbows, so that the sticks dangled in the air like the front legs of an insect. The guards whisked the old man around the backs of the assembled guests and set him down directly in front of the Duke.

'Well, now, Messer Salviani,' the Duke said. 'You know that you are here because you remember Simonetta Vespucci when she was alive. Tell the people how well you knew her.'

The old man Salviani gazed at Angelina. I suspected that, like many elderly people, he could still see well at a distance. Angelina seemed to be smiling back at him, but he was not fooled.

'She is smiling, but not at me,' he said.

'Never mind that!' the Duke bellowed. 'Compare her with Simonetta Vespucci. Remember the story of the Judgement of Paris, who had to decide which of three goddesses was the most beautiful.'

'I have only two goddesses to compare,' Salviani said.

For the first time I noticed how strong his voice was. He considered Angelina again for a few moments, and then gave his assessment. 'In the beauty of her face, she is not the equal of Simonetta,' he announced, obviously not fearing the Duke's anger, 'but she is so different.'

'Different?' Duke Cosimo echoed. 'What do you mean, different?'

'Simonetta always looked so intelligent, so interested, Your Grace,' Salviani explained. 'When you conversed with her, she made you feel, not merely by her replies, but by her very expression, that you were the most fascinating person in the world.'

Like everyone else in the room, I suspect, I found myself awed by the fact that here was a man who had talked to Simonetta Vespucci when she was a living woman and not merely a wonderful image in paint.

I dared to interrupt the old man. 'It is unfair to judge Angelina on her conversation,' I said. 'It isn't her fault that she can't speak.'

'If you please, young apprentice,' Salviani replied, to a general growl and murmur of approval, 'I had not yet finished praising your Angelina.'

I fell into an ashamed silence, while Salviani continued.

'Angelina does not have Simonetta's wonderful presence, but what she has is a kind of wonderful absence. She is with us, and yet she is elsewhere. I could believe that she really was a pagan goddess.'

Duke Cosimo stopped him. 'Splendid, Salviani! Conduct Messer Salviani to my kitchens for a good meal, and when you conduct him home take enough food with you to give his family a supper as well.'

For the first time, as Salviani was led away, I noticed that his fine clothes did not fit him properly. They had not been made for him, and I suspected that before he reached the kitchens the robes would be torn off him and sent back to the Duke's staff wardrobe. Duke Cosimo addressed us all.

'Angelina will be the face of Florence through all ages, for as long as this city is remembered. Bronzino is already painting her in a picture of which I will not yet speak.'

That, I knew, was the Duke's signal to Bronzino, Pontormo and myself that we were not to speak about it in that company either.

The Duke continued. 'Bronzino is the first to paint her, and Bandinelli will be the first to sculpt her. Bronzino!'

'Your Grace,' Bronzino replied, bowing.

One of the crazy irrelevancies that afflict one's mind in moments of great stress came to me: Bronzino could not have learned his manners from the kindly but unsociable Pontormo, so Pontormo must have sent the boy Bronzino to a tutor in etiquette and deportment.

'When you have finished your painting,' the Duke told Bronzino, 'Angelina will leave your house, and you will place her in the care of Baccio Bandinelli. You are dismissed, and my guards will take you home.'

All Bronzino said as we walked out was, 'Even that old wreck Salviani was given a supper. I didn't even get a bread roll.'

14

Although it was late, we had to call at Bronzino's house first, to change Angelina out of her fine clothes. She sat unresisting while I extracted the silver tiara from her tightly bound hair, which I allowed to fall loose. Pontormo and I made the guards leave the room while we removed her gown and shoes, and dressed her in her ordinary garments.

Pontormo told me that there was no need to accompany him and Angelina back to his house. 'The Duke's guards will be with us,' he said, 'and they'll be standing outside all night. I don't think I've ever been in so little danger in my life.'

'Won't Angelina be upset by the change to her routine, Signor Pontormo?' I asked. 'I've always come with you.'

'Oh, she'll be all right with me,' Pontormo replied, and to my chagrin he was proved right. Angelina went off with him in the middle of the squad of guards with no sign that she had noticed anything unusual in the arrangements, or that she cared, if she had.

Bronzino had shut himself up in his room in a sulk. I was unsure whether the sulk was mainly over Bandinelli getting the services of his model for Venus, or whether it was still about not having been offered a free supper at the Palazzo.

Eventually, when I had put out all the lights except for a single candle in the studio, and closed the shutters against the night insects, Bronzino stalked out of his bedroom dressed only in a piece of linen around his hips. As far as I know he had invented this garment himself, tying it around himself with skill so that it looked as neat as the loincloth worn so stylishly by St. Sebastian in which to be shot full of arrows.

Bronzino walked over to the half-finished painting and contemplated it.

'This picture has been a burden to me,' he remarked. 'I can't accept any other commissions until it's finished, and I can't tell anyone what it is. Meanwhile, my competitors are poaching my portraiture business.'

I felt that the real tragedy of the painting was the fate of the innocent Angelina, but I said nothing because I was unsure whether Bronzino was talking to me or to himself. It turned out that he was talking to me.

'This is all your fault, Giuseppe!' he said. 'It was you who picked out that woman.'

'I have sincerely regretted that I did so, Master,' I said, 'but we did go out to search for a model to be Venus, and many people would be surprised that you should rebuke me for finding you a beautiful Venus.'

'A beautiful but a mindless Venus,' Bronzino replied. 'I must finish this painting as soon as possible. I'll need your help.'

'How, Master?' I asked.

'I won't be able to keep Sister Benedicta and Father Fleccia coming back here again and again,' he replied. 'I'll have to work partly from memory, so while they're sitting for me you must make your own rough portraits so that I can refer back to them later.'

That was bad news, because it meant that I would have fewer chances to ask Sister Benedicta and Father Fleccia what we could do to save Angelina. I wished that I could have spoken to Pontormo about it, but of course he had gone home, and he and I had never been alone since we had left the Palazzo. I folded Angelina's new clothes and put them away carefully in a painted chest that Bronzino used for his own best clothes. I noticed that we needed some more dried leaves and stalks to protect the clothes from the moths. I held up the silver tiara, turning it in my hands next to the single candle. The pearls glowed in strange, unexpected colours as they caught the light of the little flame.

'Where should I put this, Master?' I asked Bronzino. 'It's so valuable.'

I still had no idea where Bronzino kept his own wealth, and I thought that it might be at some goldsmith's where the tiara could be stored safely.

Bronzino surprised me by his response. 'Make a sketch of it tomorrow, Giuseppe, so that I can remember what it looks like. Store it anywhere you want. It's not ours, and I haven't accepted responsibility for it, so it doesn't matter if someone steals it.'

'May I keep it in my own room, Master?' I asked.

'I told you,' Bronzino replied, 'put it anywhere!'

I took the tiara upstairs and hid it under my own work clothes. Nobody would expect an apprentice to own anything of value. I came down again in case Bronzino had any more tasks for me, but he waved me away without a word. He was still in his St. Sebastian underwear, contemplating the painting.

'Go to bed, Giuseppe,' he told me. 'I'll put the candle out myself.'

I was relieved that he had no further use for me that night, whether legitimate or immoral, and I went up to bed.

I checked that the tiara was still where I had hidden it, as if anyone had known it was there and broken in silently to steal it within the previous few minutes. I was so nervous that I even thought about closing my window, in spite of the heat which was still oppressive although the summer was coming to an end.

As I lay sleepless on my bed, watching scrappy clouds sail by in the light of the moon which was shining in through other windows but not through mine, I tried to imagine how Angelina was spending the night in Pontormo's house. I found it strange that I had never tried to picture it before, but because I had seen nothing of the interior of the house I had no basis for guessing what it was like. Imagination cannot start from nothing: even the most creative painters build their images, whether they know it or not, on the basis of their own memories.

I hoped that she was not lying on some filthy sack stuffed with the dried leaves of a summer that had baked the city years before. Pontormo would never think of changing them every October. Even if Angelina's conditions were as bad as I feared, I would rather she were there than in the Palazzo della Signoria, or, worse, yet, at Baccio Bandinelli's house.

While I wondered what I could do to help Angelina, my own personal devil whispered into my thoughts that I was not responsible for her. She was neither my wife nor my relative, and I owed nothing to her. I knew, though, that all of this was my fault, for having drawn Bronzino's attention to Angelina's beautiful face looking down on us from that upper window. I was to blame for everything that had happened to her since, and now she was going to be taken away from me, almost certainly for ever, to places where she would receive even worse treatment, and where I would not be able to give her any more help. Then I wondered when I had ever given Angelina any help at all.

I forced myself to remember that moment when I had first seen her. It was like a scene from a romance in which a young knight riding by sees a beautiful maiden looking out from the tower where she is imprisoned.

One difference was that although Angelina was held at Sister Benedicta's house without her consent, it was the happiest home she had known.

The other difference was that a gallant young knight could not have ridden into Sister Benedicta's house and carried Angelina off on his horse. Oh, I could steal a horse, I supposed, although I had no idea how to ride one; but where could I take Angelina? The image of Bronzino and Bandinelli jointly riding in pursuit of me was laughable, but the fact that the Duke would send his brutal soldiers after me was terrifying.

They would follow me anywhere the Duke's power held, not stopping until they recaptured Angelina and killed me.

I was staring through the open window above me. I saw that the heavy clouds that had retained the day's heat and humidity like a sponge had cleared, and a few stars were decorating the little square of darkness in the ceiling. I wished I knew the names of some stars, and how to find my way by them at night. I dismissed the thought by reasoning that there was no point in knowing how to navigate if I had no idea where to go. I had never been out of Florence.

I must have fallen asleep soon afterwards, because I found myself looking at a square of pale blue sky instead of at the stars. Far away, somewhere in the city, a church bell was tolling to summon the pious to a very early Mass.

When Bronzino appeared for breakfast, he had a wad of

paper in his hand. He gave it to me as I served out his grapes and cheese, and I saw that it was a letter, which he had sealed with wax. He must have done it in the early morning, because the wax still smelled of the smoke and fumes which it had given off when he had held it to the candle to melt it. The wax bore his own seal, bearing in irregularly edged letters the legend: 'BRONZINO PAINTER TO THE DUKE'.

'Deliver this to Sister Benedicta at once,' he ordered me. 'Don't wait until you've cleaned the house or bought the groceries. Take it now, and push it through the grille in the door.'

'Why don't I just tell her your message, Master?' I asked.

'Because the message is for her, not for you!' Bronzino replied. 'Leave now, and hurry.'

While I carried the letter over, I of course wondered what was in it. The misshapen congealed lump of the sealing wax felt unpleasant against my palm. Fortunately it was Maria and not Sister Benedicta who answered the door and opened the grille. I thrust the letter through, making poor Maria leap back in surprise.

'For Sister Benedicta, from the painter Bronzino,' I explained, and then I ran off before she could open the door and question me.

When I arrived home, not only was Bronzino already at work on the painting, but he had cleared away the remains of his breakfast and even bought fruit, bread and vegetables from the street vendors. He had not carried out either of those tasks himself since I had first come to live in his house. I expected him to say something to me, but he did not, so I had to ask him what his next instructions to me were.

'Clean yourself up, and find some scrap paper for

sketching,' he said. 'Sister Benedicta and Father Fleccia will be with us later.'

'Angelina will be so happy to see them!' I replied.

'She won't see them,' Bronzino answered. 'The Duke has forbidden it. My master Pontormo will take her back to his house before they arrive.'

'That's unbelievably cruel!' I cried.

'The Duke's cruelty has given us peace in Florence for seven years,' Bronzino said. 'I don't question his orders. He's not interested in pleasing me or you. Indeed, I would say in his defence that he's not even pleasing himself. He's doing what he believes to be in the interests of the Florentine state, and I think that so far he's shown good judgement in assessing where those interests lie.'

'Damn the Florentine state!' I shouted, and then realised that if there were any of the Duke's guards outside our house they would have heard me. Well, it was too late to call back my words. 'What about Angelina?'

'What indeed?' Bronzino said. 'She's an impressively beautiful body, and usually no trouble to anyone, and that's all one can say for her.'

I shamed myself by bursting into tears of rage. Bronzino watched me with the kind of unemotional interest with which Father Fleccia might observe one of his alchemical experiments.

'Giuseppe, this is part of your apprenticeship,' Bronzino said, coldly and without any sign either of compassion or of anger. 'If you are to be an artist in Florence, you must learn that your only power is being able to create paintings that rich people will want to buy from you. In all other things, the Duke and his guards hold the power, quite literally, of life and death over you. Be content. It's a much better life than being a peasant, or a day labourer or a craftsman.'

'What about Angelina?' I cried again. 'I love her!'

'I know,' Bronzino replied, to my astonishment, and then he went on to enrage me by adding, 'but you love her as you might love a dog or a cat or a bird singing in a cage.'

'I love her as a woman, Master!' I protested.

'She has the body of a woman, but no mind or soul,' Bronzino said. 'Anyway, what do you know about loving a woman? You know even less about women than I do.'

'I know Angelina!' I said.

Bronzino turned away from the painting and looked at me with suspicion.

'Giuseppe,' he said quietly, 'if you've dishonoured that woman while she was in my care –'

'No, Master, I swear it!' I said.

'My anger would be nothing compared to what you would receive from the Duke,' Bronzino said. He put down his brush. Even in his anger, he put it down neatly and carefully in the proper place among his painting tools.

'Giuseppe,' he said 'fetch some wine and two cups. Bring the best wine, the one we serve to guests.'

I was mystified, but I hurried down to the cellar and brought up the wine. I set the cups down on the table, but before I could pour the wine Bronzino took the jug away from me.

'Sit down, Giuseppe,' he ordered me. 'I'll serve us both.' He filled my cup first, and then his own.

'Giuseppe, why do you think I took you on as my apprentice when I had turned away so many applicants?'

I considered my reply for a moment. I had often believed that Bronzino had taken an evil fancy to my body when he had seen me, but then he could have procured willing boys in Florence for much less than it would cost him to keep me as an apprentice. I also did not believe that he had fallen into an unnatural love upon his first sight of me. That happens to poets, not to painters, even if Bronzino was also a poet on the side.

'Master, you felt you had a duty to educate a boy as Pontormo educated you,' was the reply I came up with.

'Half true,' Bronzino agreed. 'I did feel such a duty, but why did I choose you instead of one of the swarms of other boys who were always being presented to me?'

'Well, Master,' I said, 'it couldn't have been because you really were impressed by the little drawing that my father showed you as a sample of my work. Even Signor Pontormo has told me, in his honest way, that I will never make a first-class painter.'

Bronzino gulped down most of his cup of wine.

'But, Giuseppe, you see, it was the drawing! I could see that your father wanted to get rid of you, but I didn't take you in out of pity. You are not the only boy in Florence who was mistreated by his father, and I had no responsibility to rescue you from your misfortune.'

'The drawing, Master?' I said. 'What was good about it?'

'Oh, it was of no great merit in itself,' Bronzino said, 'but you had made it on your own initiative, out of an artistic impulse that had come from your own spirit. All the other boys presented themselves carrying elaborate drawings and paintings that they had obviously worked on for a long time because their families had forced them to. That little charcoal sketch on a scrap of wood was worth more than everything that your rivals could produce.'

'After all that, though,' I replied, 'both you and Signor Pontormo agree that I've proved not to have a major talent as a painter. I must be a great disappointment to you.'

'Not at all,' Bronzino replied. 'Here, have some more wine. Oh, you haven't finished your first cupful. No, you're not a disappointment. If you reach the summit of your talent you need never feel ashamed of yourself. I can teach you all the techniques you need to achieve that.'

Now I did drink up the wine. All the memories of my apprenticeship flowed through my mind in a rush, in the way that the memories of an entire life are said to stream through one's mind at the moment of death.

'Master,' I asked, 'will I ever be a good enough painter to be granted the status of Master by the Guild of St. Luke?'

Bronzino refilled my cup with wine. 'No,' he said, 'you'll never be good enough. You simply have no style of your own.'

Pontormo had told me that same thing, and I had no doubt that they were both right. Once again I felt despair overwhelm me like a wave of black water.

'My life is pointless, Master,' I said. 'My father judged that I would be useless, I'll never be a good painter, and I can't do anything to save Angelina. Why am I in the world at all?'

'Go to the church on the corner and ask the priest,' Bronzino suggested.

'He's even more useless than I am,' I said.

'Ask Father Fleccia, then, when he arrives,' Bronzino said. 'I am your master in the art of painting, not your guide in morals and philosophy.'

I cannot imagine who would have selected Bronzino as a guide to morals, except my father, and that was only because he wanted me to be trained in immorality. Bronzino certainly kept his side of the bargain with my father there. I still could not calm myself.

'Father Fleccia cannot tell me how to save Angelina,' I said, 'and I can't stop thinking about her.'

'I can solve that problem for you,' Bronzino replied.

'She doesn't need saving. Wherever she goes, the Duke will ensure that she gets a bed, her meals, her clothes and regular washing. She never knew she was at Sister Benedicta's house, and she never knew she was here or at Pontormo's house. What are you trying to save her from?'

'From being treated like a thing, Master!' I cried. 'Like a plaster bust to be set in various angles of light to study the effects of sunbeams and shadows!'

'What plaster bust is fed and dressed as well as she has been?' Bronzino said. 'You'll forget her. When you're older you won't even remember this painting, let alone remember her. She won't forget you, though, because she never noticed you at all.'

I had to swallow to prevent Bronzino's best wine from coming back up my throat. I had thought that he had some concern for my feelings, but the only reason he had served me his wine and sat me at the table like an equal was because he wanted me not to make any trouble that might impede his career. The price of even my shabby soul was higher than a cup and a half of wine.

'I will always remember Angelina, Master,' was all that I said, 'even if I forget all your paintings.'

Bronzino flushed so deeply that I could see it in his face even though it was silhouetted against the morning sunlight in the studio window.

He stood up, and went back to work on the painting, leaving me to clear away the mugs and the jug of wine. I carried the jug down to the cellar. Bronzino would expect me to return the wine to the bottles, but instead I poured it down the well. I hope the rats enjoyed it. Painters' apprentices are powerless boys of no consequence to anyone; petty revenges are the only kind of revenge they can enjoy.

When Pontormo brought Angelina over, he planted her in one of the chairs like a parcel and hurried over to examine the painting.

'You are going too fast, Bronzino,' he admonished his former pupil. 'You'll damage the quality of the work.'

'I must finish this painting quickly, Master, on the orders of the Duke,' Bronzino replied. 'I'm sure I can maintain the quality. Anyway, nobody will ever see it except King François and his court, and the king will be too polite to complain about any faults.'

'The Duke won't be polite about them,' Pontormo replied.

'He's too interested in getting the painting on time,' Bronzino said.

He asked Pontormo to take Angelina back with him after lunch, and Pontormo agreed.

When Pontormo took her down to go, Angelina stopped and resisted for a moment. She turned round and looked at me.

'It's all right, Angelina,' I said. 'Go with Signor Pontormo. He'll bring you back.' Angelina kept gazing at me for a few moments, and then she lowered her eyes and let Pontormo lead her away.

As it happened, if they had been delayed for just a little longer, they would have met Sister Benedicta and Father Fleccia in the street. I was sorry that it did not happen, although the Duke's invisible spies would certainly have reported it to him. I spotted our two guests from the studio window. Father Fleccia was red-faced and sweating in the heat. Sister Benedicta was looking all around her like a village peasant seeing Florence for the first time. I rushed downstairs to open the door to them, calling to Bronzino, 'Master, Sister Benedicta and Father Fleccia are here!'

Of course, Father Fleccia's first words when he saw the studio were: 'Where's Angelina?'

Bronzino replied to him. 'She's in a safe place, Father, protected by the Duke's own guards.'

By now Sister Benedicta had come into the studio as well. I waited for Bronzino to add to what he had said, but he remained silent, so I spoke myself.

'Angelina is at Signor Pontormo's house. The Duke has –'

'Be quiet, Giuseppe,' Bronzino ordered.

He could silence me, but Father Fleccia was no apprentice to be told to keep quiet.

'What has the Duke ordered, Signor Bronzino?' he demanded. His strange accent became stronger in his anger, and I could hardly hear the 'r' in Bronzino's name.

Bronzino waved his hands like a stallholder who is pretending to have been worsted in a bargaining session.

'Father,' he replied, 'the Duke has commanded that the woman –'

'Angelina!' Sister Benedicta said.

'– the woman Angelina,' Bronzino continued, as if he had intended to speak her name all along, 'is to sit as a model for other painters and also for sculptors. The Duke wants her to become the face of Florence in the sixteenth century as Simonetta Vespucci was in the fifteenth century.'

Sister Benedicta was not interested in the Duke's plans, except in how they affected Angelina. 'So Angelina is not going to come home when this painting is finished, as was promised?' she said. She was peering past Bronzino's shoulder at the painting itself, where she could see both Angelina and myself in a state of public nudity.

'She will be staying with the sculptor Bandinelli after she leaves here,' Bronzino told her.

Father Fleccia exploded with anger. 'Bandinelli! That

man's bad character is known all over Florence.'

'And also far beyond,' Bronzino agreed. 'Nevertheless, it is the command of the Duke. He will not allow Bandinelli to mistreat her. To put it vulgarly, her beauty must not be spoilt.'

Father Fleccia was not pacified. I was sure that he had heard all this before he came to our house. 'Bandinelli's idea of good treatment may not be the same as ours,' he said.

Bronzino stepped over and knelt before Father Fleccia like a penitent. I wonder whether Bronzino ever truly repented of a sin in his life, but Father Fleccia seemed willing to listen to him speak from that posture.

'Father, none of this was my intention,' Bronzino said, which I believe was true. He would not have wanted to share Angelina with anyone else. 'I believe that your best chance of protecting – Angelina – from worse harm is to remain absent from the Duke's list of those whom he considers not be his obedient supporters.'

'I am neither a supporter nor an opponent of the Duke,' Father Fleccia replied. 'Indeed, I am not even one of his subjects, because I am an Englishman, not a Florentine.'

'If the Duke becomes hostile to you,' Bronzino replied, 'I doubt that your king will intervene to protect you.'

'That is true,' Father Fleccia admitted. 'I must put my trust in God, and in the hope that I can please the Duke. Now, what must I do to model for the painting?' He looked at it, and seemed less displeased by it than Sister Benedicta was.

'Please, Father,' Bronzino said, 'I must show you some hospitality first.'

I served our guests with wine, cakes and fruit. Bronzino showed the best of his skilled (and insincere) charm. He convinced Sister Benedicta that he was concerned about Angelina's welfare, and he urged Father Fleccia to talk at length about the voyage he had made as a young man to the island of Terra Nuova.

Eventually Bronzino declared that it was time for work. He sent me to fetch the pale blue cloth that was the background for most of the composition.

'Father Fleccia, Giuseppe will hold one end of the cloth. Will you hold the other? I would like you to strip –'

'What!' Father Fleccia exclaimed. 'Am I, also, to be naked in this painting?'

I saw Sister Benedicta smile.

'No, Father, of course not,' Bronzino reassured him. 'I want to show your arms and shoulders. Your musculature is amazing, particularly, if I may say so, in a man of your age.'

Father Fleccia was already unlacing his shirt. 'My father thought I was a bookish and impractical youth,' he remarked, 'but I became stronger and harder as I grew up.'

I held out the blue background cloth, and Bronzino showed Father Fleccia how to hold it. I was to hold the other end.

'Master, will I appear twice in this painting?' I asked Bronzino. 'Once as Cupid, and once holding the cloth?'

'No,' Bronzino replied. 'I'll use another mask. Only your hands will appear. This time I'll paint your own hands.'

So it was that Angelina's hands appear attached to my body as Cupid, while my own hands are in the top of the painting, holding up the left corner of the blue cloth. When I saw my hands as Bronzino painted them, I was forced to admit that Bronzino had been right, and that my hands could never have passed as the hands of Cupid.

We set up chairs, hidden behind the cloth, to support

Father Fleccia's arms. He could never have held the pose for more than a minute or so.

He was Saturn, the god of Time. He is pulling back the blue cloth, which has previously hidden the scene, to reveal Venus, Cupid, and the other elements of the painting. The meaning of his gesture is that all is revealed by time.

At the end of the day's work, Bronzino dismissed Father Fleccia and Sister Benedicta back to their homes, speaking with all courtesy, but treating them as if they were his servants. For as long as he held Angelina, he knew he could command them to do what he wanted.

Bronzino did make sure that they left before Pontormo returned with Angelina. She came in rather dishevelled. She must have lain down for a nap in Pontormo's house, and he would not have known how to tidy her up. Perhaps he had not noticed. When she sat down at the table for supper, I wondered how she would have felt if she had known that Sister Benedicta had been there.

Angelina was still seeing Father Fleccia when he came to celebrate Mass, but I hoped she remembered Sister Benedicta, who had taken care of her for so long. She had been so delighted to see Father Fleccia when he had first come, that I was sure she would have been at least as happy to see Sister Benedicta again.

The routine of the next few days was like something out of one of those simple rough comedies one sees played in the streets of Florence, except that it was not funny, which most of them are. (Even when the performance is not funny, the players still demand coins from the involuntary audience.)

After Father Fleccia had finished posing as Time, and I had finished posing with him as a disembodied pair of ugly hands helping him to hold up the blue background cloth, it was the turn of Sister Benedicta to sit as Bronzino's model.

Bronzino had sent me out to buy a honeycomb. He even instructed me to bargain hard for that one small item. At the same time, I bought the snakeskin that he had told me, months before, he would need one day.

As it happened, Bronzino did not want Sister Benedicta to hold the honeycomb.

'I want only to paint your face, Sister,' Bronzino said, 'so I will not take up as much of your time as I did of Father Fleccia's.'

Bronzino was now working very late. I was impressed that he dared to paint such an important picture by the light of candles and lanterns, which distort colours and throw unstable shadows, to say nothing of attracting the insects of the night who are moved to fling themselves to their deaths upon the sticky fresh paint.

One evening, I was using the unusual amount of light in the studio to help me clean and polish Angelina's silver tiara. I looked down upon the beautiful assembly of silver and pearls, the crown of Venus, and I suddenly saw to what use I could put it.

15

Bronzino painted Sister Benedicta's face all in shadow. He had posed her in the corner of the room, away from the light of the window. That was surprising, because he usually loved his portraits to show modelling created by soft light playing upon a face, a pair of hands or upon a whole body. When Sister Benedicta looked at his work, I could see that she was surprised, too, but for different reasons.

'You have made me look younger, Signor Bronzino,' she said. 'No wonder you are in demand as a portraitist.'

'I am not creating a formal portrait, Sister,' Bronzino replied, 'but if I were, I would do my best to represent your character and your appearance.'

That would have been a departure. All Bronzino's portraits have one thing in common: they rarely reveal anything of the character of the sitter. Nobody could tell anything about Angelina or myself by looking at the painting in which we appear. The only exception that I know of is the representation of Father Fleccia as Time, and neither King François nor anyone else who sees the painting would ever know who it was.

I disliked Bronzino's likeness of Sister Benedicta, if you can call it a likeness; not because he had made her look a few years younger, but because he had made her look stupid. The half-closed, downcast eyes were meant to express deceit, but Bronzino was never strong in representing human emotion. Perhaps that was because he had none of his own, except for anger and lust, which are both sins rather than emotions. In any case, his insult to Sister Benedicta was less successful than the one he had committed against Captain Da Lucca. Few people will examine her face; they will be much more struck by the fact that the figure has the body of a great serpent, and the rear legs of a lion. (Bronzino used the same snakeskin upon which the young boy is dancing.)

It is perhaps even stranger that the hands of the figure, one holding a honeycomb and the other one cradling an asp, are the wrong way round: the left hand is on the right and the right hand is on the left. I suppose that it is part of Bronzino's scheme for communicating the idea of deceit, but I think it is a clumsy device.

While Bronzino was working, I was working too, making sketches and little splashes of colour to help Bronzino refine the images in the painting. While I scribbled lines and smeared paint, I hoped for some interesting conversation with Father Fleccia and Sister Benedicta, but neither of them was willing to talk. They did not want my company: they wanted Angelina, and I felt the same.

Eventually Bronzino remembered that I existed. 'Giuseppe,' he told me, 'here's an exercise for you. Make a study of the crown of Venus. It will be a test of your ability to represent metal with light shining upon it from a single direction. See if you can also represent the roundness and hardness of the pearls.'

I brought down the tiara. I knew that Sister Benedicta must have seen it before, because she had sent it to me, but I wondered whether Father Fleccia had seen it. He gulped for a moment, evidently suppressing words of surprise that would have been unseemly coming from a priest.

'My word!' he finally said. It must be an English exclamation of surprise. 'Is it real?'

'It certainly is,' Sister Benedicta told him. 'Her parents can afford the best for her, and they always pay for it.'

If only they had been willing to give her a welcome in their home, instead of sending money and rich gifts to keep her at Sister Benedicta's, where she would not embarrass them.

I decided to risk raising the question: 'When we took Angelina to the Palazzo the other evening, there were many great ladies and gentlemen who saw her. I looked at all their faces, trying to guess whether her parents were among them.'

'Perhaps they were,' Sister Benedicta replied. 'I know who they are, but I don't know whether they were there last night, and if I did, I wouldn't tell you. What would you have done if you had been able to pick them out?'

I had not thought about it at the time, but now I lied and pretended that I had. 'I would have brought Angelina forward, and asked everyone present to congratulate the parents on the beauty and sweetness of their daughter,' I said.

'That would have been the end of Angelina living with me,' Sister Benedicta replied. 'Where do you think she would go then?'

'I don't know,' I admitted.

Father Fleccia gave me the glare that he must give to unrepentant sinners who disregard his preaching. 'When you're older,' he told me, 'you'll know what would have become of Angelina with nobody to take care of her.'

'I know what will become of Angelina now, Father,' I replied. 'You know that Baccio Bandinelli is a bad man. His son Clemente has a good heart, but he's only ten years old, so he won't be able to help Angelina. After Bandinelli, who next? Florence is full of painters and sculptors, and even Bandinelli isn't the worst character among them.'

Bronzino intervened at that point. 'Giuseppe! You must not argue with Father Fleccia. I apologise, Father. I flattered myself that I had taught my apprentice some manners.'

'Oh, I took no offence, Signor Bronzino,' Father Fleccia replied. 'Giuseppe was speaking out of kindness and concern, and the world could well do with more of both.'

'Can't you think of something, Father?' I begged him. 'You are so much wiser and more knowledgeable than I am. I've never been out of Florence, but you've seen so many places.'

'No, I wouldn't say I have travelled widely,' Father Fleccia replied. 'I spent that winter in Terra Nuova when I was a very young man, but I never left England again until I fled from King Henry's heretics. There was a time when I would have been exhilarated to cross France and to struggle over the Alps, and then to come down through the great lakes of the north of Italy, but my heart was too heavy.'

I noticed that Bronzino was studying us both. He interrupted again.

'I come from the village of Monticelli, close to the city, Father, and I have never wanted to travel.'

'Nor did I,' Father Fleccia replied. 'I have made only two long journeys in my life. I went to Terra Nuova forty years ago because our King Henry the Seventh was offering forty shillings to a priest who would spend a winter with the fishermen. I came to Italy six years ago because his son King Henry the Eighth wanted no more priests in England. As you see, I have travelled on other men's orders, not on my own. I could have spent my life happily in my father's town house in London, except that God called me to be a priest.'

'I wonder who called me to be a painter, Father?' Bronzino asked. 'I'm not sure it was God.'

'Satan calls men to vocations as well,' Father Fleccia replied mysteriously.

In my entire life up to then (all seventeen years of it) I had never considered the idea of leaving Florence. I was interested in hearing about other countries, and I had listened eagerly to Father Fleccia's reminiscences of the great seas and forests of the island of Terra Nuova, but I had never wanted to see anywhere outside Florence. I must have had more of an artistic temperament than either I or anyone else had thought, because Florence seemed to me to contain more art and superb culture than any other place in the world. It still does seem to me so, although I have for so many years been prevented from entering the city.

I asked Father Fleccia what his first impressions of Florence had been.

'I didn't notice as much as I should have done,' he admitted. 'I'm no poet, so I wasn't alert to my feelings. I was looking inwards all the time, thinking about how I had been forced to leave England. I do remember being amazed by the Alps, as anyone would be. I had never seen anything like them.' Father Fleccia stared at the wall, as though it had miraculously become covered by a painting, or by words spelling out a terrible and shocking message. 'When I saw the great lakes of the north, before I left the territory of the Holy Roman Empire, they reminded me very much of the landscape of Terra Nuova. They're not identical, because the landscapes are greener and the climate is warmer, and the country has been transformed by human works. In Terra Nuova, you could believe that men had landed there for the first time only that morning. I did take in a memory of the mountains around Lake Garda.'

'Is Lake Garda like Terra Nuova, then, Father?' I asked. 'I didn't know that Florence had such exotic sights in her territory.'

'Lake Garda isn't in your territory, Giuseppe, I'm sorry to say,' Father Fleccia replied. 'It's in Trento, which is part of the Empire. Only the water and the mountains reminded me of Terra Nuova. I stayed there for a few days, and when I looked up at the forests covering the high rocks I could have believed that I could climb up there and my old friends from the Beothuk people of Terra Nuova would come out of the trees to greet me, as if I were there again and forty years had never passed.'

I put down the silver tiara, and Sister Benedicta picked it up.

'I told Angelina's parents that they could trust you with it, Giuseppe,' she said, 'because I had seen how I could trust you with Angelina herself.'

I wondered if Sister Benedicta would have felt the same had she known about the hot, still afternoons that I had passed with Angelina in a close embrace on my bed. The good nun would hardly have been pacified if I had told her that I had never attempted the final intimacy with Angelina.

Bronzino laid down his paintbrushes. 'Thank you, Sister, and you too, Father,' he said. 'Can I offer you some more refreshment before you leave?'

'No, thank you, Signor Bronzino,' Sister Benedicta replied. 'We'll leave now.' She did not want refreshment: she wanted to see Angelina, which she knew that Bronzino would deny to her.

That evening, when Pontormo and Angelina returned

for supper, I wished more than ever that I could converse with her. Oh, I could talk to her, of course, and Bronzino made it clear that it looked to him that I was talking to Angelina as one might talk to a cat or a dog, not expecting to be understood. Yet I still hoped that she could understand even if she could not reply, and so I wished I could talk to her alone.

Pontormo did have one interesting item of news. 'The Duke has become bored with guarding my house, or rather he has found more interesting tasks for his guards to carry out.'

I suspected that those tasks consisted mainly of beating men who had offended Duke Cosimo in some way, but I could not help the Duke's victims, except for two of them: Angelina and myself.

'Has he taken the guards away completely, then, Signor Pontormo?' I asked, much too eagerly.

Bronzino reprimanded me. 'Be quiet, Giuseppe! It is not your place to initiate conversation with my master.' For a moment I feared that Bronzino suspected what was in my mind, but he turned away and ignored me. Pontormo, on the contrary, willingly answered my question.

'No, the guards are still there at night and when Angelina is with me. They've gone back to the Palazzo now, but another guard will come out before we go home.'

My idea of breaking into Pontormo's house by night and leading Angelina away collapsed into ruins like a badly built house that had been struck by an earthquake. I sat in silence as I had been ordered to do, and contemplated the callow foolishness of my scheme. How could I, an ignorant seventeen-year-old apprentice who knew nothing of life and had never even been out of the city, rescue Angelina and take her to a place of safety?

The painting was so far advanced that I knew Bronzino would soon have to hand Angelina over into the care of Baccio Bandinelli. Even Bronzino feared for her welfare when she would be in the custody of that brute. If anyone was going to rescue Angelina, they would have to do it in the next few days.

Early the next morning, when I prepared to order our food from the vendors down below in the street, I took the purse of money that Bronzino had given me for housekeeping expenses and counted it all out, quietly, so as not to wake him. It was hardly a fortune, but it might be enough to get us out of Florence with new clothes and the means to buy food and lodging on the journey to wherever we might go. I contemplated the money. For the first time, I would have to make a decision, the effects of which would stay with me for the rest of my life. If I took the money, I would be forced to run away, and it would be the end of my apprenticeship with Bronzino. If I left the money and abandoned Angelina, I would bear the guilt for whatever would happen to her. I was already to blame for everything that had already happened, because it was I who had noticed her at the upper window.

I heard the cries of the vendors coming along the street and approaching our house. I knew that this was going to be the most important moment of my life, and I prayed with desperation that I might make the right decision. By the time the vendors were calling up to our windows, I had made up my mind, and may God and man forgive me, because I do not believe that any woman would judge me to have sinned. I bought the normal amount of food, and counted out the money that was left. I calculated what would remain after I had bought the next day's food. It would have to be enough to send us on our way.

Bronzino had declared that he had no further need of Sister Benedicta and Father Fleccia, so Pontormo brought Angelina over in the morning as he had used to do before.

In the afternoon, he and Bronzino retired together as had been their custom since they had first been master and apprentice. As had become my custom, I took Angelina upstairs, but I lay next to her only until she had fallen asleep. She did not wake up when I left her. My plan depended upon my being able to leave the house without awakening either Bronzino or Pontormo. I needed to rehearse that, to make sure I could do it successfully. I stole down the stairs, opened and closed the door to the street, and hurried off towards Pontormo's house.

To my relief I saw that there were no guards outside. I put my shoulder to the door and pushed at it. Nothing happened, which will not surprise anyone who sees me as Cupid and observes the childish weakness of my shoulders. Let that same viewer, though, look at my big hands holding up the blue cloth to the opposite end to where Father Fleccia glowers at me in his character as Time. My hands were strong.

Knowing Pontormo as I did, I surmised that although he was punctilious about locking the door, it would never occur to him to check the condition of the wood of which it was made. I looked about.

The street was empty, and the shutters were closed on all the windows. With one hand against the door jamb I pushed at the door, and slowly prised it apart. I heard something snap, and the top half of the door swung inwards.

I was able to jump over the bottom half of the door, and I landed on a bare earth floor. I could smell paint and stone dust, and the sour stink of a house where too many mice live. I looked around in the darkness, and nearly cried out with fear. The Virgin Mary herself was looking right back at me. It was a wonderful painting, in the style of the earlier part of this century. Pontormo must have painted it when he was a young man, but why had he kept it hidden in his house instead of selling it for a good price, or at least exhibiting it for good praise? I looked around again. There were only three rooms in the house, and I had not expected it to be so small. All around there were sketches for paintings, and little clay figures postured and posed in the shadows, waiting to be transformed into great marbles and bronzes that would now never be created.

I wondered what Angelina could have understood of all this, but she could not have told me, and of course I could not question Pontormo about it myself. I realised that not even Bronzino would ever have seen most of these wonderful things. Even though I had no right to be in the house, I felt privileged to be there, as if Pontormo had invited me in to witness his secret works. I peered into the next room. There was a disordered knot of blankets on the floor, next to a surprisingly neatly-made bed. I was enraged to realise that Angelina had been sleeping in the same room as Pontormo during all those nights, even though I was certain that he would never have touched her. I was equally certain that he had yielded his bed to her, and the old man (fifty years old, but an old man nevertheless) had been sleeping on the hard, uneven floor.

The final room in the house was Pontormo's kitchen. There was very little food to be seen, and I knew I had been wise in making sure that both Angelina and Pontormo were fed properly at Bronzino's house.

While I was looking round for evidence of food and drink, I saw a sheaf of papers lying on the kitchen table. I had to hold the top sheet of paper close to my eyes to read it, because the light was so dim in the house. The top line said, in bold capital letters:

TUESDAY MORNING, OCTOBER 14, 1544.

It was Pontormo's diary! I read on, eager to read the man's thoughts. I have never known such mingled feelings of astonishment and disappointment.

TUESDAY MORNING, OCTOBER 14, 1544.

Had a slight headache when I woke up. Ate half a bread roll, drank a cup of wine left over from yesterday.

I shuffled through the pile of papers and read another entry.

WEDNESDAY EVENING, JUNE 11, 1544.

Fried an egg and had a lettuce which I bought this morning, together with some vegetable soup. I think it all cost me two pennies.

I tried an entry about halfway between those two dates.

FRIDAY EVENING, AUGUST 15, 1544.

I felt quite unwell this morning. It was an oppressive and thundery day. At Bronzino's house I had a good salad of cold meat and a pancake afterwards.

I put the pile of paper back on the table, and as I did so I saw similar piles of paper stacked in the corners of the room, covered with dust and cobwebs made by spiders who had lived years before. I took up another sheet and examined it in the dim light.

THURSDAY, 12 MARCH, 1538.

I had some mutton and half a loaf of bread. I paid three pennies for it.

I admit that I felt wounded that there was no mention of me: after all, who was it at Bronzino's house who had made that good salad of cold meat and the pancake? I was also hurt on Angelina's behalf that the recent entries contained no mention of her, even though she was staying in that very house with him. Every other man in Florence would have boasted of it.

I had no time to read much more of Pontormo's diary, and it seemed that there would have been little point to it anyway. All it contained were accounts of his meals, sometimes with a note of how much he had paid for the ingredients, accounts of his illnesses and accidents, and occasional mentions of visits to Bronzino's house. Sometimes Pontormo recorded having seen another artist or a famous client, but he wrote down no details of their conversation.

I knew that I had no right to criticise Pontormo for the sketchiness of his diary. I had no right to be reading it in any case, and if he meant it only for himself then he was entitled to write what he pleased, however thin and eccentric it might seem to any intruder who read it without permission.

I placed all the sheets of paper back where I had found them. I could never speak of it to Pontormo, of course, and I would never be able to ask him why he, who had witnessed more than thirty of the greatest years of the artistic life of Florence, should have chosen to record nothing of it. I wondered whether he ever re-read the entries himself, and why he would want to read of his meals, his headaches and his sprains years later.

There was nothing more for me to do. I had established that I could leave our house without being noticed, and that I could force my way into Pontormo's house. By taking Bronzino's money, I had committed myself to running away and abducting Angelina. I was as confident as I could ever be that I could carry out the plan, but I was not enough of a fool to believe that it could not go wrong, and I had enough of an artist's imagination to picture only too well what would be my fate at the hands of Duke Cosimo de' Medici if he caught me trying to steal Angelina from him. After looking up and down the street to check that nobody was about, I propped up the damaged door, and hurried back to our house.

I succeeded in getting and climbing back up to my room without Bronzino or Pontormo waking up. Angelina was still asleep. She was lying on her side with her arm thrust out, and her hair flowed across her shoulder. No painter could have arranged her limbs or her hair in a more perfect composition. Not wanting to wake her yet, I sat down on the floor and watched her sleep. How strangely fascinating it is to watch someone you love sleep, in the same way that you can lie in still and silent embrace with them for a whole afternoon.

I could not speak, so I had to think instead. I kept asking myself whether I was right to take Angelina away, and whether perhaps I should simply run off by myself instead. The answer was that there would have been no point to pursuing either option: I was in no danger, and I could stay as an apprentice in Bronzino's house for years to come, with nothing to fear except his indecent assaults. No doubt even they would soon stop when I become more of a man and less of a boy, and Bronzino would seek a pretty youth to replace me. It was Angelina who was in danger, even if she seemed not to know it.

As quietly as I could, I made sure that the crown of Venus was still where I had put it for safe keeping. Bronzino thought that I was keeping it safe for him. Sister Benedicta thought that I was keeping it safe for Angelina's parents. I would disappoint them all. I had no sympathy for Bronzino, who had misused me so cruelly and so often, and I knew that Sister Benedicta would get no blame. As for Angelina's parents, I was glad of the chance to strike a blow against them for the rejection of their daughter. Angelina was strange and silent and unusual, but she could have loved them if they had allowed her the chance.

It was not I who woke her up. It was Bronzino, who came out of his bedroom and bellowed 'Giuseppe!' from below. Angelina sat up with a cry. I calmed her, washed her face, and tidied her hair and clothes before we came down to the studio for supper.

In spite of my intention to steal as much of Bronzino's money as I could, I had spent it generously on food that morning. I wanted Pontormo to record in his diary that I had prepared a good meal for him that evening, because it was probably the last one that I would ever give him. I hoped that he would not starve to death after I disappeared, because of his own neglect and that of Bronzino.

While I made and served supper, I planned our escape from Florence. I would do it on the first afternoon when Bronzino let me take Angelina upstairs, while he slept with Pontormo. If I were lucky, the chance would come on the next day. For the first time, I looked around the studio and the house. I remembered how intimidating they had seemed on the day when Bronzino had first taken me in as his apprentice. Suddenly everything looked unfamiliar again, and the studio seemed to have grown larger. I was seeing it as I had seen it the first time, because I knew that within the next day or two I would be in Bronzino's studio for the last time.

That night, when I escorted Angelina and Pontormo back to Pontormo's house, I watched to see whether Pontormo would detect any sign that someone had broken in. The night guards greeted him politely, and made no mention of having noticed any damage or intrusion. Pontormo turned the key in the lock, and the top half of the door fell back on its broken upper hinge.

'Here, Giuseppe, give me a hand,' he asked me. 'Why do things always break without warning?'

I held the door vertical while he opened the remaining lock, and supported it while he and Angelina went inside.

'I don't need to lock it tonight, anyway,' Pontormo called from within. 'I've got my own private guard, by courtesy of Duke Cosimo himself! Good night!'

'Good night, Signor Pontormo,' I replied, wondering whether it was the last time that I would ever bid him good night.

Pontormo had never done me any direct unkindness, but I blamed him for not having been a strict enough master to Bronzino and failing to correct Bronzino's behaviour in youth. I also knew that Pontormo had introduced Bronzino to vice, although Bronzino must have taken to it willingly, unlike myself.

'Please don't tell anyone about the broken door,' I asked the guards.

'We never noticed it ourselves,' their corporal replied. 'Please don't tell that to the Duke!'

I hoped sincerely that I would never have occasion to speak to the Duke again.

When I came back to our house, Bronzino was working late on the painting, by candlelight, always a sign of anxiety in him or in any other painter.

'You can go to bed now, Giuseppe,' he told me, but I did not want to.

'I need to do some cleaning around the house, Master,' I replied.

'You'll disturb me!' he snapped, and then he said 'Oh, well, I'll go to bed myself, then.'

I wanted to stay up so that I could contemplate the painting. I knew how Bronzino planned it to look when it was finished. I studied it carefully, indeed desperately, because I wanted to keep it accurately in my memory for life. I had never seen some of the details that I knew Bronzino would add. The two theatrical masks would lie on the floor, looking upwards with their empty eyes, the old man's mask to the front, and the young woman's mask to the rear, looking up between Angelina and the youthful dancing boy who was my childhood self, although I am sure that I never had such a foolish expression as a boy. Well, I hope not.

The young woman's mask would appear again as Oblivion, in the top left-hand corner of the painting, where my own hands were already holding up the blue cloth. Father Fleccia was recognisable at the other end, with a face that condemned everything that he saw below. Sister Benedicta's face awaited her chimera of a body. The dove was already in place in the bottom left-hand corner. After

Bronzino had painted the dove, it had given its life for Art, and its body for his supper. The poor bird did not even, as far as I know, gain a mention in Pontormo's diary.

The most complete part of the painting was the two central figures. To the left I appeared in that painful posture, something between kneeling and squatting. My bare bottom stuck out at the viewer, my left hand (Angelina's left hand, really) supported the back of her head while my right hand straddled her breast. I wondered whether King François, or any of his Court, would be able to tell that Angelina had never spoken a word to me?

Even though I had chosen to seek a career as a painter, and I knew that life paintings must have models, I could not help feeling resentful that Angelina would be seen in her nudity by the king, his courtiers and those who passed through his palace. (As it happened, the painting never found its way to Paris, but was lodged in the château of Chambord.) I found little consolation in knowing that at least the painting would not be on public display where anyone could see it.

I saw that Bronzino had done a good job of depicting the crown of Venus. I was glad that he had finished it, representing the silver beautifully and the roundness of the pearls, because if I succeeded in my plan he would never see that tiara again.

16

For the first time in my apprenticeship, I had to be woken up by Bronzino shouting at my bedroom door.

'Giuseppe!' he roared. 'Wake up! The men with the groceries are nearly here!'

I dressed myself as quickly as I could, and went to the studio window to let down the basket. Bronzino was watching me from the other side of the room. I prayed that he would go away. I did not want him to be there when I took his money out of its leather bag and put it in my doublet. I had to spend more than I had intended to, so that Bronzino would not become suspicious. I brought the food into the kitchen, and started to make breakfast. Bronzino did leave me then, to wash and dress. I had meant to take the money immediately, but I did not dare to do so with him staying so close to me. It meant that I would have to move the coins later in the morning, with much more risk of him detecting me doing it.

Bronzino was unusually chatty over breakfast, talking to me as though he were another man as young as myself, a friend of mine. Of course, I had no other young man as a friend. I had only Bronzino, who was forty-two, and Pontormo, who was fifty, but who seemed much older. The only younger person whom I could perhaps claim as a friend was Clemente Bandinelli, and he was only ten years old. Perhaps other young men of my age would have found me strange. I had no idea how a seventeen-year-old Florentine of my day was supposed to behave. Bronzino had kept me a boy beyond my time, and Pontormo's influence was towards making me a middle-aged man before my time.

I wished I could tell Bronzino to be quiet, but before I lost my patience Pontormo arrived with Angelina, accompanied by the guard.

As Pontormo had become more accustomed to the Duke's men, he had begun to enjoy their attendance upon him. Poor Pontormo never saw that if he had exploited his talents properly, and made the same amounts of money that lesser painters amassed and still do, he could have had his own guards, wearing his own uniform. He could have been carried through the streets in a curtained litter, and people would have pointed to it and said: 'There goes the great painter Pontormo!'

It was difficult for me not to communicate my apprehension and excitement to Angelina. She might not understand words, and she usually could not understand other people's behaviour, but she could often detect strong emotions. I pretended that it was a day like all the other days we had spent in the studio. Because Venus and Cupid were finished, we did not have to pose, but I had to run around fetching brushes, knives and paints for Bronzino while he worked on the other figures.

Angelina had nothing to do, and sat where I had placed her at the table, still working her way slowly through her breakfast. I realised that meals for Angelina must seem much more important parts of her day to her than they did to other people, because it was the one activity that she could share with them.

While I scuttled around the studio for Bronzino, I kept

studying the painting, because I knew that, whatever might happen, I might never get another chance to see it. I was genuinely sorry that I would never see the painting in its completed state.

'Master,' I asked Bronzino, 'have you settled on a title for the painting yet?'

'No,' he replied, 'and I don't intend to give it one. Let King François give it whatever name pleases him.'

'What if the Duke demands a title for it?' I persisted. 'He may want it to be put on the frame, or mentioned in the letter presenting his gift.'

'In that case, I'll give him whatever title comes into my mind at that moment,' Bronzino said. 'Why should you care? You appear in it twice, as Cupid and as Folly. What more do you want?'

What I wanted was for Angelina to be removed from the painting, and be taken home to Sister Benedicta's house, to live there in peace and safety for the rest of her life, even if I had to say goodbye to her for ever.

'I was merely curious, Master,' I replied.

'What title do you suggest?' Bronzino asked. 'You can say anything you like, because I won't use it.'

I gave him the title that sprang into my mind, just as he had said he would do if the Duke were to insist upon a title. 'I would call it Cupid and the Silent Goddess, Master,' I replied.

'Why "silent"?' Bronzino demanded. 'Venus isn't silent. That's not one of her attributes. Of course, perhaps the world would be a better place if Venus were to be silent, and if Cupid were to be disarmed of his bow and arrow.'

I looked away from the painting, and stared at the studio window, trying to empty my mind of the memory of the half-finished artwork, so that I could construct the finished painting in my imagination. I composed the vision with as much care as I could, placing all the incomplete and missing figures and faces in their correct places, and putting all the mysterious assorted objects where they would appear when the painting was presented to King François. The king was noted as a great humanist and a man of learning. He would certainly receive the painting politely, but I wonder whether even he would understand what it meant.

Bronzino had been given no choice of subject when Duke Cosimo had ordered him to paint a picture showing Venus and Cupid, but it was Bronzino's own choice that the theme of the painting was to be the deceptions of love. He denied that the painting had a theme, but it was there to see nevertheless, and both Pontormo and I had been struck and disturbed by it. Who had deceived Bronzino in love so deeply that he had painted what was his greatest work yet to illustrate that painful subject? The guilty party was certainly not Pontormo, who had loved Bronzino since he was a boy, with a mixture of paternal and perverted love. Perhaps it was me after all, although I still did not believe Bronzino's declaration of love to me.

Staring at the incomplete painting, I realised how everything concerned with it was incomplete as well. Angelina and I, who were the main figures, would never see the painting in its finished state. Bronzino would lose his unrequited lover, myself, and never find another lifelong bond as he had known with Pontormo. I would never be able to say a proper goodbye to Sister Benedicta and Father Fleccia. Duke Cosimo de' Medici would never be able to have his artists and sculptors reproduce the image of Angelina all over Italy and beyond, as the new Simonetta Vespucci. Angelina's parents would, if all went well for her and myself, never get back their tiara of silver and pearls. I was sorry for some of these incompletenesses.

The morning seemed to last longer than any other morning I had ever known. At last it was time for me to make lunch, and I tried to make it a good one, in the hope that Pontormo would finally feel moved to award me a mention in his diary. I also wanted to make sure that Angelina and I would make our escape with the fortification of a generous meal beforehand.

I found myself actually trembling with excitement as the afternoon arrived. Bronzino fortunately did not notice, but Pontormo asked me whether I had a fever. I could have told him the truth and answered that, yes, I did have a fever, but instead I told him that I would be all right after my siesta.

At last Bronzino and Pontormo retired to Bronzino's bedroom. It seemed somehow disappointing that what I planned to be my last sight of Bronzino was so unaccompanied by any drama. He shut the door behind them, and I heard him murmuring to Pontormo for a few moments.

I led Angelina upstairs, and she lay down on the bed while I took the tiara out from its hiding place. While I was unwrapping it, I saw that she was looking at me. I knew that she was expecting me to lie down beside her, as I had always done. I ignored her while I wrapped the tiara up again, this time in some old rags, but she held out her arms to me. It was almost the first time that she had shown any initiative in wanting me. She had almost never shown any sign of understanding other people's feelings. I put the tiara down with the bundle of clothing that I had made up, and slid into her embrace. What better way in which to wait for Bronzino and Pontormo to fall asleep?

When there had been silence in the room below for a

long enough time, I pulled myself as gently as I could from Angelina's arms. She awoke quietly and stayed lying there while I crept to the door. I opened it, and went downstairs to listen at the door of Bronzino's bedroom.

There was still no sound. Now I had to get past one of the most difficult stages of our escape: I had to get Angelina downstairs and out of the house without making any noise. If she were to stumble clumsily, as she so often did, or, much worse, if she were to protest and throw one of her wailing tantrums, I would have to put Bronzino's money back in its rightful place and try again another day.

When I came back to the bedroom, Angelina was still awake. I collected together everything that I would take with us, which did not amount to much in addition to Bronzino's coins and the silver tiara.

Angelina stood up quite willingly, and let me lead her down the stairs. I heard Bronzino mutter in his sleep as we passed the first floor where the studio and his bedroom were. Even in the muffled murmurings and meaningless words of complaint that a sleeper utters, I could tell that it was Bronzino and not Pontormo who had spoken.

We reached the ground floor. I opened the door, which squeaked and clattered, but no more than it usually did. I was sure that Bronzino's sleeping mind would not notice it. The door closed with the same low noises. After four years, I was back where I had started, standing outside Bronzino's door, not knowing what was to happen to me. This time, of course, I had more responsibilities than merely to worry about myself.

I took Angelina's hand and led her toward the north side of Florence.

I wondered where she thought I was taking her. I prayed that she did not believe that I was returning her to Sister

Benedicta's house. I also prayed that everyone in the district was either sleeping, fornicating or sodomising, so that they would not happen to be looking out of the window as we passed.

All this had come about because Angelina had been looking out of a window one morning in the spring, and because I had looked up and seen her. I wanted no more faces at windows, and I resolved that I would never again look up from the street to investigate such a sighting.

I wanted to leave the city by one of the north gates, but we had to take a long way round because I wanted to get there by passing through districts where we were not known. Well, I was not known, but the tall silent beautiful young woman who had been abducted by an artist was certainly known to everyone in our quarter.

I hoped that Angelina's fame had not spread further. I could not hide her, and news of our passing would reach the Duke's spies quickly enough, but not as quickly as if I had led Angelina through the flower market and the street of the perfumers.

By the time Florence was waking up from its afternoon sleep, we had reached a part of the city that was not far from one of the gates. We had to stop to rest after walking all through the afternoon. I paid for some eggs, bread and salad with Bronzino's money, as well for some wine, which I mixed with equal parts of water as Father Fleccia had taught me. It makes bad wine less sharp and pushy, he would say.

Everyone noticed Angelina, for her height and her muteness. I told them that she was my sister and that she was partly deaf, and had never learned to talk. I did not say that she was completely deaf, because they would have become suspicious when they saw that she could hear even if she could not understand. I could have told them that she was an idiot, of course, but I could not bring myself to do it. I wanted to keep feeling the tiara through the thick mufflings of cloth in which I had hidden it, but I did not dare to draw any more attention to ourselves. We were enough of an unusual and noteworthy sight as it was.

By now, in the late afternoon, there were crowds of people in the streets, all moving in the same direction. Because the city gates close at sunset, I guessed that they were non-Florentines (what a strange word), heading for the gate so that they would not be locked into the city for the night. I was right. We joined the columns of farmers, pilgrims, thieves, friars and beggars who had risen like Lazarus when the time came to go home.

The guards stopped everyone, but they let them all pass after a question or two. They asked me who I was and where I was going.

'My name is Giuseppe,' I said. It would be easier to remember the truth under questioning than to try to keep a set of lies consistent. 'I'm taking my sister home. She's been staying in Florence with some nuns whom we hoped might be able to cure her of her dumbness, but it hasn't worked.'

'Where is your home?' one of the guards asked me.

In spite of the heat, a cold wind seemed to blow through my body. I knew nothing of Italy outside Florence, and I had prepared myself only to get us out of the city and somewhere out of Duke Cosimo's domains. I had not thought of a particular place to go, but now I had only a moment to name one. Bronzino and Pontormo had travelled a little, including their stay in Pesaro on the Adriatic Sea, but I would not go anywhere they had been in case they thought of looking for me there.

The guard interrupted me just as I remembered Father

Fleccia's account of how he had made his way to Florence.

'Well, you must be going somewhere!' he shouted, and I was able to reply with complete confidence.

'We're going home to Riva, on Lake Garda, in the Prince-Bishopric of Trento.'

'Go on, then,' the guard responded, and we passed through the gate.

When I led Angelina out into the unknown countryside, we stood aside from the road for a few minutes while the procession of other travellers passed by us. Angelina still seemed to trust me, but I was now in territory that was as unfamiliar to me as it was to her.

There were two vital needs to be met: to get away from Florence, and to find somewhere to spend the night. I approached the next group of travellers, which was made up of families rather than groups of craftsmen or farm workers. I told them that we were travelling north, and asked for some advice on where we might stay on the journey. With a kindness that surprised me, they invited us to join them, and expressed great sympathy for my 'sister's' muteness.

When Angelina and I woke up the next morning, in the corner of a room which we were sharing with a dozen other travellers, the first thought that came to me was that by now the alarm would have been raised in Florence. I had to count on the near-certainty that the news would travel only around the city and towards the south, and not towards the north. Fugitives are supposed always to travel to the warm, corrupt lands of the south, and not to the harsh peoples and mountains of the north.

I helped Angelina to wash, and bought her some breakfast before our group set off again. We had to keep travelling now. If we were caught, I would be imprisoned and probably tortured, and possibly executed. Angelina would become a slave of the Duke, and be kept locked up until he tired of her and threw her out.

Even after days on the road, Angelina had still not shown any signs of fear or distrust. Wherever we slept, she embraced me tightly. I resented the laughs that this caused, and I was sure that nobody in our group believed she was really my sister.

Eventually we were travelling on our own, trying to mingle with other groups so that we would not be obvious victims for robbers. All my attention was taken up by guiding and caring for Angelina. I hardly noticed the cities of Bologna, Modena, Mantua and Verona, except for experiencing brief disappointment that they resembled Florence. I cannot imagine what else I should have expected.

We were now in open country, with fruit orchards among the fields, and mountains on the northern horizons. I had never been in open country before. I had known only the narrow streets of Florence, and my only sights of greenery had been courtyard gardens and distant views of the hills beyond the city walls. I felt conspicuous and exposed in the open landscape, and of course Angelina was even more noticeable. I hoped that we were safe. If anyone who saw us now were to realise who we were when they reached Florence and heard the news, we should be out of the Duke's domains before any pursuers could ride up and catch us. From conversations around us I knew that we were close to the frontiers of the Prince-Bishopric of Trento, which was part of the Holy Roman Empire, as Germany and northern Italy sometimes like to call themselves and sometimes not.

Angelina and I were washing beside the banks of a fast-flowing river, which I was told was the Adige. It would have been too dangerous to bathe in the river, but we could splash ourselves with its cold, clean water. I had chosen the spot because there were bushes and trees to hide us while we washed. Suddenly I heard a sound that I had never heard on that road, which was full of plodding walkers and oxen hauling carts. There were horses coming, galloping on the road, ridden by men who shouted at everyone to get out of the way. I pushed Angelina down and peered through the bushes. Eight horsemen wearing the livery of the Duke's guards rode past towards the castle at Rovereto, which was our first destination. I jumped down again and hid us both. The guards could not actually go into Rovereto, which was the frontier post of Trento and completely inside Trentine territory, but if they captured us inside the Duke's domains we were done for.

There was no way to go back towards Florence. We could not go off the road, because we would be wandering in hills and fields that we did not know, and we would certainly be reported and taken. We hid for hours beside the Adige until the guards came again, riding back the other way. I counted all eight of them, so I knew we might have a chance of escaping if we hurried on to Rovereto as fast as we could.

We inserted ourselves again into the ordinary procession of people, oxen and the occasional horse going north on the road. Nobody seemed to be going south. I knew that I had to take the chance that the horsemen had asked other travellers to look out for us, but it seemed that they had not. Paradoxically, Angelina's distinctive appearance had protected us from that. The Duke's guards were so sure of seeing her that they had not asked people to report a tall woman with a curly haired young man. My fear now was that the horsemen would come back, but, having made one pass to the north, it seemed that they were now searching to the south. We slept in another crowded inn that night. At least, Angelina slept. I was too frightened.

When the dawn came, I thought of rousing Angelina and leaving early before anyone else, and then I realised that doing this would only attract more attention. I struggled with my impatience, and we left when everyone else started moving after breakfast.

By the afternoon we were approaching the frontier of the Empire, and I asked the people around me to point out the castle of Rovereto when it came in sight. In the end, they did not need to. I saw it in the distance, set just off the road where four soldiers stood, armed with halberds and bulky armour on their chests. They were stopping and checking everyone entering the Empire.

I prepared to wait, and then I noticed another set of soldiers, closer to us, who were also speaking to people before allowing them to continue up the road. This was another danger that I should have foreseen. Our flight from Florence had taught me what a narrow experience of life I had. Of course I had heard that frontiers were guarded, and that all rulers tried to control who left and who entered their territory, but I had not allowed for it. We might still be safe, though, because the Duke's horse troopers would not have told the frontier guards to watch for us. I decided that the best course was to walk up to them openly, trying not to look in any way unusual.

When they challenged me, I told them my story about taking my mute sister back to our home in Riva, trying to make them feel sympathetic over the failure of the treatment for which I had taken her to Florence. Fortunately, Angelina chose this moment to bestow her beautiful smile upon everyone. I was trying not to look longingly at the castle of Rovereto, only a few steps away but within the Empire and safe from the Duke. The guards waved to us to pass on. I thanked them, Angelina smiled at them again, and I was relaxing with relief at how easy it had been when I heard the approaching sound of shouting and hoofbeats.

'Stop them!' called a voice. 'That tall girl and the boy!'

I grasped Angelina's hand tightly and tugged at it. 'Run with me, Angelina!' I cried. 'Run! Like me!'

I glanced over my shoulder, and saw that the Florentine frontier guards were starting to run after us. I began to run, hauling Angelina with one hand, and clutching the precious bundle which held the silver tiara in the other. The uproar of voices coming closer behind us made the castle of Rovereto, only a few paces away, seem as unattainable as a castle in dream.

It was then that Angelina let go of my hand. My heart, which was pounding like a blacksmith's hammer, nearly stopped from shock and fear. I had an instant to decide whether to go back with her and take my punishment in Florence, or try to run away on my own and seek sanctuary in Trento. I never had to make that decision, which would have revealed, especially to myself, just what kind of moral character I was made of. Angelina did not fall back. She had let go of my hand in order to run past me. Where had she managed to learn to run, confined in Sister Benedicta's house and courtyard? It must be that those long legs of hers were made to run. Angelina sprinted away towards the castle like the Ancient Greek Princess Atalanta, who could outrun any man.

Fortunately my legs had kept working while my mind was paralysed with astonishment. I ran past the Trentine frontier guards, believing that I was now safe, but the

Florentine guards, who were much more numerous now that they included the horsemen, came over the frontier with me. I did not believe that the Trentine guards would risk an incident with Duke Cosimo on my behalf, so I knew I had to get to the castle without help.

Angelina, now well ahead of me, had stopped at the open door leading into the guard chamber. With the Florentines still baying for me like dogs, I snatched at her arm, dragged her through the door, and flung myself upon the mercy of the Prince-Bishop of Trento, knocking out two of my teeth in the process.

The loss of those two teeth began my transformation from the pretty youth in the painting to the bald fat man that I am today, forty years later. If I had not managed to pull Angelina in through that door which led to the Holy Roman Empire, the Florentines would certainly have carried her back to the city and to degradation at the hands of Baccio Bandinelli, and of men even worse than him. I sold the silver pearl-encrusted tiara in the town of Trento, at no more than a quarter of its value, but it was after all a fair price for fencing stolen goods. The money paid for a little house in Riva del Garda, at the very head of the great lake. It also paid for an unofficial extra fee to the town priest, who was unsure about whether Angelina could really give her consent to our marriage. I do not know whether she could consent under the terms of the laws of the Church or of the province of Trento, but I know that she wanted to stay with me.

When I fled from the power of Duke Cosimo de' Medici, I also escaped from the power of the Guild of St. Luke. In the little town of Riva, there was no guild of powder-grinders and pill-rollers to control who carried on the trade of a painter. I was able to set myself up as the local jobbing artist, doing little altarpieces for small churches, and painting portraits of merchants and prosperous farmers, always with the same views of the lake and mountains in the background. When the flow of commissions was slow, I used to paint that standard background on panels, so that I could simply add the portrait of the next customer who came along. I did acceptable work at a low price, and because there had never been a painter in Riva before, I found that I had a secure living to support both myself and my wife.

Pontormo had been right, of course. I would never have made a great painter, even if I had spent my whole life in Florence. Nevertheless, I had a small talent, and I owe everything to my hostile father who was the one who spotted it. I have taken care of my little scrap of painterly talent, and looked after it as a poor family might polish and venerate the only gold coin they possess. I know that Duke Cosimo raged over the loss of Angelina, and I hope that Angelina's parents were distressed over the loss of the tiara. Perhaps they were simply relieved that their strange daughter had been removed from them for ever.

As the years passed, news came to me from Florence, often years after the event. Although Bronzino continued to gain commissions from the Duke and his court, he found it expedient to spend two or three years away in Rome after we absconded. Bronzino never did achieve his ambition of being appointed as official court painter, although most people in Florence came to believe that he had, so perhaps that was enough to satisfy his vanity.

Clemente Bandinelli did follow his father in becoming a sculptor. I wish I could have seen some of his work. In the end, Clemente, weary of the constant and vicious abuse that he received from his father, went off to Rome to establish himself as a sculptor. He showed great promise, but sadly he fell ill and died within a year, but not before half-completing a sort of variation of the traditional Pietà, where the dead Christ is supported on the lap of the Madonna. In Clemente's sculpture, though, the dead Christ is held by Nicodemus, who brought linen and spices to help Joseph of Arimathea to wrap the Saviour's body.

Baccio Bandinelli hurried to Rome, and when he saw the work that Clemente had left there, he determined to finish it, as a memorial to the son whom he had mistreated and tormented throughout his short life. Some of the work was done by other sculptors, but Bandinelli himself carved the head of Nicodemus, to whom he gave the face, not of his dead son, but of himself, so that it is Baccio Bandinelli who holds the dead Christ. Perhaps he was thinking of the legend that Nicodemus, too, had been a sculptor, and that he had carved a likeness of Christ.

Bronzino must have been made bitter by the fact that he had to complete the painting so that it could be sent to King François. However, when it was delivered to the château of Chambord, the king apparently received it not merely with diplomatic politeness, but with real joy, and with delight at the prospect of spending many hours working out the philosophical meanings of the various strange figures and objects in it.

As for Angelina and I, we became as rooted in Riva del Garda as though we had always lived there, and, indeed, we spent most of our lives there. The vast lake comes to an end at Riva, in a neatly squared-off basin of rock that looks like a great artificial work but which is natural.

Even though she never learned to move gracefully, I often took Angelina for walks up the slopes of the overhanging mountain, from where we could look down on the town, the lake and, to the north, the first of the great mountains beyond which lie Germany, France, and Father Fleccia's England and the island of Terra Nuova, none of which I shall ever see.

Since Angelina died I have not returned to the heights of the mountains, but they hang over the town of Riva so dominatingly, just as the lake spreads out before it, that I cannot escape the sight of them. I see them from the window of my solitary bedroom, just as the empty skies of Florence once were the only view from my bedroom window in Bronzino's house so many years ago. I know that when I lie in bed dying, I shall be looking at those great vertical walls of rock, as tall, fascinating, and mysterious as my lost Angelina.

The End

Alan Fisk is the author of *The Strange Things of the World* (1988), *The Summer Stars* (1992), *Forty Testoons* (1999) and *Lord of Silver* (2000). A member of the Historical Novel Society, he has lectured on subjects including 'Writing Historical Novels' and 'Story Theory'.

Printed in Great Britain
by Amazon